PRAISE FOR S

"Sasha has done it again! I devour ... them to come out because I kno... should be on your must-read author list if you are into sports romance."

"You want a sizzling soccer romance??! This is for you! I could not put this book down! I was hooked from the second I started reading!!"

"Sasha Lace has fast become one of my favorite authors! The world she exposes, the world she builds, has me glued to my screen from the first word to the very last!"

"This is everything that I love about contemporary romance: strong male and female main characters, romance with instant chemistry."

"A witty, flirty, and a little bit of everything else romantic story. The sizzle was awesome too. Read it in one sitting, it was such an easy read."

"30% in and Sasha Lace became a one-click author."

"I am loving that an author is giving women their shot in the world of sports romance!"

"Gabe needs to be added to your list of book boyfriends, he is handsome, knows what he wants and my heaven, knows his way around a woman. The spice in this was beautiful and fun. It was delicious."

"I left each chapter wanting more and more and MORE. Well written, fast read that gives readers everything they are looking for."

"As with any book by Sasha there was a point where I was reduced to a crying mess and wanted to throw my Kindle at a wall . . . which led to having to stay up all night to get to the HEA."

"Would I recommend this book? Yes! Would I recommend everything written by Sasha Lace? Yes!"

Playing to Score

TITLES BY SASHA LACE

Playing the Field series

Playing to Score

SASHA LACE

 Montlake

Published by Montlake, Seattle

First published as *Scoring the Doctor* by Sasha Lace in 2023. This edition contains editorial revisions.

www.apub.com

Amazon, the Amazon logo, and Montlake are trademarks of Amazon.com, Inc., or its affiliates.

ISBN-13: 9781662526138
eISBN: 9781662526145

Cover design by The Brewster Project
Cover image: Cover image: © LadadikArt © Dmytro Aksonov / Getty Images; © Vadim Gouida © cristapper / Shutterstock

Printed in the United States of America

CONTENT WARNING

Anorgasmia (difficulty having an orgasm)

Verbal and emotional abuse (the FMC has an ex-partner who verbally abused her)

Pregnancy health concerns (premature birth and bleeding during pregnancy)

Swearing

Explicit sex

For my mum

Chapter 1

SKYLAR

Sean's hard body covered mine. A faint odor of mud and cut grass hit my nose. The scent of the pitch always clung to him. Once, I'd loved that smell. Not so much anymore. His hot breath fanned my ear and his hips snapped hard and fast. My limbs ached from practice, but I tried to muster some enthusiasm to match his rapid thrusts.

My mind wandered to the day's events, no matter how hard I tried to rein it in. The team manager, Claire, had made us do extra laps after discovering a couple of the younger players were hungover. Claire wasn't happy until she'd had some of the girls throwing up on the sidelines. I'd called her out afterward, but she'd doubled down. If we were serious about promotion to the Women's Super League, then this was the time to knuckle down and work.

As the captain, I wanted to keep the girls happy, but Claire was right—this year was too important to fuck things up. We had to be tough on them. Calverdale Ladies finally had everything we needed to succeed: a great team and a billionaire director who wouldn't stop until we got promoted to the Women's Super League. We were two points ahead of our closest rivals in the league table. Three wins would do it.

This was our year.

Sean planted his elbows, panting and grunting as he increased his pace. The ceiling needed to be painted. Dust lined the top of the lampshade. We could do with another one. In fact, the whole bedroom needed redecorating. We'd moved in together five years ago and we still hadn't got round to putting up new wallpaper. I flicked my gaze to the eggshell curtains. It was time for a change. A new color scheme entirely. Maybe lilac. I was definitely having a lilac moment after I'd found those perfect lilac football boots to match my hair.

Sean groaned and buried his face into the pillow next to my head. The bedframe rattled against the wall. Maybe we should get a new bed, too. One with a more stable headboard.

Sean's voice was ragged in my ear. "You like that, don't you? You're filthy, aren't you? A dirty girl."

I patted his clammy back. Sean's idea of sexy talk always left me cold.

His huge arm stretched over me as he gripped the headboard. "Are you close?"

Everything inside of me tensed at those dreaded words. No, I wasn't *close*. I was never *close*.

He groaned. 'Fuck, Sky. You're going to have to hurry up. I can't last . . .''

I squeezed my eyes shut, trying to clear my mind. A rush of thoughts swept in.

Just switch off.

Stop getting in your head.

Try and relax.

My fingers dug into the covers. All I wanted was to be clawing the sheets with pleasure for once, and not frustration. This should

2

have been the most natural thing in the world. I wanted the kind of sex the girls in the locker room talked about—the excitement, the connection, and the bone-melting orgasms.

There had been times when I'd almost been able to relax enough—on the nights when Sean was out, and it was just me, a glass of wine, and a hot bath—yet still something always held me back. Sometimes your greatest opponent wasn't any of the players on the pitch, it was you, and the bullshit in your own head. Knowing that didn't make it any easier to let go.

Sean grunted in my ear. "For fuck's sake, Sky. Come on . . ."

It always came down to this moment. It had been terrifying that first time I'd faked it. Drama had been my worst subject at school. I'd been so certain that Sean would roar with laughter at my exaggerated moans, but he hadn't. He'd looked pleased with himself, puffed up with male pride, and although I'd expected to feel guilt, there had only been relief. Faking saved me from the awkwardness afterward. The recriminations. The name-calling. It was just so much . . . easier.

Sean's voice quivered with frustration. "Sky! Are you done?"

No point dragging it out. I took a few deep gasping breaths and readied myself to put on a show. Sean held perfectly still atop of me, panting. He was always so easy to read, but his tense demeanor gave me a rush of anxiety.

"You're not even close, are you?" His breathless voice was loaded with irritation.

My mouth filled with the usual lies, but the intimacy of the moment caught me off guard—he was still inside of me, his hot breath fanning my face, his critical eyes burning into me.

"I'm . . . I'm trying."

"Trying?" His frustrated expression slipped into mockery. "You're not supposed to *try*. It's supposed to just . . . happen. I thought you were going to talk to someone about this?"

3

"I did. The doctor said there's nothing wrong with me."

"And you let them fob you off again?"

Sean's weight on me felt suddenly like a sack of bricks. His sweaty tang filled my nose, overwhelming me.

"I'm not letting them fob me off. I just don't know what I'm supposed to do if they tell me there's nothing physically wrong with me—"

"Of course there's something fucking wrong with you. This isn't normal. You need to stop being so pathetic. Go back to that doctor, and tell them you want answers. How am I supposed to enjoy this if I'm not getting anything back from you?" He pulled out, and lifted away without looking at me. "Not good enough. You need to do better than this with me, Sky. I deserve better."

He barked his words as though I was a junior on his team who didn't have what it took to make the cut. I stared at him in disbelief. This is why I'd started faking, to dodge these conversations. If I'd been quicker off the mark with the act, we could have avoided this whole discussion.

He gave me his back. The silence rang loud. He stretched and admired his impressive muscular frame in the mirror above the dressing table.

"You remember I'm going to my parents' for dinner tonight?"

I smoothed my expression at his abrupt change of subject. Fine. I was done with the conversation too. The whole thing made me feel so shitty about myself. Talking about intimate stuff had always been awkward for me. I didn't even talk about these kinds of things with my friends. After a few pints in the pub, no topic of conversation was off limits with the team, but I always held back on the personal stuff. I was there to lead. The girls needed to see me as someone sensible to lean on. A bit of distance on personal topics didn't hurt.

"What time are we going to your parents' place?"

I watched his face in the mirror as a small frown creased his brow and then disappeared. "Don't worry about it. It's a family thing."

Sean's parents had always disapproved of me. It was fine for their son to be a football player, but they'd never liked the idea of him dating a female footballer. I wasn't blind to their narrow glances whenever I went round for tea. With my tattoos and piercings, I wasn't the kind of girl Mr. and Mrs. Wallace wanted for their superstar son. God knows who would be suitable. The Virgin Mary, maybe?

I fiddled with the silver ring in my nose and pasted a smile onto my face. "Fine. I have plans tonight anyway."

He didn't even try to mask the relief in his expression. The powerful muscles in his back rippled as he strode to the bathroom. I moved to the mirror and pulled my faded lilac hair into a ponytail that revealed the shaved edges of my undercut. The sound of the shower filled my ears.

I rested my palms on the dressing table and let my head drop. What the fuck was wrong with me? Sean was the captain of the top football team in the Premier League. Teenage girls throughout England had posters of my boyfriend on their walls. If I couldn't have an orgasm with a man that looked like Sean Wallace, what chance did I have?

A harsh buzz made me jump. Sean's phone flashed and vibrated on the bedside table. Strange that he hadn't taken it into the bathroom. Sean was surgically attached to his phone. Sometimes it made me nervous, but I trusted him. Sean had girls throwing themselves at him. It came with the territory when you dated a famous footballer, but we'd been together since school. He always told me I was the only girl he could trust to want Sean Wallace the *man* and not the football icon.

Unease gnawed my gut, and I always trusted my gut. It only took two attempts to crack the passcode and unlock the phone. Sean had never been creative. I read the first message.

Last night was amazing. When can you get away again?

The sender had no name, just an initial, M. I scrolled through an endless slew of messages until I reached a bunch of faceless nudes. The messages dated back a year. A fucking year!

Sean strolled back into the bedroom, naked and toweling his golden hair. He raised a questioning brow. "Everything okay?"

I held up the phone. I managed to keep my voice level. I even managed not to throw the phone at his face. "No. Everything is not okay."

He paled. The towel dropped from his hand. "She messaged me first. They always message me first."

They.

He swiped his towel from the floor. A cold, dark expression settled over his handsome face. "I've got needs, Sky. If you're not going to give me what I need, I have to look elsewhere."

His nonchalant tone made my voice harden. "I'm not enough for you?"

He wrapped the towel around his waist in a violent movement. "Don't try and make me feel guilty. This isn't on me. You should have tried harder to fix whatever it is that's wrong with you."

A lump of anxiety rose in my throat. Sudden heat pressed behind my eyes. That's why he'd done this. He wanted a woman without my issues in bed. A better woman. He turned back to the mirror and scanned his row of expensive skincare lotions, selecting a bottle.

"I mean, look at you." He pumped moisturizer into his hands and slathered it over his face. "How am I supposed to take you to my parents' house when you embarrass me every time? It wouldn't

6

hurt you to tone it down a bit. Wear something more respectable. Your hair is a mess. This is what happens when you dye it so much."

My chest felt like it would burst. "Get out."

He raked a comb through his hair, angling his chin to admire his reflection. "I'm not going anywhere. You just need to cool down. We'll talk about it when I come home."

My fingernails cut into my palms. "Get *out*."

"You're acting crazy. This is what you do. You blow everything out of proportion. This doesn't have to be a big deal."

I choked back a cry. Fine. If he wouldn't leave, then I would. I scrambled around the room, picking up clothes and throwing them on.

Sean watched me. "Where do you think you're going?"

"I'm leaving."

A muscle quivered in his jaw. I braced myself for whatever nasty words he was about to spew, but a tense silence enveloped the room.

He sighed, and his voice took on an unbearable softness. "You're being ridiculous, as usual. Come on, Sky. We get each other. We can find a way through this."

We had understood each other once. We both knew what it meant to dedicate your life to football, to give everything to your team, and to deal with all the nonsense that came with a life in the public eye. I'd put up with so much from Sean over the years—the nastiness, the name-calling, the moods—but this was too much. This was a betrayal, and a humiliation. If word had got out to the press, it would have made headlines.

We'd have to find a way to handle a separation discreetly. If things got messy on social media, it could affect the teams. The logistics was a conversation for another time. For now, I needed to put all my efforts into not falling apart.

"It's over, Sean."

He shot me a look of amused contempt. "Over?"

"You cheated on me." I stormed to the door.

"I'm not the problem here. I've never been the problem." The bitterness in his tone held me frozen. "This has never been enough for me, but I stuck it out with you. You're broken, Sky."

His words landed like fists in my gut, stealing my breath. Maybe I was broken, but I was also tired of being treated like dirt. Enough.

Sean spritzed himself with his overpowering cologne. He stared at his reflection, as though enthralled by what he saw. His voice was soft and mocking. "You think you can do better than me? No man would be willing to put up with you the way I have."

I forced the words through gritted teeth. "I'll take my chances."

Chapter 2

REECE

I stepped into the hallway and tripped over a pair of heavy black boots. My shoulders tensed and I rolled them loose. I'd have to talk to my sister Frankie again about leaving her stuff everywhere. I found her in the kitchen, stirring a pot of something beige and unidentifiable on the cooktop.

"What is it?" I rolled up my shirtsleeves. "Chili?"

Frankie wrinkled her nose. "It started like that. Now it might be curry."

Miri and Gabe would be here any minute. I'd told Frankie to let me deal with the food, but she'd insisted I take a break from the stress of cooking. She didn't get that it was more stressful watching someone else do it wrong.

I washed my hands at the sink. "I'm taking over."

I took the wooden spoon from her hand and tried the unappetizing concoction. Overwhelming heat made my eyes water. I tried to keep my face level. "It's great. It just needs a little . . . salt."

A blackened cake sat on the window ledge. Ribbons of gooey dough shone in the charred volcanic surface. It shouldn't have been possible to both undercook and overcook something at the same time, but somehow she'd managed it. Too late to do anything about it now.

I smiled. "This looks great."

"Thanks." She brightened and took a seat at the table. "How was Laurel?"

"Who's Laurel? Don't tell me Dr. Forster is getting some?" The cool, crisp voice drifted from behind.

Gabe Rivers leaned against the doorframe. My sister's billionaire husband had taken ownership of Calverdale Ladies last year. He'd pursued Miri for his team and signed her as a striker. Since then, I couldn't go a day without him leaning in a doorway—with a smirk and a sassy comment—somewhere in my vicinity. I'd long itched to get him in the therapy chair and find out what lay beneath that cocky grin. He appeared well adjusted for someone raised with every material whim catered for. Underneath the dazzling smile and designer suits, he was actually quite normal—and by normal, I mean as fucked-up as the rest of us.

Gabe and Miri had surprised everyone with their low-key wedding ceremony—a tiny, family-only gathering—at the town registry office. Gabe had offered to buy us a new house, but Mum wouldn't hear of it. She'd only just accepted the separate annex that we'd had built so she could have some privacy. With the rehab nurses and specialist physiotherapists, Mum was making incredible progress. She'd been lucky to survive a heart attack when she'd already been weakened by a stroke.

Gabe grinned and squeezed my shoulder. "So? Spill the beans, Doc. Who's the unlucky lady?"

Frankie pushed me away to the table; her gaze transferred to Gabe. "Laurel is Reece's supervisor. She's also about a hundred years old."

Gabe raised a wry eyebrow. "An older woman? Nice."

Miri chuckled and walloped him on the chest.

Frankie stirred the chili so violently she splattered the white-tiled backsplash above the stove. "Shrinks need their own shrinks and then they have shrinks, like weird nesting dolls. They have group sessions where they all talk about emotions until it all gets too overwhelming."

I rolled my eyes and snatched the spoon from Frankie before she made more mess and gave *me* a heart attack. "I'm a clinical psychologist, not a psychiatrist."

"Same thing."

My jaw clenched. "It's not the same thing."

Frankie always left the kitchen in chaos. I opened the cutlery drawer to put the knives back in their correct place. She had no respect for any of the systems I'd instigated to keep everything neat. The fridge was always full of empty cartons and food on the wrong shelves, even though I'd clearly labelled where everything ought to go. Most unforgivably, she'd taken every single spice jar out of the rack after I'd sorted them alphabetically. I couldn't wait to get everyone out of here so I could bring some order back.

Miri's floral perfume filled my nose as she planted a light peck on my cheek. "Where's Mum?"

"She's having a nap. How are you?"

Miri grimaced and rubbed her pregnant belly. "My indigestion has indigestion. You?"

I flashed a meaningful glance at Frankie. "Irritated."

Miri smothered a grin and lowered her voice to a whisper. "She's only trying to help."

"I know. It's fine."

It was categorically not fine, but it was also my issue, not Frankie's.

I couldn't help but glance at Miri's growing bump. "You're blooming."

She winced. "That's what people say to make pregnant people feel better. My pregnancy sheen is sweat from all the vomiting."

"Can you eat anything? Are you drinking? I read an article last week about the efficacy of ginger for hyperemesis during pregnancy. It was a randomized controlled trial. I'll go and dig it out now—"

"Please don't science me. I'm not in the mood." She waved a dismissive hand that came to rest on her swollen belly. "I've seen the midwife today. It's all fine."

Frankie grabbed a serving spoon and dispatched the chili/curry in messy scoops. Miri watched me with the shifty look she always wore when she wanted to say something that I wasn't going to like.

Frankie cleared her throat dramatically and threw her hands up. "We wanted to wait for Elliot, but there isn't going to be a better time than this. We're staging an intervention."

Miri flinched and pulled Frankie to the kitchen table. "At least sit down first, and no, we're not doing anything that dramatic. It's not an intervention. It's a . . . discussion. We wanted to talk to you, about a delicate issue—"

"You're driving me mad, Reece." Frankie lowered herself to sit and raked both hands through her dark pixie hair. "I'm walking on eggshells. I can't even finish a cup of tea before you've picked the mug up and washed it."

My shoulders tensed, but I kept my tone even. "I'm sorry you feel like that, Frankie. I like things to be neat."

Miri raised her hand in the air. "It's not just Frankie. You're also driving me mad."

I took a calming breath. It wasn't my fault nobody in this house picked up after themselves.

"And me." My younger brother, Elliot, glided to the table and took a seat.

Miri surveyed the food on the table with a grimace, then pushed her seat back. "We know you like things to be done . . . in a certain way, but you're even more uptight than usual." Miri's voice softened. "You look tired. We're worried about you. Is something going on?"

My jaw clenched. I *was* tired. Shattered, actually. These past months, a heavy weight had pressed my shoulders. Every morning, I woke up far too early and still exhausted. Everything in my life had changed after Mum's stroke. Once we'd got over the shock, all that had mattered was the practicalities. We'd all thrown ourselves into getting Mum home and organizing the caring arrangements.

Miri had taken the lead, and I'd been so tied up with work, and trying to sell the house to release my finances to help, that I'd had no choice but to let her. It had put too much on her shoulders. Moving back home to take care of Mum had been a greater adjustment than I could have anticipated. I could never regret it. My family had needed me, and I'd done what any son would do, but it had cost me a house I'd loved, and my relationship. It had been a relief when Megan had walked away. My life had become so messy overnight. That's not what Megan had signed up for. I cared about her enough to spare her. It was too much to ask of her to stick it out with me under these circumstances. Too much to ask of anyone.

The constant guilt and worry about Mum were suffocating me. The one night I hadn't been here, she'd collapsed. If Gabe hadn't broken in and given her CPR, then she would have died. Gabe had saved her life that night, so I could forgive his smirking and leaning.

It wasn't just my personal life that stressed me out. Work at the hospital, covering for absent colleagues, had become unmanageable. I had patients back to back. No time for lunch. No breaks. As a mental health professional, I knew exactly what this was: burnout. I'd ignored it in the hope it might resolve itself. I'd been kidding myself.

Miri covered my hand with hers, her skin cool on mine. "Is there anything you want to talk about?"

"Isn't that my line?"

"You don't have the monopoly on listening."

My siblings stared back at me in waiting silence. An intervention? This was intense even for this lot. If it had got to the point that they felt the need for something so dramatic, then I owed them honesty. I talked to people about mental health for a living, but even I could admit I preferred not to burden my family with my problems. I sighed and cleared my throat. "I should have been here. I keep thinking about how long Mum was lying on that floor on her own."

Instead, I'd been going round in circles with Megan, and I'd let my whole family down.

Frankie watched me with shrewd eyes. "This is basic self-care, Reece. You're being unfair to yourself. You know all this. You can't pour from an empty cup. Isn't that what you tell your patients?"

Miri took a sip of water. "When did you last take time off? Can't you take a sabbatical? Add some more letters to that alphabet soup after your name?"

I turned my face to the window. If I took a break, I'd return to more work. And it wouldn't be fair to my patients. They relied on me. Still, Frankie was right. I'd been emptying my cup for so long, there wasn't anything left to pour. I needed a break, whether I wanted to admit it or not.

I arranged my silverware in a neat line. "I need to do something. I'll be bored out of my brain."

Gabe chirped up from across the table. "What about a change? That's as good as a rest."

"A new hospital will be all the same problems in a different place."

"Then why not do something different with your skills? We could use you at the football club," Gabe said.

For a moment, I was too startled by the suggestion to reply.

"You want me to play football?"

"You? Play football?" Gabe chuckled darkly. "Not as a player, as a psychologist. The girls have been stressed lately. The next couple of games will decide whether we earn promotion. You could do some coaching. Get them into the right mindset. All the top teams have sports psychologists. I've been thinking about bringing someone in for a while."

Miri shot Gabe an impressed glance. "That's actually a great idea."

Gabe raised a smug eyebrow and squeezed her hand. "I'm not just a pretty face, my love."

Miri smiled and returned her attention to me. "You should think about it. Mindset is everything in football at this level. You have skills we can put to use. It won't be the same pressure as the hospital. You might enjoy it."

Frankie nudged me in the ribs. "Sounds like a cushy gig to me."

My fingers felt clammy around my fork. It was a big change. I'd always worked in hospitals. Besides, I'd been packed shoulder to shoulder in that rowdy stadium before, and it wasn't my cup of tea. Too many people. Too chaotic. The team always struck me as a rabble. Would they be receptive to this kind of thing?

Elliot scoffed. "You want Reece to do sports psychology? He doesn't even understand the offside rule."

Technically, that was unfair. It wasn't that I didn't understand it. I just didn't care enough to understand it. As nice as it was that my family wanted to help me, this idea was a hard pass. Now I had to get them to move on.

"I help people in distress. Sports psychology is not my area of expertise." I smoothed a hand over the tablecloth and kept my tone light. "I find my attention span is limited with sports. I prefer more intellectual pursuits."

Elliot balled up his napkin and threw it at me. "My attention span is limited when I have to listen to your voice."

"I'm sure you'll have something to offer," Miri said.

Nope. How long would we have to go down this road before they gave up? They'd obviously been scheming to get me to leave the hospital. This was going to be a long evening, but I wouldn't back down. Boundaries were important and, unfortunately, my family always delighted in trampling over mine.

Miri rested her hands on her huge belly. "A few of the girls have been getting nervous lately about taking penalties. Even Skylar seems off. If the pressure is getting to the captain, then it's getting to everyone." Miri's lips puckered thoughtfully. "I swear, something weird is going on with Skylar. It would be good if she had someone to talk to . . . if all the girls had someone to talk to."

Skylar Marshall.

A curious heat spread through me. We hadn't spoken since school, but I'd crushed on her hard throughout my teenage years. Not that she'd known I was alive. Sean Wallace and Skylar Marshall had ruled the school, and I was the kid eating lunch with the librarian.

I tried to keep my voice from appearing unduly interested. "What do you mean, something's wrong with Skylar?"

"I don't know. She doesn't have her head in the game." Miri studied the chili on her fork before wrinkling her nose and pushing her plate away. "Weren't the two of you in the same year at school?"

"Were we?" I busied myself rearranging my silverware. "I don't remember."

Frankie poured herself another glass of wine. "Ah, Skylar Marshall is so cool. You know, she has three million followers on Instagram. That's more than some of the men's team. Did you know that? How many have you got, Miri?"

Miri smoothed a smile onto her pale face. Poor Miri. This pregnancy was tough. She'd moved in with Gabe, but when he went away for work, she always came home. She must have liked the comfort, even if we all drove each other up the wall. "I don't know. I don't care about that sort of thing."

"One hundred fifty thousand," Frankie said, pointing her wineglass at Miri for emphasis. "You've got one hundred fifty thousand. That's embarrassing."

A little frown flitted across Miri's face.

"It's not a competition, my love. Don't worry." Gabe squeezed Miri's hand and flashed a faux-sympathetic smile. "But if it was, I have ten million followers. Just putting it out there."

Miri gave an indignant snort, but amusement flashed in her eyes. "Well, you've just lost one."

What was up with Skylar? She'd always been so confident. Every weekend, I'd watched my old crush from the sidelines. I was there to support Miri, but I couldn't help it if my eyes occasionally drifted to Skylar Marshall. It wasn't my fault. Whose eyes wouldn't drift?

During her last match, Skylar had scored a winning penalty but instead of celebrating the victory with her team, she'd dashed to the opposition goalkeeper to console her. That moment had gone viral, and Miri told me Skylar had been so embarrassed to see it played over and over. That was the thing about Skylar, her compassion wasn't virtue signaling. She was a genuinely caring person. I'd gleaned as much from the odd snippets Miri dropped. It was Skylar who always remembered her teammates' birthdays, and organized the trips to deliver gifts to the local children's hospital. It was Skylar who had taken Miri under her wing when she first started at the club.

It shouldn't have surprised me. Skylar had been that way at school—always volunteering to help. When I'd organized a school

17

litter-pick, Skylar was the only student to turn up. I'd crushed on her so hard back then. I hadn't mustered the courage to speak to her. I'd hardly dared lift my eyes from the ground. The school yard had never been cleaner by the time we were done.

If Skylar needed something, I wanted to help. The back of my neck itched. Well, not just Skylar. The whole team. I could help the whole team. This wasn't just about Skylar. Definitely not.

"Fine. I can help you at the football club," I said.

Miri frowned. "Really?" She exchanged a look with Gabe. "I thought that would be a harder sell."

I sat a little straighter in the chair. "No. You're right. I need something else to do. A sabbatical is a great idea. It sounds ideal."

Yes. This was about taking a break from the hospital for a while. It was the best decision for me. I could help Skylar. Well, the whole team. It wasn't just about Skylar. It was the right decision for me. In fact, it had very little to do with Skylar Marshall.

"Come by my office when you're free and we'll talk." Gabe held up his wineglass. "Welcome to the team, Doc. Good to have you on board." He raised a sardonic eyebrow. "Let's hope we can hold your attention as much as your . . . intellectual pursuits."

Chapter 3

SKYLAR

The team gathered in one of the meeting rooms on the training ground. My eyes burned with exhaustion and my stomach ached and grumbled. I'd hardly slept. Hardly eaten. Still, I had to carry on as normal. No one in this room needed to know that my life had imploded. This year was too important.

Everything hinged on the last three games. Three wins and this was in our hands. It didn't matter what any of the other teams in the table did, we'd be promoted from the Championship League to the Women's Super League, the top league in England. We were so close to victory I could almost taste it. If the team lost faith in the captain, then we were screwed. No matter how my guts churned or how my heart ached, I had to inspire confidence. I didn't feel confident. Not one bit. Thankfully, I'd always been good at faking.

Gabe entered, followed by a tall, dark-haired man. Thick-framed black glasses shielded the man's dark eyes and a perfect swoosh curl fell across his forehead. A smart tweed blazer wrapped around his broad shoulders. He looked the type to be found tucked away in the corner of a bookshop with a cappuccino and a notepad.

His eyes met mine briefly as he scanned the room, and my stomach gave a curious lurch.

Gabe clapped his hands to get our attention. "This is Dr. Reece Forster. He's our new team psychologist. We've brought him in to help with mindset. I know this has been a stressful season, and we've got a lot riding on moving up to the next league. Reece is going to run sessions to get our heads in gear. I trust you'll all give him a warm welcome."

A team psychologist? Well, wasn't that fancy? Gabe was sparing no expense. A luxury like a team psychologist would have been unthinkable a year ago. Until Gabe arrived, we hadn't even had our own gym. I couldn't stop my eyes from roving over the new guy—very nice if you liked that kind of thing and you didn't hate all men in general since they were all lying, cheating scumbags.

My phone buzzed in my pocket. I pulled it out to see another missed call from Sean. Speak of the lying, cheating scumbag devil. I'd told him I needed space, but he didn't understand the concept. My thumb hovered over the delete key. What more did he want from me? We'd agreed over text to keep everything quiet until we'd put together a joint statement.

At least he hadn't bothered me at work. The last thing I wanted was him turning up and causing a scene in front of the girls. Our paths usually crossed in the gym when the women's training sessions overlapped with the men's, but I'd skipped out on gym sessions this week. I'd have to face him again soon so we could put our heads together on the statement, but not yet. The press had styled us into the golden couple of English football. They were going to relish every moment of our downfall. My guts churned.

Lana leaned in next to me, her breath warm against my ear. "I'm calling dibs on the hot doctor."

My breath caught in my throat. "What?"

She cocked her head to appraise him. "It's the glasses." Her lips curved in an unconscious smile. "I've always liked a man that looks like he knows his way around a spreadsheet."

"But he looks so . . . straitlaced, like a librarian."

"Right?" she whispered under her breath. "A smoking-hot librarian. Dr. Straitlace. I'm into it."

Lana's chuckle raked through me. If she had her sights on him, he didn't stand a chance. She'd screwed her way around most of the men's team and half of the women's. She wasn't shy about going after what she wanted. Not that I judged her for that, of course. Just because I'd been with Sean since school didn't mean I begrudged other people having fun. Anyway, what did it matter to me? If Lana wanted the new guy, she was welcome to go after him.

Lana smirked and leaned in again. "I might see if any of the other girls are up for a bet on who can score with Dr. Straitlace first."

I couldn't keep the annoyance from my voice. I liked to have fun with Lana, but that was way too far. "What? No. Absolutely not. He's a professional, here to do a job."

Lana snorted. "Don't spoil our fun just because you're wifed up."

Wifed up.

Not anymore. I loved this team, but sometimes they were a bunch of messy bitches, and a sniff of the news about me and Sean would send them wild. They'd want to know all the details, but worse, they'd worry about me. If they sensed weakness or lost faith in the captain, we'd all be in trouble. I needed to keep a lid on it until we got through this season and got promoted.

The team is all that matters.

Lana smoothed a hand over her gleaming auburn ponytail and leaned in again. "Yeah. We could do with a bit of fun to lighten the mood around here. We'll each put twenty quid in the pot. First to score with the doctor takes the prize."

I put a finger to my lips. "Shh. We're supposed to be listening."

Slowly, Dr. Forster slipped off his tweed jacket and hung it on the back of his chair. He rolled his shirtsleeves up to the elbows. His forearms were tanned, and more muscular than I would have imagined for someone so buttoned up. These were the arms of a man who worked outdoors with his hands, not a man who sat in a chair scribbling in a pad all day. These were arms that could wrap around you and protect you. The kind that made you go weak at the knees. Now it was almost impossible to take my eyes off him. Every movement was so measured and elegant. So controlled. Silence swirled in the room. The girls never paid this much attention to me when I did a team talk. They never paid this much attention to anyone. It was the way he stood, so still and composed—that, and the forearm porn. I couldn't be the only one who appreciated such things.

Dr. Forster stepped forward. "Thanks, Gabe. It's good to be here, and I'm looking forward to getting to know everyone better. I'm also offering one-on-one coaching sessions."

His low, considered voice was as level and soothing as the rain that tapped against the window. My whole body leaned in, listening.

"We can work on mindset, confidence on the pitch, or any worries you might have that affect performance. I don't know how much interest there would be in that kind of thing. Could I get a show of hands to see if it's worthwhile?"

I watched as every arm in the room shot skyward. I kept my hands pinned in my lap. The last thing I needed was to spill my guts to a shrink.

His steady gaze flicked to me for the briefest of moments and, for some strange reason, my heart pounded. His expression and tone remained level. "That looks like most of you . . . great."

Lana surveyed the room and leaned into me again. "I'm not the only one who fancies a one-on-one with the new guy." She rubbed

22

her hands together and raised a mischievous eyebrow. "This is going to be a good prize fund."

Lana was my best friend, but she'd always been a handful. The press called her the "bad girl" of women's football. I had no doubt that she enjoyed that moniker. If she had herself set on something, I wouldn't be able to talk her out of it. She was an amazing friend— the life and soul of every party and loyal to a tee. Still, she was also the only person I knew who was more stubborn than me. With Lana, you had to choose your battles carefully.

"Do what you want, but if Claire and Gabe find out about this, then you're on your own," I said.

A small smirk lit Lana's face. "Fine. Let the games begin."

Gabe glanced at his fancy watch and rested a hand on the doctor's shoulder. "Let's wrap this up. I have another meeting." Gabe beckoned me. "Skylar, can you help Reece get settled in?"

An inexplicable unease washed over me. "Me? I've got training. Can't Claire do it?"

"Claire's in this meeting with me."

Lana elbowed me out of the way, her voice like silk. "I'd be happy to do it, Gabe. It would be a pleasure. I've always had a huge interest in psychology."

Dr. Forster's face remained level. "You have? Which areas of psychology interest you?"

Lana smiled sweetly. "All of it. The brain is so fascinating, isn't it? I mean, how does it do everything? Thinking. Telling you what to say. Controlling how you move around and things. Just all of that . . . stuff . . . mind-boggling. All that brain stuff. Wow."

If he found that response as ridiculous as I did, his inscrutable face didn't betray him. "Yes. Absolutely. The brain is an impressive organ."

"It is." Lana's eyes twinkled with mischief. "A very impressive organ."

This poor man. She'd eat him alive. It was only his first day. I'd have to rescue him.

I stepped in front of Lana. "No. It's fine. I'm the captain, so I'm happy to do a tour. I'm also interested in psychology."

Gabe looked over our heads as though searching for a more interesting conversation. "Fine. It doesn't matter who does it. Somebody needs to show him around. Make Reece feel welcome, won't you? This is Miri's brother. She's going to want to know that we've been nice to him."

Lana tossed me an amused glance, but I folded my arms. *Yeah, mate. I'm pulling rank.*

I transferred my gaze to the doctor. "I'm Skylar. Lovely to have you here, Dr. Forster."

He shook my hand, his palm warm against mine. "It's just Reece."

A tingle crept up my wrist at his touch. "Reece."

Heat stroked my cheeks. I gestured toward the door. "This way, Reece. Let me give you the lay of the land."

"Thanks. I'd love to talk more about your interest in psychology."

Shit. I plastered a smile onto my face. "Great. That sounds . . . perfect."

Chapter 4

SKYLAR

Reece fell in step alongside me as we traversed the training suite. Music pumped out from the gym. I glanced at my watch and my stomach dropped. The men's team would be in there working out. The last thing I wanted was a run-in with Sean. Reece lingered at the entrance to look inside.

I hurried past, forcing him to catch up with me. "Do you like to work out?"

"Me?" A rueful smile pulled at his full lips, but he dashed it quickly. "Not really. My younger brother is a dancer. He's taken it upon himself to whip me into shape. Exercise is Elliot's love language. I wish it was hanging up the towels after he's used them, but sadly that's a no."

I laughed. "Tell me about it, I grew up with three older brothers."

He was being modest. He definitely worked out. His tall, well-muscled body moved with easy grace under all those starchy clothes. He carried himself with a commanding air of self-confidence. Not that I had any business noticing.

We walked down a long glass corridor with the vast expanse of green training pitches to our left. I pointed out the dressing rooms, the swimming pool, and the cafeteria.

As we passed by the trophy cabinet, he flashed me a curious glance. "You don't remember me, do you?"

"Should I?"

"We went to the same school."

I couldn't keep the look of surprise from my face. "We did? I knew Miri went to the same school. She was a couple of years above."

"We sat next to each other in Geography."

Really? I would have remembered sitting next to a man that looked this good. I racked my brain, struggling to remember. I'd messed about in school. Sean had always convinced me to bunk off and hang out in his bedroom. What a waste of time.

The back of my neck warmed with guilt over not remembering him. I slapped my palm against my forehead. "Reece Forster? Geography, right? Yeah. I do remember."

"It's fine. I don't expect you to remember. You were popular and I was . . . quiet."

"It looks like you've done well. Dr. Forster, huh? You must have been listening in class more than me. You went to university?"

His shiny brogues tapped on the stairs as he followed me up to the next floor. "Cambridge."

"No shit. Well, look at you. Very fancy."

A faint smile crossed his lips, but he stayed silent for the rest of the journey along the second-floor corridor full of offices. A gold plaque gleamed on the last door in the row.

Dr. Reece Forster
Psychologist

He slipped a key from his blazer and unlocked the door. A huge walnut desk dominated the large office. Bookcases teemed with neat rows of heavy tomes. He inclined his head toward the open door. "Do you have time to talk? I'd love to brainstorm about future group sessions . . ."

There was a tentative edge to his voice. How had I sat next to this hot-as-hell guy at school and not noticed? A strange tingling lit the pit of my stomach. I scuffed the tip of my trainer on the floor. "I should really be hitting the gym."

"Of course. You must be busy. I don't want to keep you."

His intense, keenly observant eyes made my heart pound. "No. It's fine. You're not. I'm not busy. I mean I am busy, but not too busy . . . I can brainstorm . . ."

I snapped my mouth shut. I didn't get nervous. Why was I rambling like an idiot?

His face held perfectly level. "Come in, then."

I followed him inside and closed the door behind us. Two armchairs sat in the middle of the room, facing each other. My gaze fell on the leather doctor's couch pushed to the back wall. I couldn't help the playful smile that pulled at my lips. "Do I get to lie on the couch?" I drifted over and smoothed a hand over the buttery leather. "This all has a very Freudian 'Tell me about your mother' vibe."

His tone was impassive. "Do you want to tell me about your mother?"

I hopped up to sit on the couch. "She's a delight. A wonderful, caring woman. No deep-rooted psychological trauma."

"That's a shame. I live for deep-rooted psychological trauma."

I couldn't help my laugh. He didn't look like he had a sense of humor, but it was there, even if it was as dry as the Sahara. Maybe Dr. Straitlace wasn't as straitlaced as he looked.

I swung my legs over the edge of the couch, letting them dangle. "Sorry to disappoint. I'm the picture of sanity. If you've ever wondered what total emotional stability looks like, then look no further."

He hovered by the window. Sunlight streamed in, making his dark hair gleam with shadows of rich chestnut. "I don't ask my patients to lie on a couch. Gabe had this room furnished. He's seen too many TV psychiatrists."

I crossed the room and sat in one of the chairs in the center of the office. He lowered himself smoothly into the seat opposite. His intense gaze burned into me. He hadn't taken his eyes off me since I'd stepped in the room. I had no doubt he was watching and analyzing me. It was unnerving, but in an odd way it gave me a little glow to be observed. To be the center of someone's attention.

He relaxed back in the chair, his brow smooth, his slight smile bland and noncommittal. Silence swirled around us. I twisted a tendril of damp hair between my fingers. I wished I'd bothered to dry and straighten it after my shower.

I cleared my throat. "Are you sure we had Geography together? Mrs. Baxter?"

"Mrs. Butler, and yes, I'm sure."

"Oh." I clasped my fingers together in my lap. Reece sat still and composed. It made me intensely aware of my own fidgeting. "I bunked off a lot. I regret it now. I wish I'd knuckled down. Sean hated going to classes. Do you remember Sean? Sean Wallace. He plays for Calverdale United. He was in our year, too."

He stared back levelly. "I remember."

"We live together. Well . . . we did, before . . . we're taking a break . . . I kicked him out, actually."

His expression remained unchanged. Heat climbed my throat. Why had I blurted that? It had to be the silences and the clinical, detached way he studied my face, like a scientist might examine an interesting specimen in the lab.

"I haven't told anyone on the team. Please don't tell anyone. You're not going to tell Miri, are you? Or Gabe?"

His level tone softened. "Not if you don't want me to."

"I don't."

He nodded. Silence fell between us again.

"Sean's been texting other girls."

I felt Reece's eyes on me, but I couldn't look up from my fingers gripped tightly in my lap. "You're sure you won't tell Miri, will you? Nobody can know about this. Sean is a big name. This isn't just about me. It's about the men's team as well. If the story blows up, it's going to be a media circus. The football club is all that matters. Sean feels the same. We're dealing with it discreetly."

"I understand."

Reece smoothed his tie and crossed his legs at the knee. His brogues gleamed like polished wood. I'd never seen a man dressed so immaculately. With that pristine button-down shirt and artfully disheveled hair, he was flawless.

"You haven't told anyone at all? That must be difficult. A breakup can be stressful. I'm sure there are people here that would want to support you."

"It would be terrible for team morale. Everyone is relying on me to get them to the end of the season. We're so close to getting promoted. Everything is hanging on these last three games. I need to look like I'm in control."

He cocked his head, his tone somehow soft yet uncompromising. "Are you in control, Skylar?"

"Yes. Always. I'm the captain. I don't lean on the girls with my problems. They lean on me."

"Even captains have problems."

I pasted a rueful smile onto my lips, despite the ache in my heart. "Not me."

Silence swirled between us. I'd told him too much, but my confession had made the horrible scratchy gnawing feeling inside loosen its grip a little. I hadn't told anyone, not even my parents. Still, this guy was here to do coaching and motivational stuff, not counsel me through a relationship breakup. I didn't need a therapist. This was Miri's brother, for goodness' sake. A sudden awkwardness came over me and I stood. "Anyway, this isn't why you're here. You've got better things to do than talk to me."

His intense eyes met mine. "No. I haven't, and I'm here because my family wants to get me out of the house because I annoy them."

"Why would you annoy them?"

He kept his expression perfectly level. "I don't know. I'm the picture of sanity. If you've ever wondered what total emotional stability looks like, then look no further."

So dry. So deadpan. Not even a hint of a smile. I couldn't help my chuckle to hear my words parroted back to me. His eyes were riveted to my face and it made my pulse pound.

"Do you promise you won't tell anyone any of this?"

"I promise."

"It's a relief, honestly. It doesn't even feel real. Me and Sean are over."

"How does it feel to hear yourself speak those words?"

"It feels . . . great. Is that weird?"

"No. Not if the relationship wasn't working."

"It wasn't. Not for a long time."

A suffocating silence enveloped us again. This was what he did. The long pauses made you say more than you wanted to say. I needed to run before I gave him more messy facts about my messy life. This man was dangerous. I wouldn't be back in a hurry.

I moved to the door. "Anyway, I should go. Time to hit the gym. If you need anything or you get lost, give me a shout."

"I will. Come back if you want to talk again." His dark, inscrutable gaze locked with mine. "My door is always open to the captain."

Chapter 5

REECE

Frankie shielded her eyes from the sun and surveyed my vegetable garden. She plunged her shovel into the ground, dangerously close to my rhubarb plants.

A shadow of alarm went through me. "Be careful."

She yanked the spade out, sending soil everywhere. I drew a deep breath. By some strange miracle, the twins had volunteered to help me with the garden. It was good of them, and it had never happened before. I'd have to suck it up and be grateful for the "help."

Frankie bent down and fingered a slug-eaten cabbage before looking up at Elliot. "I don't understand how humans have even evolved, since it's impossible to grow vegetables without things eating them."

I moved around the vegetable patch, ripping up the odd weed. Frankie's gaze burned into me. Something was up. There was no other reason for them both to be outside with me. "Come on then. What's going on?"

Frankie cleared her throat. "I've got someone I want to set you up with. A friend at university."

I suppressed my eye roll. "No. Thank you."

Elliot smirked. "I've told you not to risk introducing anyone you know to Reece. I reckon he's a full-on freak. I'm talking manacles, masks . . . the whole lot. Why else would he have put up with Megan for so long? She had to be fulfilling some specialist kink."

I sighed. "Can we get through one day without the two of you speculating about my love life?"

Frankie angled her trowel at me. "What do you say? Do you want me to set you up?"

"No."

"Why not?"

"Because I'm not interested in meeting anyone at the moment."

Frankie raked over the fresh earth she'd turned over. "Why not? You've looked sad since you split with Megan. Fuck the pain away, I say."

"Sure. Why not? That's the first thing we learn when we train as psychologists. It's followed by 'eat the pain away' and 'inject the pain away.'"

Elliot flashed me a glance. "You should do it. I've never seen anyone more in need of getting laid. See if she'll remove the stick from your arse while you're at it."

I drew a calming breath. "I appreciate your concerns, but respectfully, I don't want to talk about my love life with either of you."

Is this why they'd volunteered to help out? So they could tag-team in annoying me? Frankie threw a weed into a bucket with a heavy thud and slid me a glance. "I bumped into Megan the other day. She's cut her hair short. It doesn't suit her. She asked how you were . . ."

I kept my gaze on the strip of lighter soil where I'd planted my corn. I didn't need to hear about Megan.

"I told her you have a hot new girlfriend and you're fucking each other's brains out all day. She looked mortified. She made that little squeaky noise she makes when she's about to cry."

I kept my voice flat despite my rising stress. "I wish you hadn't done that."

"I know, but it was too fun not to. Megan was the worst." Frankie slammed her shovel into the ground. "She left you when you needed her the most, and she was so dull. She wasn't good for you. You need someone with a bit of life. Someone a bit . . . wild."

My siblings had the wrong end of the stick about Megan. She'd broken up with me, and it had hurt like hell, but it was for the best. I'd given her an easy out, and she'd jumped at it. Megan had a ten-year plan, and her boyfriend moving back home to look after his sick mother wasn't part of it. She hadn't wanted to deal with my baggage. The past six months had been . . . a lot. I couldn't blame her for walking away, even if it had hurt to watch her go.

"Megan made a choice. I respect it. You should respect it too. And I don't need wild. I like a quiet life."

"No. You need someone to bring you out of your shell. There's more to life than books and gardening. You have the hobbies of a pensioner."

"I like my garden, and I don't want to talk about Megan. I come down here for peace and quiet."

Frankie swiped a muddy hand across her sweating forehead. "When shit got real with Mum, Megan jettisoned out of here. Be angry about it. It's okay to be angry about it. Isn't that what you bang on about all day anyway? It's okay not to be okay? Or is it okay for everyone else and not you?"

I pulled out a potato and scraped away the dirt before tossing it into a wheelbarrow. I drew another calming breath. Birdsong filled my ears. I tried to relax the tension in my jaw.

Frankie trampled over my strawberry plants to pick up a watering can. She showered water over a patch of weeds. "Anyway, I've signed you up for a couple of dating apps. You've already had a few matches."

34

My blood turned to ice. "You've. Done. What?"

She tugged off her gardening gloves and pulled her phone from the pocket of her dungarees. A smile crept onto her lips as she scrolled, then she twisted the screen in my direction. My face stared back at me. Despite my exasperation, I tried to keep myself together as I scanned the profile that had been created without my knowledge. I read it out loud.

"My name is Dr. Forster. I might look like a geek on the street, but I'm a freak in the sheets. I'm a love doctor, looking to set hearts racing with some no-strings fun."

Elliot sniggered and turned his face away.

My teeth gritted, but I kept my tone even. "Please tell me this is a joke."

"What? No. It's real. This is perfect. You have a photo looking professional and then Elliot got a couple of shots of you without your glasses at the gym." Frankie flexed her bicep and grinned. "You need to show off the goods if you want to attract the ladies."

Anger made my guts churn. I swiveled to Elliot. He merely shrugged. I took a deep breath, but even Buddha wouldn't be cool about being put on dating apps without permission. "What are you thinking? What if a patient sees me on there? This isn't funny. This is my job and my reputation on the line."

Frankie frowned. "Don't be overdramatic. You're allowed to date, aren't you?"

"Not like this. It looks completely unprofessional. Dating apps are for casual hookups. I don't want people to see me on there looking for something shallow."

Elliot snorted. "Hey, don't knock casual hookups until you've tried them. Shallow is exactly what you need. It's the only way you're going to get over Megan. This is why you're so wound up. It's going to make all our lives easier when you get some action."

Absolutely not. I held my hand out. "Give me the phone."

"No." Frankie slammed the phone back into her pocket.

"Delete me from everything immediately."

Frankie sighed and exchanged a look with Elliot. "I told you he'd be weird about it."

"I'm being serious. Delete everything *now*."

Frankie held her hands up in mock surrender. "Fine. Don't get your knickers in a twist. I'll delete them. Let's contact the matches you have first."

"Delete it immediately. I'm not messing about here, Frankie."

Frankie rolled her eyes and pulled her phone back out. "We're just trying to help." Her glittery fingernails tapped at the screen. "You're no fun, you know that?"

"Hey, I didn't know you were all down here."

I looked up to see Miri waddling toward us.

Frankie pouted and stuck a hand on her hip. "Reece is making us delete him from the dating apps."

Miri's face dropped. "Why? That profile was amazing."

My shoulders bunched. "You knew about this, too?"

Miri shrugged. "It was my idea."

So, all three of my siblings had teamed up to humiliate me. Great.

Miri slung an arm around my shoulder. "It's just a bit of fun. We're trying to help you. How did things go with the team?"

"The team was fine."

Miri smiled. "I want to hear all the gossip. How is everyone?"

My mind drifted back to Skylar. It had been odd to talk to her again after all this time. She had more tattoos now. Two colorful sleeves full of intricate designs peeped out from beneath her T-shirt and a string of yellow roses inked the length of her collarbone. More piercings, too. With her bright blue eyes and delicate features, she was still stunningly beautiful. More beautiful close up than I could have ever remembered. Not that I had any business noticing.

We were colleagues now. Clearly, she was going through a difficult time and needed support.

Frankie ripped up another perfectly healthy strawberry plant. I leaned in low to Miri and whispered, "Please take Frankie away, for the sake of the vegetables."

Miri's expression brightened with amusement. She beckoned Frankie. "I'm prepping Gabe's place for the birthday party. He gave me his credit card. Do you want to help?"

Frankie paled and her mouth dropped open. "You have a billionaire's credit card?"

Miri laughed. "Yes, but that doesn't mean we can go crazy."

Frankie transferred her gaze to me. "I'm sorry, Reece. Can you do without me?"

"I'm sure I'll manage."

Miri flashed me a look. "You're coming to Gabe's birthday party, aren't you? Mum's still up for it. She wants to pop in, depending on how she feels."

I tried to keep the grimace from my face. Gabe's parties were full of celebrities and loud, pretentious people. Parties were overwhelming at the best of times, but Gabe's were another level.

"I think it's too much for Mum," I said.

Miri's face dropped. "She wants to. She's been doing so well. Come on. Please. It's important to Gabe. I can't do it for long either. I need to be in bed by 8 p.m. these days."

So much for using Mum as an excuse. I'd thought that would be watertight. It wasn't fair to stop Mum from going if she wanted to. It meant a lot to Miri too. It wouldn't hurt to pop in. Usually, I went to hide in the library, anyway. That was the one perk of Gabe's mansion. He had a library with a sliding ladder like you'd see in a movie.

I pasted a smile onto my face. "Fine. If Mum's well enough, then I will. But only an hour."

And don't expect me to leave the library.

Chapter 6

Skylar

I yanked the hem of my tight plum-hued dress and frowned at my reflection in the clear microwave door. Sophie, one of my teammates, passed me an orange juice. She wrapped her arms around the thick neck of her football player boyfriend, Aiden. Aiden smiled and kissed the top of her head. God. Just my luck to get stuck with the most loved-up couple at a party. We weren't supposed to drink to excess in the season, but we didn't have training in the morning. I needed to find someone equally as miserable to drown my sorrows with. These two lovesick puppies weren't going to cut it.

Miri waddled into the kitchen and threw an arm around my shoulder.

"Hey, is this too low cut?" I tried to tug my dress up over my boobs, but the sweeping neckline wouldn't budge. "Sean always said this color doesn't look good on me."

Miri flashed an incredulous grin. "Are you kidding me? You look amazing. Every color looks good on you."

"I don't know about that."

Miri scoffed. "Excuse me. Do I have to remind you about the thirst tweets? You had twice as many as Sean, as I recall."

I covered my hands with my face. "Oh God. Don't."

Last year, some guys had curated a bunch of comments on social media about me and Sean, and thought it would be hilarious if we read them out for their YouTube channel. The deal was that all the comments would be complimentary, and they were, albeit *too* complimentary.

Sean had loved every second of hearing about how the whole world lusted after him. Me, not so much. It had been funny up to a point, and then it had just been embarrassing. I didn't like any of that stuff. I always turned down the fashion shoots and modeling offers. I wouldn't let the PR team talk me into any more of that sort of thing after that YouTube shitshow. I liked to play football, and that was it. Sean might have enjoyed the billboards of him posing in jockstraps that barely contained his junk, but I had no aspirations to make a fortune from pretentious perfume commercials and push-up bras.

Miri glanced over my shoulder. "Where is Sean?"

I waved a dismissive hand. "I'm sure he'll be along later."

But hopefully not.

"Come on. Let's find the birthday boy." Miri linked her arm through mine and pulled me toward the door. "We need to set up the karaoke."

A barrage of music and laughter hit us as Miri led me into the revelry in Gabe's mansion. People crammed every inch of the ginormous sitting room.

Miri smiled when her gaze landed on Gabe. "Ah, there he is."

She waddled off, leaving me standing alone. I scanned the room, looking for someone to talk to. The music pulsed too loud in my ears, and no matter how much I tried to adjust my dress it felt overly tight and revealing. I drifted back to the kitchen and downed another tequila, the alcohol hot on my tongue as I chased it with salt and bitter lime. Where was Sean? Would he come here? He'd said it was over with his other woman.

You're the problem.

At least the other girls can give me what I need.

Not good enough.

The booze made my stomach roll, but at least it would take the edge off this horrible, numb, scratchy disquiet I'd had since I found those messages on Sean's phone.

"Skylar Marshall? I was hoping I'd get a chance to speak to you."

The unfamiliar American accent stopped me in my tracks. I turned to see a tall, dark-haired man in a smart suit. He flashed a smile and presented his palm. "Evan Lewis. Chairman of the LA Halos."

The LA Halos? What on earth was he doing here? That was one of the best women's football teams in the US. I'd thought he looked familiar.

He raised his beer bottle to his lips. "Your form has been amazing this season. Twenty shots on goals. No misses."

"Thank you."

Where was this going? Why was he reciting my stats to me as if I didn't know them? Everything was muted and sharp at the same time. I had to get out of all this noise and activity.

"Excuse me, I was just on my way to the bathroom."

Not true, but I couldn't deal with a conversation right now. I wanted to be alone.

He nodded. "I hope we can catch up later."

I pasted a smile onto my face. "Sure. Great."

I weaved my way through the sitting room to the entrance hall. There were still too many people. My teammates crammed every corner of the hall and the stairs, but I headed up through the crowd of limbs and chatter. Too much. Too many happy, smiling faces.

I tried the door to a room and slipped inside. The moonlight illuminated a huge library. Bookcases lined the walls. There was even a ladder to reach the highest shelves.

"Skylar?"

A startled yelp erupted from me. Silvery moonlight illuminated the tall figure of a man sitting on the shadowy window seat with a book in his hand.

"Reece?" I scanned the empty library. "What are you doing up here?"

He raised a dark brow. "Hiding."

I couldn't help my chuckle. "What do you mean?"

A hint of a rueful smile played on his full lips. "This isn't really my scene."

Music drifted in to fill the silence between us.

I bowed my head. "I'll leave you to it. I'm sorry I disturbed you."

"You didn't disturb me. What are you doing up here?"

I had no idea. Usually, I loved parties. Tonight, it was just . . . too much.

Before I could figure out an answer, Reece inclined his head to the opposite end of the window seat. "We could hide together, if you like."

Did he really want company or was he just being polite? Music and chatter pulsed from the party, making my teeth grit. Nope. Still too loud. I pulled the door closed behind me. An intense relief swept through me, and my body relaxed into the silence and stillness of the library. I joined Reece on the window seat, pulling my knees up to my chin. Outside, a vast expanse of dark grounds spread under a blazing white moon. A fire roared and crackled in the hearth.

I snuck a glance at Reece's reflection in the tall window next to us. The moonlight played over his proud, handsome features, and I

41

drank in the comfort of having somebody near. I'd been on my own at the house since Sean left. I'd always been an extrovert. Usually, I would have been at the center of this party, dancing the night away, enjoying every moment. People gave me life. I didn't want to be alone, but I couldn't be around anyone tonight either. Anyone but this man. His solid, quiet presence and measured, rational manner soothed me somehow.

"Are you okay?" he asked.

"Fine," I lied. "What were you reading?"

He lifted his glasses and rubbed the bridge of his nose. "Oh. Nothing. It's a book of poems. You'd probably think it's boring."

"Maybe I like poetry."

"Do you?"

I found myself lost in his intense eyes. The back of my neck heated. No. Except, for some reason, I didn't want someone as smart as Reece to know that. Anyone else and I would have admitted it.

"Sure. Which one are you reading?"

He turned the book over in his hands. "Yeats."

Yeats? What the fuck? I'd heard of Keats. Not Yeats. I stayed silent.

He opened the book and cleared his throat. "How many loved your moments of glad grace / And loved your beauty with love false or true / But one man loved the pilgrim soul in you / And loved the sorrows of your changing face . . ."

I closed my eyes, savoring his low, gentle voice and the tender words that washed over me. A sudden ache pressed at my throat. "'Pilgrim soul'. That's beautiful."

I opened my eyes to find him watching me.

"Yes. I think so, too."

A thick silence swirled between us. We were silent for so long I could almost hear the wood in the ancient bookcases that lined the library creaking under the weight of their heavy tomes. I kept my face turned to the window and watched Reece's reflection in the dark glass. I had the strangest urge to shuffle closer across the window seat toward him, but I didn't dare.

He cleared his throat. "People say that Yeats wrote this for a lover he was infatuated with. Lots of people loved this woman for her external beauty, but he sees something deeper—the restlessness inside of her, the sorrow—and he promises that he will always love her, even as she grows old."

The crackling fire in the hearth grew loud. The moonlight dancing over his strong, proud profile entranced me. "What happened? Did they end up together?"

Reece's voice was as soft as a kiss. "No. I don't think so."

A sudden pain speared my heart. The words spilled out of me, unbidden. "All those years together and I don't think Sean ever cared for me like that. He treated me like I was another football trophy in his cabinet. I loved him . . . at the start, anyway." My voice wavered, and I took a breath. "Not anymore. Not for a long time. I don't know why I didn't have the balls to end things sooner. I don't know if anyone will ever love my 'pilgrim soul'."

Reece closed the book, his face still turned to the window. "Why would you think that?"

"Sean says I'm not easy to love. I'm loud. I'm stubborn. I work too many hours at the club. I'm easily irritated. Sean didn't want me to meet his parents because I have all these tattoos. Sean says my cooking is no good. My hair sticks up at the front. I have all these scars on my cheek. There are lots of things wrong with me—"

"I don't see a single thing wrong with you."

I couldn't help my derisive snort. I had to put a stop to this conversation, because something weird had happened to me. The stress of the party and the words of the poem had made my heart ache when I'd been working so hard to keep things together. If I

43

wasn't careful, I could burst into tears at any moment. "You're just being nice."

"No. I'm being honest. You're perfect. Just as you are."

My eyebrows shot up. Surprise at his admission held my lips glued shut. Reece thought I was perfect? The fire in the hearth grew loud again, the heat licking all over the bare skin of my arms. Reece opened his mouth as though he was going to say something, but closed it again. Unease flickered in his dark eyes, but he regained his composed, measured demeanor so swiftly that perhaps it had been imagined.

I spoke just to fill the awkward silence. "Whoever that woman was, she was an idiot. If someone wrote a poem like that about me, I wouldn't let him get away."

"Maybe there were reasons they couldn't be together." Reece kept his gaze fixed on the book he gripped in his lap. "Sometimes love is complicated."

"Love is the only thing in this world that isn't complicated. Whatever the problem, love will always win."

The reflection of flames from the fire danced in Reece's glasses. "Do you think so?"

"Yes. Even after everything that happened with Sean, I still believe in love. Don't you?"

A slight frown pulled at his brow, but only for a fraction of a second before he held out the book to me. "Here. Gabe doesn't mind me borrowing the books. Nobody reads anything in here. I'm sure he wouldn't mind if you want to read this."

His elegant fingers brushed mine as he passed me the book. A delicious tingle—hot and charged like electricity—sizzled up my bare arm at the light touch. My skin erupted with goosebumps. My shocked gaze met Reece's.

A cold wind rushed inside, making the fire hiss.

"Skylar?" The low, familiar voice drifted from the open doorway.

The book slipped from my fingers with a heavy thud. Sean stood watching us. I hadn't spoken to him since I'd kicked him out. A sudden flash of guilt at being caught alone with another man made my shoulder blades cold before a torrent of righteous indignation swept over me. No. Fuck that. I had no need to feel guilty. I could talk to whoever the hell I wanted. Sean didn't get a say anymore. I jumped down from the window seat and smoothed my dress.

Sean weaved toward us on unsteady legs. His overpowering reek of liquor hit my nose. How drunk was he? Had he said anything about me to the girls downstairs? Reece's hand brushed mine. He towered next to me, somber and silent.

Sean stumbled forward. "I've been looking all over for you. Who the hell is this guy?"

Warmth crept into my face.

Reece held out his hand to Sean. He kept his tone light and affable. "I'm Reece, the new team psychologist."

Sean glanced at Reece's hand but didn't shake it. Reece didn't need to be stuck in the middle of this. I needed to get Sean out of here before he caused a scene or said anything to my girls.

I turned to Reece. "I'm sorry I disturbed you. I'll see you on Monday."

I grabbed Sean's elbow and tried to pull him to the door, but he held firm, refusing to budge. His glassy eyes fixed on Reece and he squinted. "Don't I know you? It's you, isn't it? Reece Forrester. We went to the same school! We had some laughs, didn't we, mate? Remember that time the guys hung you up on your locker by the hood of your duffel coat? How long were you hanging there before the caretaker had to be called to get you down?"

Reece's lips pressed flat. "It's Forster, and yes, I remember."

"Forster. That's right. Weren't you railing the librarian? What was her name? Mrs. Franklin?" Sean let out a roar of drunken laughter. "Wasn't she about eighty years old?"

Reece stayed silent, his face a mask of pained tolerance.

My throat tightened. "Stop it, Sean."

Sean shook his head high, his drunken eyes wide with animation. He pointed his beer bottle at me. "Really, Skylar? You're into geeks now?"

I swallowed hard, trying not to flounder at Sean's ugly words. His behavior was always worse when he was drunk. I turned to Reece. "I'm so sorry about this."

"You're sorry?" Sean threw back his head with a nasty laugh. "What are you fucking sorry for? It's a free country. I can say whatever I want. It's just banter. Me and Forster are fine, aren't we?"

The silence turned chilly before Reece inclined his head in a nod. "Of course. We're fine."

I needed to get Sean moving. I gripped his elbow and tugged him, but he wouldn't budge. If I couldn't get him out of here, then I'd have to go and hope he followed. I needed to get him away from Reece before he said something else insulting. I moved past him. "I'm going home. You're drunk. I suggest you do the same, Sean. I don't have anything to say to you."

Sean gripped my wrist, holding me in place. He yanked me toward him. His beer breath hit my nose, making me recoil. "And where am I supposed to go? You've kicked me out of my fucking house."

Reece was at my side like lightning. "Let go of her."

I tried to shake Sean off, but he wrenched me in tighter.

Reece's voice was firm, and an icy confidence blazed in his level gaze. "I mean it. Let go now."

Sean released his grip so quickly I stumbled sideways. "What the fuck are you going to do about it, Forster?"

Reece stepped in front of me, shielding me. Alarm buzzed through my veins. Reece was taller, but Sean was a professional athlete made of solid muscle.

Reece met Sean's belligerent gaze. "You're angry. We can see that. Alcohol is impairing your judgment right now. This conversation would be better had tomorrow."

The mocking smirk vanished from Sean's lips to be replaced by something brutal. Sean glared at Reece like a dog about to rip him to shreds. "You want to get up in my face? You?"

My whole body tensed for a fight.

Reece held Sean's menacing gaze without flinching. "You're intoxicated, Sean. We can see that you're hurt and angry, but Skylar doesn't want to have this conversation with you now." Reece's cool, measured voice was as soothing as it was laced with authority. "She has made her boundary clear. It's time for you to respect that. When the alcohol wears off, the two of you can have a discussion. I can help you if you like. We could all sit down together and talk. This is neither the time nor the place."

Reece held up both his hands before tentatively putting one hand on Sean's shoulder. "You don't want to cause a scene. You're hurting. It's not good for the team or your career. It's been a long night. Why don't you let me give you a lift home? We'll stop on the way and get a coffee."

Sean looked at him in confusion, but he didn't back away. Reece pushed his glasses up his nose. He looked so unfazed. So elegantly composed. So many guys would have run a mile with someone talking to them the way Sean was, but Reece was here talking carefully and kindly, trying to defuse him. He'd taken control of the situation with calm assurance. It only made Sean look like a bigger idiot. My ex was a grenade, stuck so far up his own arse he couldn't see that he had blown up his own life. I'd never been surer that we had no future.

Sean blinked hard before his expression darkened and his drunken gaze slipped over me. He'd probably never encountered a man like Reece before. Kindness had confused him. He blinked a few more times, then stumbled backward. A couple of books fell off the shelves where his broad back hit the bookcase.

"Forget it. You're not worth it, Skylar. There's something wrong with you, anyway. It's not me, you know. It's you. You're frigid or something . . . it's not normal. Of course I'm going to look elsewhere."

Icy shame shot through my system. I did my best to stand tall despite my embarrassment.

Sean shook his head and let out a bitter, hollow laugh. "Fuck you, Forster. You're welcome to her. You deserve each other."

My heart pounded. White noise roared in my ears. Sean sauntered toward the door, and I wanted to run after him and throw myself on his back and drag him to the ground, but shock froze me in place. I held my tears rigidly in check.

There's something wrong with you.

Not good enough.

Chapter 7

REECE

Skylar's scent of watermelon perfume, liquor, and lime filled my car. The night flashed by outside, but still she hadn't said a word. I stole a glance at her, noting her set jaw and her mouth tight with frustration.

Skylar's words rattled through the stillness. "Sean bullied you in school?"

"He bullied everyone."

A memory flashed through my mind.

Books surrounded me on the floor of the school cafeteria. Sean's laughter rang harsh in my ears, even as he disappeared around the corner with his sycophants. Pain burned in my ribs from his sly punch. A couple of students sidestepped me before Skylar dropped in front of me.

She picked up my glasses from the floor. "Are you okay? What happened?"

My neck warmed with embarrassment. "Nothing. I slipped. Ketchup on the floor . . ."

I held out my hand to take my glasses back, but her warm fingers brushed my face as she propped them back in position on my nose. My heart almost stopped beating. Her beautiful face came into sharp focus.

"And I thought the salmonella-burgers were the most dangerous things here." She smiled and held out a hand to haul me back to my feet. *"Be careful, yeah?"*

Everyone had stepped over me, but Skylar had stopped to help. Not that she remembered. This moment of compassion had burned into my brain. It had made me fall for her so hard, but I'd never even made it onto her radar.

Skylar cleared her throat. "I'm sorry about Sean."

"No apology necessary. You're not responsible for someone else's behavior."

It didn't look like Sean had changed. I'd worked with plenty of abusers. Usually, they'd been hurt and they were acting from a wounded place. Still, even if I could find empathy, I wasn't a robot. Sean Wallace had made my teenage life hell. He'd made those choices. It wasn't easy to forgive. The truth was that sometimes things weren't that deep—some people just weren't that nice or kind.

Skylar's hands curled into fists on her lap. "I won't tolerate bullying in the team. I hate it. If I'd have known in school what he was doing . . ."

Her head dropped and she fiddled with the piercing in her nose. I kept my eyes fixed on the road, giving her space to talk.

"I'm not expecting sympathy. I've been an idiot for too long. Deep down, I knew that he was messing around with other girls. Most of the guys on the team are. I just hoped he'd be different." She turned her face to the passenger window and spoke in a quiet voice. "I don't know what happened to me. It's like I got bent out of shape. I used to be so confident, but lately Sean has me questioning everything about myself all the time. Whenever I asked him if he was seeing someone else, he made me feel stupid for even suspecting him. The drinking had gotten worse. The names he calls me . . . the way he makes me feel . . ."

The tremor in her voice made me steal another glance at her. Her profile was proud and sad in the dim light of the car. My heart hammered foolishly. I wrenched myself away from my ridiculous preoccupation with her beautiful face so I wouldn't crash the car.

"We've been together since school. He's all I've known. Sometimes I feel like . . . like . . . I'm a spoon . . . and a spoon isn't supposed to bend, but over time the metal got weak, and I shouldn't be a different shape, but I am. I was a dessert spoon and now I'm just a . . . teaspoon." The sadness in her voice made my heart contract. "And I'm talking absolute nonsense, ignore me."

She kept her head turned away.

"No. I get it. Sometimes we bend so much to accommodate another person. It's not healthy when that happens, but you can find your way back. You can straighten the spoon back to how it's supposed to be, and you might find you can be an even better spoon that you didn't even know about, like a . . . soup spoon."

She laughed. "You ran with the weird spoon thing."

Amusement touched the corners of my mouth, but I kept my face level. "I like it. I might use it myself."

"What about you? Do you have anyone special in your life?" She dropped the question tentatively. I'd never self-disclose that information with a client, but this was a strange gray area. We were colleagues, certainly, but was she a client? The conversations we'd had felt like therapeutic ones. She'd sat in my office and opened up to me about her breakup. Trusted me with confidentiality. I'd been employed as a psychologist to help this team. This had to be a professional relationship. Anything else would be unethical.

Better to change the subject. I cleared my throat. "How much further to your house?"

She glanced at my hands wrapped around the steering wheel and turned her face away. "Not far. Ten minutes."

Silence swirled between us and made my pulse pound.

"You should be careful with the girls on the team. Everybody will be falling over themselves vying for your attention if they think you're single. Probably even if they don't."

A wry smile pulled at my lips. "The entire Calverdale United men's team is in that building. I saw all the muscles in that gym. I'm sure my arrival won't ruffle too many feathers."

She shot me a playful glance. "Oh no. Feathers are ruffled, I can assure you."

Was Skylar Marshall flirting with me? Unlikely. She'd never even known I was alive at school, and she'd been dating a man who was so good-looking he was splashed all over billboards throughout the country. Even if there was a possibility that she was, I'd have to put a stop to it. Skylar might have believed love wasn't complicated, but I couldn't think of anything more problematic than my infatuation with this woman. No matter how I tried to get rid of these feelings, I couldn't. It had always made me feel out of control.

The silence thickened until Skylar craned her neck. "This is my house. Just by this lamppost."

Skylar and Sean's house loomed enormous and imposing in front of us. It shouldn't have surprised me that they lived in such a huge place. They were football royalty. I kept my gaze on the house, fighting not to stare at her face. Something about the little wrinkle she got between her eyebrows when she was thinking mesmerized me. Her purple ankle boots matched her wavy purple hair, and colorful ink graced the milky skin of her shoulders and arms. Skylar had always had a kooky offbeat style. At school, her art folder had been covered with song lyrics and intricate doodles. I'd spent hours during lessons studying them, wondering what they all meant.

She swept her hair over her inked shoulder. Her tongue traced out to lick her candy-pink lips and my mind filled with dirty thoughts. What would it be like to kiss her? To hike that dress above her hips and drive into her? To taste her?

Stop. Absolutely not. Get a grip.

What was wrong with me? Maybe my siblings were right. I'd gone too long without sex. I had needs. There was no shame in admitting that. Still, not with this woman. It wouldn't be right.

"Thanks for the lift."

"No problem."

She smoothed her dress over her powerful, toned thighs and it made my heart beat too hard. This was basic psychology. I wanted what I couldn't have. I'd wanted this woman for so long, but now I was a grown man. This wasn't a big deal. Attraction was just a feeling, and I could put it to one side and work with her. Of course I could. I wasn't a lizard or a silverback driven only by the urge to fuck. I didn't have to lose my head over this.

I am in control.

She cleared her throat and slid me a tentative glance. "Would you like to come inside?"

Yes. More than anything.

No. No. Definitely no. Oh fuck.

The silence thickened. She was so beautiful. She'd always been so beautiful. A dizzying current of desire raced through me, and my mind filled with more unwelcome thoughts. *My hands sliding her dress off her shoulders, down her strong, inked arms. Pulling her onto my lap. Exploring the milky skin of her toned thighs with my lips. The soft close of that pretty, warm mouth around my . . .*

"Just for a coffee or . . ."

The rough edge to her voice made my heart pound. My teenage dreams had been full of this scenario. A shot with Skylar Marshall. My fourteen-year-old self would have killed me in this moment. I'd already narrowly avoided swearing my undying love to her in that library. The way she'd looked on that window seat had nearly been my undoing. The moonlight had flashed silver streaks in her lilac hair and the sadness around her beautiful eyes had bewitched me. How could she not know that she was so easy to long for?

She chewed her lip and raised a questioning eyebrow.

I hesitated, choosing my words. It would be a terrible idea. I couldn't go there with a colleague and certainly not one I'd been counseling. Skylar was going through a bad breakup. She needed space to clear her head, not a rebound guy. This was on me to do the right thing to protect both of us.

I took a breath and turned my face to the window. "No. Thank you."

"Are you sure?"

Nope.

"Yes. I'm sure."

She chewed her lip. "Right. No problem."

Her voice sounded breezy, but from the corner of my eye I caught the hurt and disappointment that darkened her beautiful face. My heart ached. The last thing I wanted to do was make her feel bad. Still, this was better in the long run. She hurried out of the car. I watched her go into her house before I pressed my forehead to the cold steering wheel and took deep breaths.

I am in control.

Definitely. Completely. Without question. I am in control.

Chapter 8

SKYLAR

Every muscle sang with pain. My nerves crackled with electricity. Eighty-nine minutes of charging around a pitch, and now everything depended on one goal. If I scored, we'd win the match. One step closer to promotion to the Women's Super League. If I missed . . .

Don't think like that.

A captain can't miss.

The keeper patted her gloved hands together. We eyed each other from twelve yards apart—enemies with fingers twitching at our hips, ready to draw our guns. She'd shoot me dead if I didn't shoot her first. I knew Bethany Lawrence's stats. The club had spent a fortune on analyzing the opposition. That was one of the perks of being owned by a billionaire who was married to our striker—an endless supply of cash on anything that might make the team better. Gabe Rivers had thrown so much money at this club, we'd have to work hard *not* to get promoted at the end of the season.

Still, it was possible to screw it up. Gabe could buy most things, but not luck. And we'd had a lot of bad luck the past few matches. Nine times out of ten, Bethany Lawrence would dive left.

That's what the data said. The best bet was to place the ball in the top-right corner.

Maybe she'd studied my stats too. It wouldn't help. Every time I took a penalty, I did something different. That was the key. Never show your hand. Don't be predictable. Don't give the fuckers anything to study. I caught Bethany's eye and then I looked purposefully at each goalpost.

Do you see that, Bethany Lawrence? Predict that.

A wild laugh rose up in me. Adrenaline burst hotly through my system, giving me an odd sense of delirium. My heart thundered in my ears. Everything was too loud and too sharp. Every part of my body tense. My teammates stood at my back. I couldn't look at them. This was too important to fail. This wasn't for me. It was for them. I owed them this. They'd followed me into battle, and now it was my time to deal a killing blow.

I just had to aim it right. Not too close to the post.

Do you know my stats, Bethany Lawrence?

Twenty out of twenty attempts on goal this season.

I never miss.

The sweat that drenched my body left my skin with racing chills as it evaporated. My breath came so hot and sharp, I could almost taste my lungs. I straightened my socks over my shin pads, taking my time, making a show of it. Bethany Lawrence always went left. The data didn't lie. Confusion clouded my brain.

Or was it right?

Shit.

"You've got this, Skylar." A shout drifted from the sidelines.

A few cheers rang out. Then clapping. Then stomping. I scanned the sparse stands. Among the handful of tense faces, my gaze found Sean. It had been a week since he'd turned up drunk at Gabe's party. Since I'd thrown myself so desperately at another man, only to be rejected.

There's something wrong with you.

Sean wore a bulky puffer jacket; his blond head was bowed to his phone. He wasn't even watching, probably too busy sliding into the DMs of another model on Instagram.

You know what it's like. They message me first.

A cacophony of sound screamed in my ears. I couldn't block it out—the clapping, the stomping feet, the howling wind. How would I even be able to hear the bloody whistle?

Do you know my stats, Sean?

One heart, broken.

My breath came in sharp, hot gasps as though I'd left the stadium entirely and floated up into the atmosphere, where the air was too thin. I scanned the sideline again and my eyes locked with Reece Forster's. His dark peacoat flapped in the breeze, but he stood perfectly still and composed next to Gabe Rivers. So poised. So in control. He'd turned me down. Of course he had. He'd seemed into me in the library, but then he'd heard everything Sean had said about me and it had put him off.

Bethany Lawrence always dove left. She tensed, ready to go. Ready to pull her pistol and take her shot. Was that a lean to the right? No. She'd go left. She always went left. A niggling sense of doubt twisted my gut. I pushed it down. The whistle ricocheted in my head like a starter's pistol. My body flinched. I took a run-up. My foot skidded on wet grass. With every ounce of strength, I aimed for the top-right corner.

For the first time, Bethany Lawrence dove right.

◆ ◆ ◆

The bathroom door swung open. Claire strode in, her neat silvery blonde bob swinging around her jaw. My shoulders clenched. Great. Everybody had gone home. I couldn't stand any more sympathetic smiles or pats on the back, especially not from my boss. I just wanted to be alone.

Claire's voice was more gentle than usual. "Do you want to talk about it, Marshall?"

The back of my neck itched with embarrassment. I braced my hands on the cool ceramic sink.

Claire's voice was tentative. "It was a good game. You did your best. It's not over yet."

"I never miss. It's over. Everything we've worked for . . ."

"The Rovers lost. They've gone down two points. We're still in with a chance. If we can win the next two games and if City loses two matches, then we can make it to the top of the league table."

"That's a lot of ifs."

Her face lit with determination. "But we're not out yet. We can still do this. It's not over until it's over."

No, but it just got a hell of a lot harder.

I splashed cold water on my puffy eyes. Claire flashed me a tight smile and offered me a paper towel. I drew a breath. She was right. A small flicker of relief warmed me. We still had a chance. The odds were slim, but while breath moved in my body, I wouldn't stop fighting for this. I'd made a promise to take this team to the top, and I'd do my best to keep that promise, even if I was falling apart.

Claire's gaze dropped to my fingers, which were wrapped so tightly around the basin my knuckles were white. I clasped my hands behind my back. A couple of purple strands had escaped my ponytail and I scraped them back. Sean's voice rang in my head.

Do better with your roots. You can tell everything you need to know about a person from the state of their hair.

Staring at myself then in the mirror, it hit me. All I could see was the things Sean thought were wrong with me: the kink in my hair that would never lie flat, my pale skin, and the patch on my cheek that had scarred after my teenage bouts of acne. It didn't matter how much concealer I put on, I knew the imperfections were there.

Heat pressed behind my eyes again and I turned my face away. I couldn't risk Claire revealing to Gabe Rivers that she'd found me weeping in the toilets. It was bad enough that she'd found me like this. What if they put someone else in charge? Lana was always there, waiting in the wings. What if they took me off the team entirely? Oh God. Is that why they'd brought a psychologist in? Were Claire and Gabe worried I was losing it?

Claire shot me a glance. "Has Evan Lewis spoken to you yet?"

"Evan Lewis?"

"He's a friend of Gabe's. He owns the LA Halos."

The memory drifted back. He'd tried to talk to me at Gabe's party before I'd run away.

Claire smoothed a perfect brow in the mirror. "Just a heads-up, but there might be a transfer deal in the pipeline if you're interested. He's been asking a lot of questions."

My heart hammered. Why was she telling me this now? She was sowing the seeds to try and get rid of me. That was the last thing I wanted. I had to shut this down.

"You want to transfer me?"

Claire watched me with a solemn expression before she nodded. "If it's what you want."

"No way." I gave a snort of derision. "No way would I leave this team. I'm the captain. This isn't even up for debate."

She watched me for a minute before she flashed me another tight smile. "Maybe this isn't the right time to talk about it. It was tough out there. You know I'm here. If you ever want to talk about anything . . . anything at all."

"I'm fine," I lied. "Absolutely fine."

Chapter 9

REECE

Skylar fiddled with the silver bar in her eyebrow. I tried to force my gaze to her eyes, but I couldn't stop myself from drinking her in. Purple leggings clung to her strong, toned legs and perfect backside. Her cheeks were pink and her purple hair loose and damp, as though she'd just stepped out of the shower. Thoughts of her naked, lathering herself with soap, scrubbing the mud from her beautiful body, forced themselves into my mind.

I dragged my attention back to her face. I had no business thinking about her undressed or noticing the color of her leggings or the perfection inherent in every delicious inch of her body. This was better as a professional therapeutic relationship, even if my brain still wanted to act like a horny fourteen-year-old.

She peered over my shoulder into my office. "Are you busy?"

"Not busy. Come in. How are you feeling?"

"I don't even know where to start." She dropped into a chair and held her head in her hands. "I might have just lost us the chance of promotion. We've worked so hard all season, and I fucked it up."

I closed the door and settled in the chair across from her. "I saw you doing your best under enormous pressure. You didn't *fuck* anything up."

She gave a small snorting laugh.

"Did I say something amusing?"

She smoothed her face. "It's funny when you swear, like hearing your dad or a teacher swear."

Is that how she thought of me? Hardly flattering, but then I supposed I was probably more like someone's dad than I was like Sean Wallace.

"What the fuck is wrong with me, Reece? I never miss. I don't panic. Nothing like that has ever happened to me before. I couldn't think straight. I just felt so . . . stressed. I usually feel confident taking penalties."

"Nothing's wrong with you. Our emotions are messages. Your body is communicating something. You're under a lot of pressure right now in your professional and personal life."

She lifted her head and her pretty eyes flashed with fire. "It's nothing I can't handle. I'm not scared of anything on the pitch. It wasn't the penalty. A captain needs to be good under pressure. We're so close to success and I'm fucking everything up. What if it happens again? What do I do now?"

"You're not fucking anything up. There are ways to manage stress. Mindfulness. Creative activities. Talking therapy . . ."

She sunk her head into her hands. "No. I haven't got time for fucking meditation and yoga. This is my team. They need me now. Everything is on the line."

"If you don't make time, then your feelings will make themselves heard however they can. You can see they won't always choose the most convenient times."

She shook her head. "Fuck! We're done for then, aren't we? No promotion. It's over."

"I thought you still had another chance at promotion?"

"We do, but it's not in our hands anymore. We need to win the next two games, and we need City to lose both of theirs."

"So you still have a chance?"

"City never lose. Three wins would have made us masters of our own fate. Now, it's out of our control." Her hands clenched into tight fists at her sides, her mouth set tight and grim. "Every woman on the team has put so much into this. This is everything to me. It's all that matters." She raked her fingers through her damp lilac hair, pulling it high and letting it fall. "This can't be happening to me right now. It just can't. I'm the captain. Everybody is relying on me to get us there."

Her chin set in a stubborn line. Everybody liked to win, but for Skylar this was all or nothing. The real question was why this mattered so much.

"It sounds like a lot of pressure."

"I can handle it."

"What would it mean to you if you didn't get promoted?"

Her brows drew downward in a frown. "That's not something I think about. We have to be the best."

"What happens if you're not the best?"

A touch of uncertainty flickered in her proud expression. I leaned into the silence until it took on its own energy and pulsed around us.

"My brothers all play football. They wouldn't let me play with them when I was younger, even though I begged them. Mum wanted me to be a dancer. She dragged me to these awful tap-dancing lessons until I threw a fit. Dad was the only one who took me seriously. He took me to training every weeknight. I was the only girl in the whole region good enough to play with the boys in the junior league. People took me seriously then."

Ah. So, she'd spent her early years fighting to be taken seriously as a footballer. Fighting to be good enough to play with the men. Always fighting to be the best. No wonder she put so much pressure on herself. It's hard to believe you're good enough when you're always striving to be better.

She rubbed her eyes and her shoulders slumped. "Football is all I ever wanted. Men don't have to prove themselves like this. I still feel like I'm fighting all the time."

I kept my tone soft, seeing if I could offer her a different way of thinking. "It sounds exhausting. Failure is a part of life. We win some and we lose some. Sometimes you're going to miss a goal."

"Exhausting, yes." She sank deeper into the chair. "But a captain shouldn't miss a penalty like that."

"Even captains miss sometimes. What if you don't have to be perfect? What if you're good enough as you are?"

She tilted her chin. "Do you think I'm good enough?"

I hesitated. The question had caught me off guard. Of course she was good enough. Skylar Marshall was perfect. As a professional, I needed to help her explore where her insecurities had taken root and help her work with them. As a man, I wanted to show her the truth. To tell her she was so beautiful it made me ache. To worship her body and leave no doubt in her mind that every inch of her was divine.

Stop. Inappropriate. She's sitting in your therapy chair.

Before I could think of a reply, she spoke again. "I was never good enough for Sean. His parents hated me. He was embarrassed to have me over to their house."

Despite her prideful dignity, a pensive shimmer lurked in the shadows under her eyes. "But fuck Sean." She fixed her gaze on her hands. "It wasn't good between us. It hasn't been for a long time. Sean's right, anyway. There is something wrong with me."

Silence swirled around us. She sniffed and I nudged a box of tissues across the table toward her.

"I can't . . . It's not something I can talk about with you. You're a man, and you're so . . ." Her eyes darted away. "It doesn't matter."

Sean's nasty words from the party drifted to mind.

It's not me, it's you.

If it was something intimate, then she might feel more comfortable talking to a woman. I fought not to let my gaze linger too long on her beautiful mouth. I'd fantasized so many nights as a teenager about kissing those perfect, pouty lips. My jaw tensed but I kept my expression level. What was wrong with me? Skylar was going through a rough patch—wading her way through a bad breakup, opening up, making herself vulnerable. If I was going to keep things professional and help her, it was my responsibility to maintain a boundary.

I'd thought my job here would be discussing mindset, not relationship issues and anxiety. If I couldn't manage these feelings, I'd have to stop seeing her like this in my office. Skylar needed time and room to find a way through this—a safe space. Not this.

She swallowed and darted a glance up into my eyes. "Anyway, I've taken up too much of your time. I'd better go."

"You don't have to go. I'm here anytime."

She moved to the door. I followed. We both reached for the door handle at the same time. Her hand wrapped around mine. Warmth shot up my wrist at her soft touch. I couldn't stop my gaze from dropping to her parted lips. Why was I standing so close to her?

She tilted her chin, a look of uncertainty in her eyes. "So, your door is still always open to the captain?"

She was so close I could feel the heat of her beautiful, toned body. My heart pounded. "My door is open to everyone on the team."

But every time someone walks through the door, I'm hoping it's you.

God. She was absolutely stunning to look at this close up. A patch of freckles sprinkled her cute nose and flecks of green dotted her bright blue eyes. All those tattoos and piercings made her milky flesh a divine, wild canvas. The yellow roses tracing her collarbone were exquisite. A turquoise and gold bird swooped down into the V of her shirt, and I had the most disturbing urge to lick it. An unwelcome stiffening in my trousers made me take a sharp breath.

Think of unsexy things.

Get a grip.

I'm in control.

Her gaze dropped to the bulge in my trousers and her eyebrows shot up. Heat swept the back of my neck.

Oh God.

I stepped back abruptly. I had to get her out of here. Shame made my teeth itch. A look of hurt confusion crossed her face as I edged her lightly out of the room. I closed the door behind her and pressed my back against it. She'd seen it. There was no way she couldn't have seen that I was aroused. Embarrassment ground in my gut. Memories of sitting at the desk next to her all those years ago drifted to mind. It had been the same then. I couldn't even be in her presence without the blood rushing downward. I'd been a horny teenager then. Now, I had no excuse.

A soft knock sounded on the door. "Reece? I think I might have left my hoodie in there."

I darted my gaze to the chair where the purple garment sat, neatly folded.

I couldn't have her back in here. "No. I don't think so."

"I'm pretty sure I was wearing it."

My heart pounded at the lie. "Yes. Sorry. Maybe. I'll look for it. It's just I have another . . . appointment to get ready for."

And a raging boner to take care of.

A pause. "You're sure I can't just come in and grab it?"

My whole body felt hot. She must have thought this was so weird. "Not right now."

"Okay. Well . . . I'll see you around. Let me know if the hoodie turns up."

My heart pounded, but I tried to keep my voice level. "I will. Goodbye, Skylar."

I waited for the sound of her retreating footsteps before I closed the blinds and locked my office door. My skin crackled with hot, uncomfortable need. I sank down into the chair that was still warm from her body. I picked up the hoodie, pressing the soft fabric to my nose and inhaling her crisp scent of watermelon perfume and fresh turf. I closed my eyes and pictured her beautiful face. What the hell was wrong with me? This woman made me feral. I couldn't stand another minute without the release. Shame ground in my gut, but I couldn't spend all day in this state. With trembling fingers, I undid my trousers and yanked them down. A groan of relief slipped from my lips as I wrapped my hand around my shaft.

I am in control.

Completely. Totally. Unquestionably. In control.

Chapter 10

REECE

The next morning, I went to see Mum in the annex. She pulled a face when I put the tea tray on the side table next to her. "You forgot the sugar."

"Remember what the doctor said?"

Mum grimaced and put the cup down with unsteady fingers. "I can't drink tea without sugar."

"It's no good for your diabetes. We've been through this. Uncontrolled blood sugar increases the risk of cardiovascular disease."

Mum raised an unconvinced eyebrow. "It's one sugar. I still need to live my life, Reece."

A muscle tensed in my jaw. Mum never listened to me. I didn't want to fight over a spoonful of sugar either, I just worried about her. I slid a couple of Frankie's books into the bookcase and gathered up some of Elliot's empty protein shakes. "Why does no one pick up after themselves?"

Mum sighed. "Please, Reece. Sit. Just for a minute. I'm exhausted just watching you."

I dropped into the armchair opposite her.

Mum watched me with shrewd eyes. "Relax. Take a breath. The world isn't going to fall apart because you sit down."

The chattering trills of the birds filtered in through the open window. A restless energy crawled under my skin. I'd lost control in my office. I'd acted like an animal. Like something dirty and wild. I'd lied about the hoodie. Poor Skylar must have thought she'd gone mad. Closing my eyes, I took a breath. A cool breeze caressed my face. I'd fallen out of my meditation habit. I needed to get back into it. Nothing kept me as calm.

I opened my eyes to find Mum watching me. "Frankie says she has a friend she wants to set you up with."

"I'm not talking about my love life with you."

Mum kept a bland, innocent tone, but her eyes were speculative. "I wonder when you're going to get back out there and join in. You've put your life on hold for a long time. Things ended so quickly with Megan. If you ever wanted to talk about that—"

"There's nothing to talk about, but thank you."

A twinkle gleamed in her eye. "Nothing to talk about? Now you've really caught my attention."

Mum had worked as a psychotherapist her whole life. She'd still be working at the addiction clinic if it hadn't been for the stroke. Nothing got past her, and now she had nothing better to do than analyze her family. I knew the urge. I'd spent many a happy hour pondering Frankie's shopping addiction and Elliot's revolving door of women. Still, Mum had enough on her plate without my problems.

Mum watched me. "How's the new job going? I hope it's slowed you down. You were working every hour of the day at that hospital. There's more to life, Reece. You're a young, single man . . ."

"I can make you a coffee if the tea is a problem."

She chuckled and pursed her lips. "Deflection. Wonderful. I'm touching a nerve, then?"

"It's 9 o'clock on a Monday morning. I thought we were having breakfast, not therapy."

"This isn't therapy." She sipped her tea and gave me a faux-sweet smile. "You can't afford me."

I laughed, but it felt hollow. Her gaze drifted down to my hands. My palms were red. I'd spent last night disinfecting every pan in the kitchen to calm myself down after my little meltdown in my office.

"Are you going to tell me what's wrong?"

I turned my face away. In the past, I would have talked to Mum about my problems, but not now. The last thing I wanted to do was add to her burden. She was doing so well since she'd come home, but the shadow of her ill health always hung over us. "Nothing's wrong."

She stilled, watching me from behind chunky, white-framed glasses. "It's not me, is it? You don't need to worry about me. The doctor was pleased with me yesterday. He was a nice young man. I thought he was going to give me a sticker."

"It's not you."

"Good, because I'm doing well. I feel good, but I'm bored. Give me something else to think about."

I sighed. May as well take the opportunity to pick Mum's brains. I didn't have to make it too personal. "Fine. Let's have an ethical debate."

"Go on."

"Hypothetically speaking, how would you handle a situation where you might develop . . . feelings toward a client?"

Mum's eyebrows rose a fraction. I regretted the question instantly. It had been clumsy and awkward.

"Feelings?"

"Attraction." My collar suddenly felt too tight. I unfastened the top button. "Hypothetically speaking, of course."

Mum stared at me for a moment longer than was comfortable before she cleared her throat. "Attraction is a feeling like any other. The therapeutic relationship can be intense. If you're doing it right, you're making a connection. We're not robots. But any kind of romantic relationship would be deeply unethical and harmful to the patient—"

"Of course. I know that."

Birdsong drifted through the window into the silence. I kept my expression level under her scrutiny. "And what about an ex-patient? If you saw somebody as a patient, and then you wanted to start a relationship with them. How long would you wait? Hypothetically speaking . . ."

Mum's brow lifted even higher before she smoothed it. "There are guidelines. Some people say after a year, maybe two years. Some people say it's always wrong. Once a client, always a client."

"Right. Of course. It's always wrong. And what would you say? Just out of interest . . ."

She studied my face for too long before she frowned. "What is this all about, Reece? You know you can talk to me. Is something going on? You had feelings for a patient at the hospital? It happens sometimes. It's perfectly natural. I'm not going to judge you. The most important thing is that you recognize it, and deal with it."

"Me? No. God. No. Not a patient at the hospital. It's not that. It's just . . . I've been talking to this woman at the football club. She's going through a rough breakup. She's opening up to me. I get the impression she doesn't do that often."

Mum frowned. "A breakup? I thought you were doing sports psychology?"

"Yes. I am, but this isn't formal. We've had a couple of conversations in my office. It happened . . . spontaneously, but it feels like therapeutic conversations. I'm trying to help her."

Mum studied my face too intently with those piercing green eyes. The slight upturn of her lips was the perfect noncommittal smile designed to invite me to say more. God. Was I this annoying when I was in the other chair?

I sighed. "Whatever you want to say, just say it."

"You seem agitated. Why?"

I raked a hand through my hair. "Who's getting agitated? I'm not agitated. I just . . . When this woman was leaving my office, her hand brushed against mine and it made me feel . . ."

Feral.

I hesitated, choosing my words. I didn't want to talk to Mum about something so intimate. Why on earth had I even let myself get dragged into this conversation? Mum was too good at this. She'd out-therapized me.

She cocked her head, studying me. "It made you feel what?"

I could be honest about it, even if this was a conversation I'd rather not be having with my mother. "Turned on."

Mum stirred her tea with a light tinkling sound. "Okay. And that's a problem, why?"

"Because she's sitting in my therapy chair pouring her heart out."

"Is she your client?"

"Not exactly, but I want to help her. She hasn't told anyone else about her problems apart from me. She trusts me."

Mum blew steam from the top of her teacup and glanced at me over the rim. "It's a straightforward question, Reece. She either is or she isn't your client. Have you signed a client agreement?"

"No."

"Does she think you're doing therapy together?"

"No."

"Then she's not your client."

"We work together. She's sitting in my chair, and she's telling me personal things. She's asking my advice. It feels like I'm counseling her."

Mum put her teacup down and waved a dismissive hand. "So, maybe she's an over-sharer, and you're a good listener. Have the conversation next time you see her. If it feels weird for you then stop having conversations in your office. Go somewhere else. Ask her out for a date if you want to get to know each other."

A panicked feeling made my shoulders tense. Ask Skylar Marshall out on a date? I'd assumed Mum would give me sensible advice, but instead she was encouraging me in something that wasn't a good idea. I tried to keep my tone level, despite my surprise. "A date?"

A smile pulled at her lips. "Yes. A date. You know. You go and do something fun together. Take her out for dinner or to see a movie. I'm sure you can think of something."

"Yes. I'm familiar with the concept of a date."

There was no planet where I asked Skylar Marshall out on a date and she said yes. She wasn't just the most popular girl in school anymore, she was a professional athlete, a bona fide celebrity.

"It's not that easy," I said.

"Isn't it?"

No, because I wanted to do the best for Skylar. She needed a friend, not a guy so desperate for her he couldn't even control himself in her presence. It wasn't appropriate under the circumstances. Besides, where would I even take Skylar Marshall on a date? If she walked into any restaurant, she'd be immediately swept off into the VIP area. I'd seen it happen with Gabe and Miri so many times. If she wanted to see a movie, she could just walk the red carpet at a premiere. Her ex-boyfriend was a professional athlete who regularly graced the cover of magazines. No. It was an impossibility even without all of the ethical stuff.

"I didn't think you'd be so . . . flippant with an ethical dilemma."

"I would never be flippant about that. A relationship with a client would be terribly unethical and damaging. There's not a lot you can do wrong in this business apart from sleeping with the clients, but I don't think that's your problem here."

"She's confiding in me, and I'm trying to help her. Her ex is trouble. She's struggling with her confidence. This feels like therapy."

Mum's gaze pierced me. "Fine. So, maybe she needs to do some work before she has another relationship. Maybe this isn't the right time for you to get involved with her romantically, but that's not about ethics. I know you, Reece. I know that you're hard on yourself. You're principled. You have high standards of what is right and wrong. All of these are good qualities."

"I'm trying to do the right thing by her. The thing is, we have a . . . history. I knew I would be seeing her, and that it would trigger certain . . . feelings. I thought we'd just be keeping things light: mindset and confidence building. I didn't realize we'd be spending so much time together talking about personal things. I had a kind of a . . . crush on her at school."

Mum pressed her lips, thoughtfully, as though I'd just delivered some huge bombshell. So what? I'd had a crush. It didn't mean anything. It was a long time ago, and we were both adults now. The silence stretched. Fine. We could sit like this forever. I wouldn't let my own mother use silence as a weapon against me. That was my job.

Mum spoke first. "A crush is fun. The butterflies in the chest. A little glimpse that brightens the day. It's a very safe place when we love from afar."

An uncomfortable feeling stirred inside, one I didn't care to interrogate deeper. I cast an eye over Mum's bookshelf. "Do you need me to bring you some more books? I can pop to the bookshop later."

"Deflection again. Interesting."

"It was a teenage crush. Not a big deal."

"The best thing about a crush is that there is no pressure. No chance of letting anyone close. No chance of being hurt."

This is why you didn't do therapy with your own relatives. I'd had enough of this conversation. I was trying not to burden Mum, and I'd ended up telling her more than I'd meant to.

"I'd better get on with it." I smoothed the wrinkles from the little lace covers on the arms of the chair and stood. "I want to get the house straight before the twins come home. I'll pop to the bookshop for you later."

Mum's gaze traveled over my face, searching my eyes. "You don't want to talk about it. I understand, but this is all very intriguing." She offered me a faint smile. "You're a nurturer. You take care of people, your family, your clients. You put everyone else's needs before your own. This is your pattern. You're a giver, but in a relationship you need to be prepared to receive, too. You must let people in, not find barriers to keep them out."

The uncomfortable feeling inside grew tighter. "I'm not finding barriers."

She grabbed my hand with her smooth palm, holding me in place. "You're very lovable, Reece. You have a lot of wonderful qualities. Don't forget that. You're worthy of love."

I thought about pasting a smile onto my face, but I didn't have the energy. A pulse beat in my temple and I closed my eyes. I'd let things slip with Skylar. Even if she wasn't my client, she was going through a lot and she needed a friend. I could be her friend. This wasn't about barriers. It was about doing the right thing. Maybe Skylar wasn't officially my client, but our conversations had felt therapeutic, and it had crossed a boundary.

I met Mum's solid gaze and lifted a sardonic eyebrow. "This isn't therapy. You can stop therapizing me now."

"I'm not. I'm your mum. I'm just mumming you." She patted my hand and gave me a wry smile. "Anyway, it's not therapy if you don't sign an agreement. Just remember, try not to be so hard on yourself all the time."

"I shouldn't have even said anything." I busied myself clearing up the cups and saucers. "We really need to get you well enough to go back to work. Your talents are wasted here."

Chapter 11

SKYLAR

In the dressing room, Lana leaned into me. Her sweat and grass scent filled my nose. "I've got some takers on the bet. Marie, Jess, Shannon, and Carmel are all in."

"What bet?"

"Who can get there first with the hot doctor. We've got a hundred quid in the pot."

Oh, for goodness' sake. Was she still banging that drum? I pulled my filthy T-shirt over my head. My legs burned with exhaustion from training and wet mud clung to every inch of my body. I had no time for bullshit. I just wanted to get in the shower.

"It's a stupid idea. Completely unprofessional. It needs to stop. He's nice. Leave him alone."

A teasing smile flitted across Lana's lips. "*Nice?* Is the bet won already? Poor Sean. Does he know?"

The back of my neck heated. "This is so unprofessional. You should be focusing on the pitch. You know this is sexual harassment? He's here to do a job. If Claire or Gabe knew . . ."

She waved a dismissive hand. "Don't be a spoilsport. It's just a bit of fun. Everyone is stressed and wound up about the match tomorrow. We're just blowing off steam. Anyway, I'm sure he'd be up for it. Look what I found . . ."

Lana pulled out her phone and scrolled to a dating app. She held the phone low, shielding the screen with her hand. She swiped through a couple of photos of a ripped guy working out at the gym. A black T-shirt clung to his tall, muscular frame and his dark hair was damp with sweat and gloriously disheveled as he lifted weights in front of a mirror.

"Dr. Straitlace is looking for a hookup." Lana raised an amused eyebrow and tapped a fingernail on the screen. "He claims to be a geek on the street and a freak in the sheets."

My brain made the connection. This was Reece? I hadn't recognized him without his glasses. I put a hand over my mouth to smother my startled chuckle. What the hell was this? *No strings fun? A love doctor here to set hearts pumping?* I'd never have expected him to have such a ridiculous dating profile. My gaze drifted back down to his muscular biceps and his strong, toned legs in shorts. He might have looked buttoned up at work, but he had a banging body under all that tweed.

The door swung open and Claire entered, followed by Reece. Reece's smooth face flashed with momentary horror as he took in the dressing room stuffed with chattering, mud-encrusted women in various states of undress. He dropped his gaze to the floor and stood stiff and upright in the corner.

Claire blew her whistle and silence fell. "Good training session, girls. We have our penultimate game tomorrow, and I know the night before a game can be stressful. Dr. Forster is here to do a quick post-training mindfulness exercise to help you with focus tomorrow."

She inclined her head toward Reece and flashed a tight smile. "I'll leave you to it. I have a few . . . things to take care of."

Claire dashed out. I didn't blame her. Claire wasn't the type to be interested in anything like this. She probably hated meditation as much as I did. The moment Claire stepped out of the door, raucous chatter and laughter broke out again.

Reece cleared his throat. "Could we have some quiet, please?"

Nobody seemed to notice him apart from me. He'd need to speak up if he wanted to be heard above this restless rabble. He scanned us, smoothing his immaculate blazer, waiting for silence. He'd have his work cut out. The girls had been wild and revved up in training tonight. Nerves were high about tomorrow. Reece tried in vain to gain some control over the team. Was he getting flustered? His hand had brushed mine when I'd left his office and it had made my insides flip. Something strange had happened, and he'd practically thrown me out of the room. Maybe I'd said something he didn't like. He was always so poised and civilized, but he'd sounded almost . . . panicked when I'd asked for my hoodie back. Had I ruffled him somehow? Why did I find the prospect so appealing? What would he look like sweaty and breathing hard? What noises did a man so starchy make when he unraveled?

Reece cleared his throat and spoke again in his quiet, composed way. "Could everybody settle down, please?"

Nobody heard him or paid any attention. Even Gabe would have struggled to get the team's attention after a practice session like we'd just had. He'd need some help. I leaped up onto the bench in front of the row of lockers and clapped my hands. I couldn't watch him suffer anymore.

I yelled to be heard above the din. "Hey! You lot! Shut the fuck up, will you? Dr. Forster wants to talk to us. Give him some respect."

The noise died down and people swiveled on the benches, turning their attention to the front of the dressing room.

Reece shot me a grateful glance. We shared a smile and I sat back down.

Lana leaned in and whispered in a teasing voice, "Freak in the sheets."

"Shut up."

"We're going to do a mindfulness exercise," Reece said.

A couple of people groaned. I suppressed my eye roll. I'd tried meditation before. I hated it. It just made me angry. It would be impossible to relax in this state. The pressure of tomorrow's match pressed heavy on my shoulders. Only a win would do. My legs jiggled up and down and my heart pounded in anticipation.

Although he addressed everyone, Reece's gaze clung to mine, his voice low and soothing. "We're going to take deep breaths together. We'll breathe in to the count of four, hold for four, then release for four, slowly."

I couldn't tear my gaze from his mouth as his full lips parted to inhale and exhale in deliberate breaths. "Imagine you're blowing out candles on a birthday cake. I'm going to count for you."

His authoritative voice was as cool as a freshwater stream running from the loftiest peaks. "Focus on the breath. Nothing else matters. You don't have to block out thoughts. Just bring your attention to where your breath is coming in and out of your body. Just noticing."

Everything about his steady, measured demeanor soothed me. I'd never noticed how incredible his eyes were, so dark and expressive, so full of kindness. They were a harbor—a place to shelter in a dreadful storm. "Just this breath and the next. That's right."

My eyes fluttered shut and I took a breath, striving to relax.

"Imagine your body is a mountain. A mountain is powerful and strong. Whatever happens, the mountain stands. It might be battered by wind and rain, or the sun might shine, but the mountain always remains the same. Unfazed. Solid. Powerful."

His calm tone had so much depth. It crackled over my skin like electricity. My mind filled with dirty thoughts. *Reece's elegant palms sliding over my stomach. His hard body atop mine.*

". . . Just following each breath. Not forcing the breath. Relaxing into it . . ."

His hands covering my breasts. His hot breath on my nipples. Sliding down onto him and riding him slowly as he whispers his praise in that low, soothing voice.

". . . Just this breath . . . and then the next . . ."

Reece easing me gently down onto a bed. His dark eyes locking with mine from between my thighs. His hot tongue probing and tasting.

My skin prickled with pleasure and my heart hammered. Any good feeling was swiftly replaced by guilt. I was supposed to be meditating, not becoming unspeakably turned on. Since when had I wanted a man this much? Sean didn't get me all hot and bothered like this. These feelings were so new. Still, I couldn't act on them. Reece was here to do a job. He didn't welcome my attention. He'd already made his position clear and rejected me. Besides, Sean had hurt me too much to start anything new.

All that matters is the team.

"When you're ready, open your eyes."

My eyes flashed open.

Reece spoke to the team, but his steady gaze rested on me. "Any questions?"

I was painfully aware that mud splattered my face and I wore only my sports bra and shorts. Usually, that wouldn't have bothered me. It was normal after a match to strip down. None of us cared in the dressing room. But with Reece looking so immaculate in his smart suit, I felt self-conscious at being half naked. What did he think when he looked at me? Did he like what he saw?

Lana leaned in and whispered in my ear. "I've got a question. Just how much of a freak are we talking?"

Her teasing chuckle raked through me as the dressing room broke into chaos and noise again. Reece's heated gaze passed over me one last time before he slipped out the door.

Chapter 12

Skylar

The next morning, we played our penultimate game. Two games between us and victory. Only a win would keep us in the running. Sweat drenched me. My lungs burned with every breath. After several attempts on goal, we had a no-score draw. The opposition was too strong in defense. I dared a glance at the giant digital display in the corner of the stadium. Two minutes before the final whistle. Two minutes before we crashed out of the league.

A season full of work and it's all about to unravel.

I shook my head. No. It wasn't over until that whistle blew. Chanting from the crowd filled my ears. Lana signaled me for a cross and suddenly the ball was at my feet. I took off, sprinting toward the goal. An opposition player flew at me for a tackle. I pivoted, holding her off and keeping possession. I'd die before I let go of this ball without a shot at goal. Then I saw it. An opening. Blood roared in my ears. My heart sang. This is what I lived for. This moment. I charged forward, leaving the rest of the pitch in the dust.

I own this fucking pitch.

My heart pounded a terrifying rhythm.

Shit. I have to calm down.

I have to be calm like . . . a mountain.

Reece Forster's velvet voice played in my mind.

I am strong and steady like a mountain.

With one hard, solid kick, I booted the ball toward the net. The keeper dove but she didn't stand a chance. It soared past her hands straight into the top corner. The crowd knew it was going in before I did. The stadium erupted in a barrage of roaring sound.

Then it was chaos.

The other girls piled on me. The final whistle blew. Hot tears pricked my eyes. A shocked laugh escaped me as my feet left the pitch and the girls hoisted me up onto their shoulders. My body filled with a lightness that could barely be contained. I could have taken off and soared above the pitch like a balloon. We were almost there. One step closer to the prize we'd worked for all season. One step closer to a dream come true.

In the shower, hot water beat down on my back. I lathered myself with foaming peppermint shower gel. My hands smoothed soapy bubbles over my stomach and the curve of my hips. My mind filled with Reece again. *His smooth, elegant hands and his velvet voice crackling over my skin like electricity. Every word from his sensual mouth dripping in authority.*

I slipped my hand between my thighs to soothe the desperate ache. I'd tried this before, but it always felt weird and unnatural. I shouldn't be doing this here. The cubicle gave me privacy, but I wasn't alone in the shower block. Still, I'd never felt this turned on before. I couldn't let this post-win bliss go. Chatter and the hammer of the showers drifted to my ears, but I closed my eyes and blocked it out. My body sang with delight at the heat on sore muscles.

Young girls across the country had posters of my ex-boyfriend on their walls, but it wasn't Sean I pictured touching me. It was Reece Forster. Dr. Reece Forster with his office full of books and his geeky glasses. Reece Forster with his elegant, handsome face and those full, sensual lips. He was so calm and composed. What would it be like to make him flustered?

Arousal built as my fingers worked, imagining it was him touching me. A shiver of pleasure sparked through me. The hot throb between my thighs became torturous. I moved my fingers, experimenting with different rhythms and pressure.

My body was half fire and half ice. Breath entered my lungs in sharp pants. Hot water pounded my skin, and I was drowning in sensation—reaching the peak of a roller coaster, so close to tipping over the edge and plummeting into God knows what lay beyond. Everything narrowed to the torturous need in me. Everything too tight and screaming for release. Whatever exquisite agony Reece Forster had put in motion couldn't be stopped.

Breathe. Just this breath. And the next.

Blood pounded my ears. Chatter and laughter swept in to fill the white noise in my head—

"Come on, Skylar. Hurry up. City have lost two matches in a row." Claire's voice boomed across the cubicles. "We've got reporters from Sports News waiting. One more win and that cup is ours. They want an interview with you."

I cursed under my breath with frustration. Every nerve was still too raw and tight with tension. As close as I was, this would have to wait.

"Hang on." I turned off the shower and sagged against the cubicle wall. "I was just coming."

Chapter 13

Skylar

Later that evening, after the cooldown and the team talks and the interviews, I danced my way through Gabe's mansion, tripping over my heels. Music pulsed in my ears. A clammy cheek pressed to mine. Jenna wrapped her arms around me in the lounge. "You fucking legend, Skylar Marshall. What a goal. You annihilated them."

She spun me around and the party blurred in a haze of laughter and smiling faces. It was supposed to be a small get-together to celebrate, but the booze was flowing and I'd got swept up in the heady feeling after a win.

The stench of liquor engulfed me as Jenna held me close. "Where's Sean?"

"I don't know. Somewhere. Maybe he'll come later."

I took another sip of wine. Drinking was better than dealing with the constant questions about Sean's whereabouts. Silky music mingled with singing and drunken football chants from the girls. I needed to slow down, but I hadn't felt this good in so long. I stumbled through the dancing throng and dropped into a seat.

My eyes were too heavy to keep open, my thoughts tumbling and foggy. I shouldn't have pulled out my phone. I definitely shouldn't have texted Sean. I deleted countless messages before I settled on: You're a prick.

No reply.

I tried again. My fingers hovered. I held my breath and typed: I'm so fucking done with you, Sean. So fucking done.

At least, that's what I tried to type. The words swam in my vision. I stumbled through a crowded hallway and down another one, using the walls to support myself. The Rivers mansion was as big as a village. I needed another drink. In the kitchen, a pair of sensitive dark eyes met mine and knocked the air from my lungs. Reece was here. Why? Didn't he hate parties? Lana sat on the kitchen island, smiling. Just the two of them? She wasn't serious about this stupid bet, was she? What a horrible thing to do.

"I need to talk to Reece for a minute . . . alone."

My tongue felt thick and heavy in my mouth. My words came out slurred. Lana raised an eyebrow and dropped down from the island. She bumped my elbow as she sashayed past. "Don't keep him to yourself for too long."

I planted myself in front of him by the sink. He raised a brow. "Are you okay?"

I opened my mouth and closed it again. Now I'd have to think of a reason for my interruption.

"I thought you didn't like parties."

"Gabe insisted I show my face."

"So you're hiding in the kitchen this time? Was the library too much excitement?"

He offered me a faint smile but didn't reply.

"What are you doing with Lana? You should be careful."

"Careful?" He frowned and studied my face. "Is everything okay?"

A laugh rose up in me. "It's great. Did you see my goal? It was you. I thought about that thing you said about being a mountain. I wanted to thank you."

"I'm glad. It was a great goal. You did well."

A ripple of warmth went through me at his praise. I shouldn't have stepped closer, but the alcohol had made me bold and I couldn't resist the heat of his body. I moved toward him, compelled by some uncontrollable desire just to be close to him. I looked up into his handsome face, drinking in the comfort of his nearness. Blood coursed hot and excited through my veins. I closed the gap between us, pressing myself against his firm chest, breathing in his woody cologne.

I stood on tiptoes and pressed my lips to his ear. "I saw your profile."

He raised a dark brow in surprise. "My what?"

"'A geek on the street. A freak in the sheets.'"

Pink tinged his cheeks. He pulled at his collar then raked a hand through his hair. "I don't know what you mean."

A warming shiver ran through me. Was he blushing? He was always so unflappable, but maybe it was possible to make him flustered after all.

"If you're looking for a hookup, you don't need to do it online. You have options closer to home."

He swallowed and stepped back. "That had nothing to do with me. It was just a prank. My sister told me she'd taken it down."

"I like it. I like the photos of you at the gym. I knew you worked out."

His face remained level, his gaze steady. "You're drunk. Are you supposed to be drinking in the season?"

I put a finger to my lips. "I won't tell if you don't. You can trust me with confidentiality if that's what you're worried about. I can keep a secret."

He turned away to the sink and poured a glass of water. "Here," he said, holding out the glass. "Drink this."

I took it. "So, you're not a freak in the sheets?"

He pressed his lips flat. I stepped forward, stumbling to close the gap he'd created between us. Adrenaline buzzed through my veins. We'd won today. Fortune favored the bold. I'd had a win on the pitch; maybe I could score again.

I leaned up unsteadily to whisper in his ear. "Come back to my place. You want some no-strings fun and so do I."

My cheek grazed his as I pulled away and I brushed my lips against his. The firm pressure of his mouth sent a thrill through me. A hot ache tingled between my thighs and I pressed myself closer to him. My hands wound into his soft hair. His jaw scraped my mouth as he turned his face away. He pushed me back, holding me at arm's length.

His voice was calm, his gaze steady. He held me away from him by the elbows. "We can't do that."

"Why? You said you want something no strings. That's fine with me."

"You're steaming drunk. Let me be clear, Skylar. This can't happen between us." He studied my face, feature by feature, before he stepped back. "We'll talk about this when you're sober. Come to my office when you're ready. I have to remove myself from this conversation now."

"You don't have to go."

I moved to follow him and tripped over my heels. He caught me before I hit the ground. His gaze passed over me and he frowned. "How are you getting home tonight?"

"Don't worry about me. I'll be fine."

I weaved through the kitchen back to the noise and frivolity of the party. Reece caught my elbow before I hit the deck again. "Come on. I'll take you home."

Chapter 14

Reece

I put the car radio on low. The night flashed by outside, and for the second time in a fortnight I was driving Skylar Marshall home from a party. As a teenager, I could never have imagined I'd ever utter that sentence. Parties and Skylar Marshall were two things that existed in a different universe from mine. She was far drunker than last time, her voice slurred and her eyes glassy. Her head dropped back on the headrest and she closed her eyes. Hopefully, she'd stay asleep. A soulful ballad drifted from the radio and I turned it off. No love songs tonight.

"I don't see the big deal, Reece. It's just a hookup."

My hands tensed around the steering wheel. So much for being asleep. "Just rest. We'll talk about this when you're sober."

From the corner of my eye, I saw her fiddling with the silver ring in her nose. A muscle in her jaw quivered. Her voice slurred. "It's me, isn't it? Sean said no man wants a woman like me."

This wasn't an appropriate conversation, but I couldn't leave something like that hanging. "It's not you, and he shouldn't have said that. That must have been hurtful to hear."

"He doesn't care about hurting me. He hurts me all the time . . ."

The back of my neck itched. Hurt her in what way? The silence stretched between us. I let it, until it was clear she wasn't going to say anything. I shouldn't have been pressing her when she was drunk, but I couldn't let that stand.

"He hurts you. What do you mean?"

She snorted and shook her head. "He's awful. He said it was my fault that he'd cheated on me. That I'd left him no choice. He made me feel so bad about myself. When we . . ." She grimaced and kept her eyes on her hands twisting in her lap. "Whenever we are . . . intimate . . . I can't stand the way he talks to me. It never feels good. He's never even tried to make it feel good for me, and then he tells me there's something wrong with me because I can't . . ." Her voice broke miserably.

The ache in my neck became unbearable.

"Every single time, I have to fake it. I've got so good at faking, I should get an Oscar. It's just easier that way because otherwise he gives me a hard time about it."

"Fake what?"

"I can't . . . get *there* with Sean." She pressed her forehead to the passenger window. "Seven years of faking orgasms. It's not normal. I've seen gynecologists. They can't find anything physically wrong with me. I just can't . . . get to the *finish line.*"

I'd had clients like this before. Women who felt sad and dysfunctional because they couldn't get off with a partner that didn't know how to satisfy them. So many men were clueless. I should have kept quiet. She was only telling me this because she was drunk. But I couldn't have her sit there feeling bad about something like this.

"Can you get *there* on your own? Because if you can climax on your own, then this is one hundred percent a Sean Wallace issue and not a *you* issue."

"What do you mean?"

"Has he ever taken the time to figure out what you like? What stimulation you need? What turns you on . . . ?"

She let out a roar of drunken laughter. "As if. We've been together since school. Nothing's changed. It started as a fumble in the dark and it's not got much better. Foreplay isn't in his vocabulary."

"Have you asked him for what you need?"

Her head sagged forward. Her voice was tired and thin. "There's no point. He doesn't listen. I've given up."

More evidence that Sean Wallace was a prick. I'd be hard-pressed to think of anything more appealing than getting Skylar Marshall between the sheets and learning how to make her come so hard her toes curled and she had to bite down on the pillow. Why hadn't he bothered to find out? Experimenting would be part of the fun.

Stop. Inappropriate train of thought. This whole conversation is inappropriate.

Yet still I couldn't keep my mouth shut. "Good sex comes from good communication and knowing what you want. A lot of men are under the misconception that all women orgasm through vaginal penetration alone. I can refer you to a sex therapist friend of mine."

She giggled.

"Is something amusing?"

"I've just never heard the words *vaginal penetration* come out of a man's mouth before. Sean looks like he's going to faint if I dare to mention I'm on my period." Her shoulders shook with silent laughter. "I don't need a sex therapist. That's too much. I don't need anything like that. I don't want to talk to anyone else. I only trust you." She dropped her gaze to her lap. "I'm a lost cause. I just can't relax enough. I can't even do it on my own."

90

"It might take time. You have to be patient with yourself."

"I've almost managed to get there a couple of times lately."

"What was different about those times?"

She chewed the skin around her thumbnail and shot me a thoughtful glance. "I was thinking about different things."

I felt her heated gaze burning into me and I clamped my mouth shut. As much as I wanted to hear about Skylar Marshall getting herself off, it wasn't an appropriate line of questioning. I stopped the car outside her house, but I didn't turn the engine off.

"Goodnight. You should drink some water before you go to bed."

She unhooked her seatbelt and lurched forward. "I'd invite you in, but you're going to turn me down again, aren't you?"

I held still with my gaze fixed on the house. "I can't go inside with you."

"So, you want all those things on your profile, but just not with me? I'm offering myself on a plate to you here, Reece, and you're saying no?"

Exhaustion washed over me. I'd craved this woman every moment of my teenage life. I was an absolute idiot to think I wasn't still infatuated with her. I should never have even agreed to work with the team. This had all been about Skylar Marshall. I'd been kidding myself to think it was anything else. This wasn't the time to get into an ethical discussion. I just needed her out of my car.

"I didn't create that dating profile. It was my siblings."

A small smile twisted the corner of her mouth. "You're no fun, you know that?"

"I've heard it said."

She chuckled. "I bet you could be, though. Do you ever loosen up?"

She turned her drunken smile on me and rested her hand on my leg, just above my knee. My breath caught and I was barely breathing in the first place. The cockiness in her expression faltered, replaced with something vulnerable and tentative. She was taking a leap. Skylar had always been brave. I didn't want to make her feel bad, but I couldn't do this. It was unethical. She was also blind drunk.

Gently, I took her hand and put it back on her leg. "Goodnight, Skylar."

"I thought maybe . . ."

I kept my gaze fixed on the windscreen. "No. I'm sorry."

"The thing is . . . I like you."

There was so much vulnerability in her voice. I kept my voice as soft as I could. "I'm not an option."

Hurt flickered in her glassy eyes. "You don't like me like that?"

If I was going to rip off the Band-Aid, it would be more effective to do it swift and hard. This wasn't the time for an ethical discourse. I just needed her out of my car. It was better for her in the long run. I'd have to extinguish any possibility in her head.

"We work together. I don't think it's a boundary we should cross."

She flinched as though I'd struck her. My heart contracted. I'd wanted to do this gracefully.

"Your loss, Dr. Forster." She chewed her lip and shrugged, but tears swam behind her eyes. "Your loss."

She flung open the car door and cold air rushed inside. I watched her weave her way up the drive and disappear into the house. I fought every instinct to run after her and drop down on my knees in front of her.

My loss.

Chapter 15

REECE

Skylar lay on the therapy couch in my office, her lilac hair soft and gleaming. She sat up, hooked her thumb under the strap of her tight purple dress, and inched it down over her inked shoulder. Her fingers danced over the top of her cleavage.

"Did you see my goal, Dr. Forster?"

She pulled the strap down and eased the lacy cup of her bra aside, revealing the soft mound of her breast and her perfect, taut nipple. Her lips parted and her head fell back with pleasure. I'd never seen a more beautiful sight.

A slow, seductive smile spread on her face. "Do you ever loosen up, Dr. Forster?" She uncrossed her legs. Her hand glided from her ankle, grazing her inner thigh and inching her dress up along with it. Her knees fell apart, revealing white lace underwear. "I can't let you see any more."

A surge of excitement heated my blood. "Yes. You can. Show me."

"Your loss." She smiled and vanished.

My eyes flashed open. I grabbed my phone. I was already late for work. I scrambled out of bed for the quickest shower known to mankind. I hadn't had a sex dream about Skylar since I was a teenager. I couldn't remember ever waking up so hard.

The hot water hit my throbbing cock and I groaned. The dirty images from the dream replayed in my mind. Skylar on the therapy couch, wet and squirming. Stop. No. This had to be professional. I couldn't think like that. I shook my head and tried to get rid of the image, but it wouldn't be removed. Every nerve pulled too hot and tight with need. I couldn't go to work in this state.

I wrapped my hand around my shaft and braced my other hand against the door. The hot water beat down on my back. I closed my eyes and played out the scene from my dream. Skylar uncrossed her legs for me again. Waves of pleasure made me groan as I palmed my length in swift strokes. She got up from the couch and crawled across the office toward me. She looked so good on her knees. What was I doing? This was so bad. So bad. I was going straight to hell for this one. Dream Skylar chewed her bottom lip and positioned herself at my feet. She licked her lips and reached for my waistband.

That's right. Good girl.

I tightened my grip, savoring the rapid soapy strokes.

Well. If I'm going to hell, I'll make it worth my while.

Chapter 16

Reece

Skylar stood in the doorway of my office. She smoothed her damp lilac hair. I fought to hide my surprise that she'd shown up after last night. I rolled my shoulders and tried to clear all the dirty images that had stacked up this morning.

She pulled her hoodie over her head and off, flashing her toned, taut stomach. "Can we talk?"

"If you like."

Her body was so strong and powerful. My mouth went dry. She must have got a new team hoodie. I had hers tucked in my office cabinet. In my weaker moments, I got it out to breathe in her scent. I'd planned to give it back to her, but somehow I hadn't got around to it.

I'm in control.

"No rush. Just take the time to arrive. Feel your body in the chair. Just settle in. Relax. Take a few breaths."

"I'm here. I have arrived." She shot me a smile.

When she smiled, she held the tip of her tongue between her teeth. It was so endearing. Everything about her had always been so endearing to me.

I'm a grown man, not a teenager. I'm in control.

She fiddled with the hem of her T-shirt. "I'm sorry about . . . all of it. I don't remember much, but I remember enough to know that my behavior was not acceptable. I'm mortified, honestly."

"You don't have to feel bad about it. It's my job to manage the boundary between us, not yours. I want to be clear that none of this is your fault. Therapy is an intense process on both sides. Clients sometimes develop feelings for their therapists. We even have a name for it: transference."

She frowned. "Is that what you think we're doing here? Therapy?"

"What do you think we're doing here?"

She wrinkled her nose. "Not therapy. I don't need therapy."

"There's no shame in therapy. One of the bravest things we can do is ask for help."

"I know. There's no shame in therapy, but that's not what we're doing here. We've had a couple of conversations. I like talking to you. It's not a big deal."

"The first rule of being in a helping profession is that you do not harm. The relationship between us has become . . . complicated."

Her frown deepened. "I don't think there is anything complicated here. We're just two people who work together having a conversation. What does it matter anyway? You told me you don't even like me."

"I didn't say I didn't like you."

She pressed her lips together. "Right. Just not like that."

I drew a breath. I'd have to reiterate this with more eloquence now we weren't sitting so close together in my car. I could be professional in here.

"Therapists aren't allowed to like their clients in that way. It's unethical."

"I'm not your client."

96

"You've confided in me. Things you wouldn't have told me otherwise."

She laughed. "Because you're easy to talk to, and I can't tell anyone else here. I've never agreed to therapy with you."

"I have strict ethical standards to follow. It doesn't feel right to me that we're talking about these personal things in here. Would you have talked to me like this if I wasn't a psychologist?"

She sat up straight in the chair. "Fine. I get it. This is making you feel uncomfortable because we're in your office. If you don't want to meet in here, then maybe we could talk somewhere else . . . over coffee or something?"

I hardened my heart. This was for the best. I had to do the right thing by Skylar, and the right thing was to let her go. "No. Thank you."

Hurt flashed across her face. She stood. "Right. I get the message. You don't want to talk to me. I have to go anyway. I have . . . things to do. Can't sit around chatting all day. I just wanted to say sorry if I made things awkward."

She moved to the door. My gaze flicked to the couch and I couldn't help picturing Skylar lying there, squirming and biting her lip.

"Here." I scribbled a note on my pad, ripped the page, and passed it to her. "These are the names of therapists that you might want to consider working with. Maybe you'd feel more comfortable with someone else."

She screwed up the note and tossed it straight into the trash can at the other side of the room. She stepped closer and looked me squarely in the eyes. So close I was barely breathing.

"Our conversation the other day reminded me of something. It reminded me who I am. You're right, I have always had to fight. I fought my way to the top, and maybe it's because I needed to prove myself. Maybe I didn't feel good enough. But you know what else it shows? It shows that I'm determined. I learned to swim against a current, and it's made me strong. When I line up a shot, I always score. I'm not afraid to go after what I want."

I didn't doubt that for one second. I might have been trying to uncover her vulnerabilities, show her that she was as human as everyone else, but it didn't mean I'd underestimated her strength. Skylar radiated power. She'd always been a goddess in my eyes. Shock and desire at her nearness held me frozen. She was so close I could see the specks of green in her blue eyes.

Her eyes dropped guiltily to my lips. "I can't believe I sat next to you in school and didn't notice you."

"Of course you didn't." My voice came out low and rough. "You were the most popular girl in the school and I was . . . a nobody."

It shouldn't have been possible for her to get any closer, but she inched nearer. "I wasn't the most popular girl in the school. I was just an idiot like everyone else, muddling along and trying to look cool. And you could never be a nobody, Reece."

"Still, you would never have looked twice at me."

Her seductive gaze raked over me like a caress. "I'm looking now."

Fire blazed in my blood. Her closeness was a drug and I'd been trying so hard to resist the craving, but Skylar Marshall made me weak. She was my kryptonite. She brushed her lips against mine, and a shiver of pleasure burst through me. She stepped forward again. My back hit the office door. Her body molded to the contours of mine. Flames of desire licked over my skin, heating my blood like a firestorm.

Her eyes searched my face, seeking permission. Standing on tiptoe, she touched her lips to mine. The whisper-soft press of her mouth sent spirals of ecstasy through me. The heady sensation of her body—so hard and athletic but so soft and warm at the same time—inflamed every nerve.

"What are you doing?" My voice barely broke a rough whisper.

"Fighting for what I want."

Her lips came coaxingly back to mine, a delicious sensation. I used every last shred of resolve I had to stand statue still. My senses reeled as though short-circuited. A strange rough groan left my mouth and my body begged for release.

Her lips brushed my ear, her breath hot against my cheek. "Yes?"

I swallowed. Words wedged in my throat.

"Tell me if you want me to stop, Reece."

Blood pounded my temple. All thought flowed from my head downward. Two treacherous words slipped from my lips. "Don't stop."

Her mouth curved into a smile against my lips. She slipped her hand low so that it grazed where I ached for her touch. A gasp escaped me, but she smothered it with a kiss. Her persuasive mouth moved against mine, urgent and exploratory. Her fingers moved with more insistence, rubbing my hard length through the fabric. A jolt ran through me and another choked, agonized noise escaped my throat. Her hand froze.

"Okay?" she whispered.

Yes. No. So much for maintaining a professional boundary.

Everything hinged on this moment. I opened my mouth and the words stuck in my throat. She studied my face and took a sharp breath. Before I could form a rational thought, she dropped to her knees. She unfastened my trousers and yanked them down, followed by my boxers. I could still say no. It wasn't too late. Why hadn't I said no yet? My heart thundered.

"Skylar . . ." I whispered the word like a benediction.

She tilted her chin to steal a slanted look at me. "Yes?"

"Please."

"Please what?"

White noise roared in my ears. I swallowed.

Tell her no. This isn't right for either of us.

I reached down and ran my fingers through her silky lilac hair. "Please don't stop."

She looked me squarely in the eyes as her hand gripped the base of my shaft and her warm, soft mouth closed around me. My breath cut off. The fire in my blood consumed me, burning me alive. I couldn't control the shudder of pleasure that ran through me. It had been so long since I'd been like this with a woman, and I couldn't have expected to break my dry spell with Skylar Marshall. I'd forgotten the exquisite ecstasy of a blow job, but a blow job from Skylar was my every fantasy made real.

Bobbing her head, Skylar worked me with her hot mouth and tongue. My hands tightened into fists at my side and her beautiful blue eyes didn't leave mine for a second. She dug her nails into my backside, pulling me forward, taking me deeper. Every part of me ached with need for this woman. My hips rocked involuntarily as I surrendered to the divine sin of the inked angel on her knees for me.

My breath came in sharp pants. "Fuck. Ah. Shit. Fuck. Oh. Oh my God."

The vibration from her satisfied laugh around my cock made my knees weak. She popped me out of her mouth and licked a long line from the thick base of my shaft to the head, teasing me with her tongue.

She chuckled. "Such eloquence, Dr. Forster. Did you learn that at Cambridge?"

Another rough groan escaped my lips. I needed her to welcome me back into the velvet heat of her mouth. Her tongue slid up and down my length and the world dissolved into nothing but raw, exquisite sensation.

She looked up at me. "Does that feel good?"

I swallowed, fighting to form coherent words. "Yes . . . so good . . . fuck . . . so good."

I gasped as she took me back into her hot mouth. My fingers tightened painfully into her hair. The torturous need for relief gripped me. For years, I'd fantasized about this moment, but no fantasy could live up to the reality of Skylar Marshall on her knees pleasuring me. She sucked rhythmically. The indecent noise filling my ears drove my arousal. Pure, stark desperation swept through me as my balls tightened. Whatever madness this was, I couldn't fight it. I was too weak. I cried out as release tore through me, but she didn't stop until she'd wrung every last moment of pleasure.

She wiped her mouth against her wrist and stood. She appraised me with an expression bordering on triumphant. In a strange way, I was proud of her for having the confidence to go after what she wanted, but then the avalanche of guilt caved in on me. What had I done? One moment of weakness had cost me so much. This was unethical, and not the right thing for Skylar. I'd wanted to help her with a breakup, not give her more problems.

She cupped my face, stroking my cheeks with soft hands. "Don't worry. It's okay. I wanted it. It's okay."

I yanked up my trousers and buttoned them with trembling fingers. "It's not okay. I should never have let that happen."

"You're being too hard on yourself. I wanted this. We both wanted this."

She reached for my hand, but I snatched it away and stepped back. "Don't, Skylar. For God's sake, don't."

Hurt crossed her face. I made my living with words, but I had none to make this situation better. Instead, I walked out of my office. It was all I could do. If I'd been a better doctor and a better man, I would have done that five minutes earlier.

Thankfully, she didn't follow.

Chapter 17

Skylar

My feet pounded the treadmill. Music roared in my ears and sweat plastered my hair to my neck. Every muscle screamed at me to stop, but I ran harder. No matter how fast I ran, I couldn't shift the adrenaline that sparked through me.

Giving Sean a blow job had always felt like a chore. It was something to do for him to make him feel good, or if I wanted to get out of having sex. Somehow, it had escaped me that giving a man pleasure was so incredibly hot. I'd never felt so turned on in my life—my nipples still pressed painfully against my sports bra. An unfamiliar heat pulsed between my thighs.

Reece, who was always so poised and in control, had been out of his mind for me. His eyes had blazed with so much lust and longing behind his glasses. Sean had never even looked at me like that at the beginning. No man ever had. I'd had the good doctor completely at my mercy. When I'd taken him deep enough to hit the back of my throat, his eyes had rolled back in his head, and he'd braced his hands against the wall as though trying not to collapse. In that moment, with his beautiful cock in my mouth, I'd had the power to bring him to his knees. His indecent groans still echoed in my ears.

Heat pooled at my core. Reece cursed so rarely, but he'd colored the air blue with his words. It was his eagerness that had turned me on more than anything. The way his hips had jerked. The way he'd fought to restrain himself. Even though I'd been the one on my knees, I'd had all the power. I wanted to satisfy him over and over. I'd never get enough.

The excitement that tingled over my skin was tempered by guilt. I couldn't strike the sad look on Reece's face after he'd left me standing in his office. He'd seemed so into it. When I'd asked him if he wanted to stop, he'd said no, but judging from the horrified look on his face afterward, he regretted it. He needed to lighten up on this whole therapist nonsense. We'd never agreed to that arrangement. He was so uptight, but I could get under his skin. I had the power to make a man so composed and put together completely lose it.

By the mirrored wall, I saw the first guys from the men's team filtering into the gym from the changing rooms. Great. Time to go. The last thing I wanted was a run-in with Sean. I tried to slow down on trembling legs. Music blasted my ears and I pulled off my headphones to stretch on the mats.

I grabbed my towel and my water bottle and headed to the locker room. If I got out now, then I wouldn't have to have a conversation with Sean. I showered, dressed, and made my way past the seminar room where we gathered for team talks. A low voice gave me pause. Nobody should have been in there at this time. Not Gabe and Miri? Had they exhausted the office and now they'd moved on to the seminar room? I couldn't help my incredulous snort. The man owned his own hotel, for God's sake. Couldn't they get a room?

I made to move by, but the low, rough voice gave me pause again. I'd recognize it anywhere. I should have kept walking, but I peeked through the keyhole. Sean leaned against one of the tables. He was talking to someone out of sight. A white T-shirt clung to his impressive torso and his black shorts highlighted his strong, muscular legs. I waited for my heart to betray me, but I felt nothing. I didn't miss him. I didn't even feel angry with him anymore. His infidelity had been the best thing for me. This relationship had been dead for so long. I couldn't care less about Sean Wallace. All I could think about was Reece.

I caught a flash of auburn hair as Sean's companion came into view. Confusion assailed my brain. Lana? Had Sean been cheating on me with one of my best friends? This whole time? How could Lana go behind my back like that?

Adrenaline coursed through my body. I should have walked away, but anger took over and I yanked the door open. They both looked up at the same time. Lana paled and jumped away from Sean. Sean rocked back on his heels and a smug smile spread over his lips.

Lana smoothed her ponytail then held her hands up in mock surrender. "It's not what it looks like."

"Don't treat me like an idiot, Lana. It's exactly what it looks like. The two of you were kissing."

Lana frowned. "Okay. It is what it looks like, but it's not as bad as it looks."

"How long?"

They both stared back at me in silence. I banged my fist on the conference table. "How long?"

Lana chewed her lip and shot a glance at Sean. "It's nothing. One kiss."

"Was it you the whole time? You've been sleeping with my boyfriend behind my back?"

Lana's eyebrows shot up and she shook her head. "No, Skylar. Honestly. No. I wouldn't do that."

"Yes. You fucking would, Lana."

Her face crumpled. Maybe that wasn't fair, but the blood roaring in my ears made rational thought fly out of my head. I shouldn't have even been this angry. I couldn't care less about Sean anymore, and it wasn't as though I hadn't moved on too. I'd been on my knees for another man a couple of doors down the corridor. Still, this was girl code. Lana shouldn't have been anywhere near my ex-boyfriend. He was no good for her anyway. Why did she even want him?

My heart hammered. "We're teammates. How could you?"

"It was one kiss. I thought you'd broken up."

I transferred my gaze to Sean. "We're telling people now?"

He shrugged. "This is bullshit, Skylar. You won't even talk to me. What am I supposed to do? I'm not a monk."

Anger surged through me. "Fuck you." I looked from Sean back to Lana. "Fuck both of you."

A hurt shadow darkened Lana's features, but I had no time for guilt. She was the one kissing my ex-boyfriend. It was messed up. Who did that to their best friend? I stormed out the exit and down the corridor. My gaze blurred behind a veil of tears. A hand wrapped around my elbow and Sean spun me round to face him. I pulled myself free from his grip and shoved him away from me.

He threw his hands up in the air. "You said we were over. You kicked me out. Why are you getting so angry now?"

I drew a breath, struggling to keep my voice low. Anyone could walk past and see us. "We agreed to put the team first. If we're out in the open with this, then we're going to need to get on to this statement. We can't put it off anymore."

"Fine. Then we issue a statement." His voice was a vicious whisper. "You can't blame me for this. What am I supposed to do when you give me nothing? You made me feel like shit. What do you expect? I had no choice but to look elsewhere—"

"Is everything okay out here?"

Gabe Rivers stood in front of his office. Had he heard this nonsense? I smoothed my hair and stood taller. The director was the last person I wanted to see me in this state.

"It's fine. Everything's fine," I called.

Sean shook his head, his voice full of contempt. "It's over, Skylar, but you don't get to end this. This is me ending it. You're the problem, not me. I don't care who knows anymore."

I fought to quell my anger as I watched him walk back to the seminar room. So much for keeping things quiet. Miri emerged from behind Gabe.

"Did you hear any of that? What Sean said?"

Miri coughed to cover her obvious embarrassment. "A bit. What's going on? Is everything okay?"

I opened my mouth to give her some line, but my heart contracted at the look of sympathy on her face. My lips trembled.

Shit. Pull yourself together.

The captain can't fall apart.

Miri put an arm around my shoulder. "Hey. It's okay. You can talk to me, you know."

She darted a look at Gabe; he coughed and mumbled an excuse before walking away.

"Is it true? You've broken up with Sean? Talk to me. I'm your friend."

The words got lost, sticking in my mouth. I'd wanted to keep it quiet. It didn't matter now anyway. Soon everyone would know. Me and Sean would be the talk of the locker room. Then TikTok. I could already imagine the hashtags. FOOTBALL'S GOLDEN COUPLE SPLIT. I tried to look dignified, but heat pressed behind my eyes. I nodded and turned my face away. Miri didn't need to see me cry.

Miri's arms wrapped around me. Her enormous bump pressed against my middle. Her words made my heart contract. "It's okay. It's all going to be okay. Gabe's away with work tonight, but you're coming home with me."

Chapter 18

REECE

I stepped into the hallway and tripped over a pair of purple boots. The recognition made my heart pound. Skylar's boots. Why on earth were Skylar's boots in my hallway? Alanis Morissette's angry vocals pulsed from the living room. Frankie had been on a 90s kick, and if I had to listen to another hour of Courtney Love or Shirley Manson, I'd be forced to go and live in a tent in the garden.

I stuck my head around the living room door and froze before a word could come out. Skylar Marshall sat on the couch, her hands clasped around a tissue in her lap.

Miri looked up. "You know Skylar, don't you?"

Do I know Skylar? Sure. I know Skylar. I know the way she dotted her i's with little hearts when she was thirteen, the way she holds the tip of her tongue between her teeth when she smiles, the way Sean Wallace broke her heart but she pastes a cocky smile on and pretends that nothing can touch her. I know the warmth of her mouth around me when I'm such a selfish piece of shit that I encourage her to give me a blow job when I'm supposed to be counseling her.

"Hi, Skylar."

She held up her hand in a wave, but she didn't look at me. Her knees were drawn up tight to her chest and her face was ashen and tear-streaked.

I dropped down in front of her. "What happened?"

She hugged a cushion and stared straight ahead with a hurt, faraway look. "Nothing. I'm fine."

"You don't look fine."

Miri shot me an odd look. "Don't fuss, Reece. Skylar needs some space."

Of course. This would look weird to Miri. She had no idea how close we'd become over the past couple of weeks. For a moment, I'd just seen Skylar in need of comfort and forgotten that anyone else existed.

Frankie sauntered past me and dropped onto the couch with a huge bowl of popcorn. "We're bingeing period dramas." She propped her bare feet up on the coffee table and relaxed into the cushions. "Are you joining us?"

I tried to keep my gaze away from Skylar, but I couldn't help myself. Dark circles shadowed her red-rimmed eyes. What had gone on to bring her here? Why wouldn't she talk to me? Was this about me? Was she upset about what had happened in my office? I had to know.

"Can I have a word, Miri?"

Miri frowned. "Can it wait? I've only seen Mr. Darcy emerge from that lake five times this year. It's not good enough. I've been slacking."

"No." I tried to relax my jaw. "It can't wait."

"Fine." Miri passed the remote control and popcorn to Skylar and held both her hands out to me. "But you're going to have to help me stand up. It took long enough to sit down."

With two hands, I hauled Miri out of the chair. She followed me to the kitchen and I closed the door behind us.

"What's going on?"

Miri sighed. "It's Skylar's business. It's not for me to say."

I busied myself filling the kettle. My heart weighed as heavy as a stone. I couldn't bear the thought that I'd made Skylar cry. I'd run out of my office and left her alone. She was probably hurt and confused. It wasn't her fault. This was all me. I planted both hands on the counter and bowed my head. I couldn't have her staying in my house, but I couldn't bear to see her in this state either. She shouldn't be alone.

"This is weird for me, Miri. I'm working at the club now. I can't have a colleague staying over in my house. It's a violation of the boundaries. I'm going to have to move out until she's gone."

Yes. Having her here was definitely the biggest ethical violation, not the blow job in my office.

Miri snorted. "Relax, Reece. It's sports psychology, for God's sake. You're just doing a bit of stuff around positive mindset, aren't you? It's not the same as the hospital. This is one night. We'll stay out of your way. You don't have to be anywhere near us. Go to the annex with Mum if you're that bothered."

"Why can't you stay at Gabe's? Or the hotel?"

"Gabe's away tonight. You know I don't like to stay there alone. Besides, Frankie's here. Frankie always cheers everyone up."

I sighed. This was no good, but what could I do? I couldn't tell Miri the truth about me and Skylar.

Miri lowered her voice. "Sean Wallace has been an absolute bastard. They've split. She shouldn't be alone."

A wave of relief relaxed my shoulders. So, they'd gone public with the news. I didn't want her to be sad, but at least I wasn't the reason.

"Trust me, Skylar needs a friend. Let me do this for her. You can stay somewhere else tonight if it's that much of a big deal," Miri said.

"Have you offered her tea at least? A sandwich? She's our guest." I took a loaf out of the bread bin. "If she's staying with us, let's be good hosts. I'll stay in the annex with Mum. Let me know if you need me."

Miri raised a sardonic eyebrow. "For the record, I think you're being weird about this."

"I don't like you springing stuff on me, that's all."

"Fine. Whatever." She grabbed a pack of chocolate cookies and headed for the door. "You've got zero chill sometimes. You know that?"

Chapter 19

Skylar

"You're filthy. Such a bad girl, aren't you? Is this how you like it?"

Sean loomed over me, sweaty and breathing hard. My heart pounded. Disgust rippled like a sickness in my veins.

"No. I hate that. I hate you."

My eyes flashed open and I tried to orient myself in the unfamiliar darkness. I scrambled for my phone and checked the time: 3 a.m. Sitting up in bed, I took inventory of my surroundings. Unpleasant memories of Sean slid away, replaced with yesterday's chaos. This was Miri's spare room. Everything was okay. My heart pounded. Restless energy made my feet itch with the need to prowl. It would be pointless to wrestle with myself trying to sleep when I felt so wired.

Quietly, I padded downstairs to the kitchen. It was the middle of the night, but only one thing could soothe me in this state. I'd always found it difficult to focus at school, so Mum had tried all kinds of things with me to channel my active brain. We'd learned to make bread together. Something about the rhythmic kneading of the dough had always calmed me down.

I rooted around in the kitchen cupboards until I found everything I needed. The ingredients and baking dishes were labeled and arranged in a neat, orderly fashion. Even the yeast had a little handwritten label on the box. Reece's handiwork, no doubt. I liked that he was so neat and tidy. I'd spent years picking up Sean's junk left all over the house and washing his filthy football kit. A sudden lightness came over me. There wouldn't be any more of that. I didn't have to deal with Sean or his filthy washing ever again.

Fuck Sean.

The door creaked and I jumped. Reece appeared, his dark hair mussed. His sleepy eyes met mine from behind his glasses.

"Skylar? What are you doing?"

"Making bread."

He picked up a pot of yeast and put it down again on the kitchen island. "At 3 a.m.?"

"I couldn't sleep."

"Me neither. I came for a glass of water. The pipes are noisy in the annex. I didn't want to wake up Mum."

"Let me." I moved to the sink and filled a glass with water.

His fingers were warm on mine as he accepted the glass. "Thank you."

His faded gray T-shirt clung to his muscular frame, and his legs were toned and powerful in shorts. Whatever his brother had him doing in the gym, it was working. Desire pooled hot and tingling in my lower belly. My nipples tightened painfully in the thin nightdress Miri had given me. A few years ago, *Vogue* had voted Sean one of the hottest men in England. Still, Sean had never set my blood alight the way the sight of this man did.

"I thought you might sleep in a shirt and tie."

His lip twitched and he raked a hand through his dark, disheveled hair. My fingers itched to touch him.

He kept his gaze on the island and cleared his throat. "We need to talk about what happened in my office."

"We will." I returned to kneading the dough. "But not now. It's three in the morning. I want to ease my stress, not make it worse."

Reece inclined his head. "Fine. I'll leave you to it."

"Don't go. Stay . . . just for a minute."

He frowned and held still. I couldn't shake the tingling pleasure I had at being so close to him when he was warm and relaxed from sleep. I took the dough from the bowl. A cloud of flour puffed up as I blobbed the mixture down on to the island. I worked the dough, pounding and turning it on the floured surface, trying to release the tension in my shoulders.

"I'm thinking about Sean's face when I do this. Is that healthy?"

His lip twitched. "It's not *not* healthy. What would you say to him? If it was Sean?"

The dough yielded under my fists, soft and sticky as I worked. "You think your hair looks so good, Sean." I landed a firm punch. "It doesn't."

Reece's voice was gentle, yet uncompromising. "What else?"

"You don't have to have an opinion on every meal I cook." I landed another punch. "Eat it or don't."

"What else?"

I drove my knuckles into the dough. "You screwed around behind my back."

Tears pressed at my eyes, and I fought to hold them back. The silence swirled around us, thick and unsettling. My heart ached. Exhaustion washed over me. How had I let Sean treat me so badly for so long?

Reece's voice was as soft as a kiss when he finally spoke. "What else?"

Before Sean, I'd been so confident. He'd wanted to diminish me. I knew that now. Maybe that's the only way he could feel good about himself. Who the hell was he to make me feel like that?

"You disrespected me and talked to me like shit. You made me feel worthless." I threw another punch at the dough, but it didn't have the same force behind it. "I don't want you anymore, anyway. I deserve better."

Sean had bent me out of shape, but I wouldn't allow him to break me. Without him, I could be whatever I wanted. I could leave all the hurt, broken parts behind and move on with the bits that suited me.

I sniffed and stood taller. Silence swirled around us as I picked the sticky dough from my fingers. "What about you? Have you got any terrible exes lurking in the wings?"

Reece pressed his lips flat. I moved to the sink to wash my hands. At least he didn't change the subject like he usually did when I inquired about his private life.

"Is that how this is going to work between us? You know everything about me, but I don't know anything about you?" I turned off the tap and dried my hands on a towel. "I can't even have a normal conversation with my friend's brother?"

"It's not normal. It can't be normal between us. The thing that happened in my office—"

"I said I don't want to talk about it."

Reece opened his mouth to protest, but I stepped forward, closing the gap between us. He snapped his mouth shut. Blood pounded in my ears. He was so close. Hot tension raced over my skin.

"Sean treated me like shit. I don't want a man like that. I want a man that respects me and treats me well."

He looked me squarely in the eyes. "You deserve nothing less."

"When I set my mind to something, I always get it. When I line up a shot, I always score."

"I don't doubt that."

"I want you, Reece."

He swallowed. "Just because you want something doesn't mean it's the right thing for you."

"It has to be right if it feels like this."

I pressed my lips to his. A shiver of pleasure ran through me at the pressure of his firm, warm mouth. Abruptly, he turned his face away. His peppermint breath fanned my cheek, warm and ragged. He buried his face into my neck.

"What are you doing to me?" Warmth brushed my throat and I wasn't sure if it was his lips or tears. "I want you so badly. I keep having these dreams. I can't get rid of you. It's like torture . . ." He cursed under his breath and pulled away. "I can't. This is my responsibility, but I can't fight it anymore. I can't—"

"Then don't."

I cupped his face and pulled him back to me. His lips crashed down onto mine. His tongue thrust its way between my lips and I succumbed to his devouring kiss. He crushed me to him. His arms encircled me and I arched my spine, seeking to press every inch of my body against him. My fingers trembled over the waistband of his shorts, then I yanked them down. He groaned as I took his length in my hand. I tried to drop down to my knees, but he grabbed my arms and hauled me back to my feet. I took his hand and pulled my knickers to one side, guiding him to where I needed his touch.

His fingers brushed the wetness between my thighs, and heat raced from his touch like flames in my blood. Then we were moving. His hands traveled up my hips. I opened my legs, wrapping one thigh high around him so that I was half straddling him. I kept one foot on the ground as he grabbed my backside and hoisted me against the wall. My hands were on his shaft, pulling him into me. We both groaned as I guided the head of his cock to my slick heat. He slid into me, filling me with one smooth thrust. The sudden fullness was delicious. The surprise on his face must have mirrored my own. How the hell had this happened? One minute we'd been talking and kneading dough, the next he was inside me. We held motionless, staring into each other's eyes, shell-shocked. I watched his throat bob and his bottom lip tremble as he swallowed. The scent of the warm rising dough engulfed me. The dim, still kitchen echoed with silence. Beyond the window above the sink, a full silvery moon blazed behind a gauze of clouds.

Reece pressed his forehead to mine, breathing hard. "Fuck," he whispered.

With one foot still on the floor, I rolled my hips, using the wall at my back for leverage. "Don't stop."

He buried his face into my neck and held perfectly still. "I can't." His words were a hot whisper against my throat. "I can't believe how good you feel."

Not dirty. Not bad. None of those stupid things that Sean used to say.

A glow spread through me. "I feel good to you?"

"So good. Fuck. Unbelievably good."

My fingers ached where I gripped his back through his T-shirt. Every nerve in me pulled too tight. "Please don't stop now."

Clutching my thigh, he pulled out and pushed inside of me in one slow torturous stroke. A low, surrendering moan escaped my lips. I rolled my hips, encouraging him to go faster. He moved in me in sharp thrusts. His breathing was ragged. His calm, poised demeanor long forgotten.

"Oh . . . Fuck . . . Skylar . . . Fuck . . . Ah."

I was the one who made him lose control like this. He fucked me hard and fast, like he was drowning and I was the only thing keeping him afloat, but it wasn't enough to relieve the desperate, tight ache where our bodies joined.

"I can't . . . It's been too long . . . I'm going to . . ."

I stroked his back. "I'm on the Pill. It's okay."

A groan left Reece's lips as his body shuddered. He sagged against me, pinning me against the wall. We held still, his chest moving up and down with his ragged breaths, and I stroked circles on his damp back through the thin fabric of his T-shirt. Echoes of all those times with Sean needled my mind. It had always been so quick with him too. I couldn't help my faint sense of disappointment. Reece wasn't a selfish lover like Sean though, was he? Reece's troubled eyes met mine from behind his sensible spectacles. No doubt he would be regretting and punishing himself for this.

I cupped his face with my hands. "I wanted this."

Footsteps on the stairs made us jump apart. Reece yanked his shorts up and smoothed his T-shirt. Sweat plastered his hair to the nape of his neck. Pink colored his cheeks and his throat. The door swung open. Miri appeared. An oversized green T-shirt clung to her enormous bump. She rubbed sleep from her eyes and waddled to the kitchen sink. My heart pounded in my throat. In silence, she poured herself a glass of water before she darted a look to the kitchen island and between us. Reece took a pile of tea towels and refolded each one in a slow, methodic fashion. A muscle in his jaw ticked—the only tell in his usual poised confidence.

Miri wrinkled her nose and raised a sardonic brow. "What is going on in here? Midnight bake-off?"

I cleared my throat. "I couldn't sleep. I was making bread."

"Of course you were. That's a totally normal activity at 3 a.m." She transferred her gaze to Reece. "What's your excuse?"

Reece rolled his shoulders. Despite his crumpled appearance, his face was a stoic mask. "I came for a glass of water."

"And to fold tea towels?" Miri frowned and looked between us for a moment longer than was comfortable. Then she chuckled to herself and shook her head.

"What are you laughing at?" I asked.

Miri smothered a smile. "Oh. Nothing. For a minute, I wondered if the two of you were up to something else down here."

Reece kept his eyes fixed on his task. Miri's thoughtful gaze transferred to me and made me suddenly aware that the nightdress I wore scarcely skimmed my thighs and that the heat between my legs was wet and uncomfortable. I needed to shower. I couldn't just stand here waiting to get busted by Miri. I tried to catch Reece's eye, but he wouldn't lift his gaze from his tea towels. Fine. I had no reason to be embarrassed. I hadn't done anything wrong.

I ran a hand over my hair. "I'm going to bed. I'll clean the mess in the morning."

I left without looking back.

Chapter 20

Reece

I paused outside the kitchen door. Music and chatter drifted from inside. Skylar's laugh was like music. My guts churned. I'd lost control last night. Again. One minute we'd been talking and the next . . . Had she enjoyed any of it? The moment I'd slid into her and realized how good she felt, I knew I was in trouble. I'd been like a sixteen-year-old virgin. It had all been so quick and unexpected.

I'd imagined fucking Skylar Marshall in every which way for years and years, and then I'd had my shot and blown it . . . literally. What must she have thought of me? If I hadn't been so caught off guard, I would have done things properly and taken my time. I hadn't even lasted long enough to give her an orgasm. I wanted her to see that there were better men in the world than Sean Wallace, but I hadn't been better.

I took a breath and turned around. I couldn't face her. Not after that. The coffee could wait. A low voice followed by another laugh from Skylar drifted from the kitchen. Elliot? What was so funny at this time in the morning? Were they flirting in there? The last thing Skylar needed was attention from my younger brother. I took a deep breath. I had no business being so jealous. Last night shouldn't have happened. It couldn't happen again. Skylar wouldn't even want me again after that performance. It was none of my business what she did . . . or who. But I couldn't stand the idea of my brother getting his hands on her. She deserved better than what Elliot had to offer.

I rolled my shoulders back and opened the door to the kitchen. Skylar was bent down in a squat. Elliot stood at her side, holding her hips to guide her. "It's all in the legs. Squeeze your backside as you come up and you'll be working your glutes too."

Skylar chuckled. "I know how to do a bloody squat, Elliot."

Her purple leggings and sports bra clung to her gloriously powerful frame and exposed her toned back and hard, muscled midriff. It took every ounce of willpower to shift my gaze up from her divine backside as she straightened and dropped down again. Every delicious inch of her was perfection. Her gaze flashed to mine and my heart jolted. A slight sheen of sweat glistened on her forehead.

My mind drifted to how perfectly our bodies had connected. Her gasps of pleasure. The scent of her sweat. The way it had felt to finally slide into her.

"Hi, Reece." Skylar flashed me a casual look, her tone light.

Right. So, that's how she wanted to play it. Carry on as normal. Pretend it hadn't happened. It would do for now. We'd have to talk about it, but this wasn't the right time. Not in front of Elliot. I needed some time to process it. I'd phone my supervisor, Laurel, and talk to her first. She'd know what to do. Heat lashed the back of my neck. Oh God. How was I going to tell Laurel about this? She'd be so disappointed. She'd have to report me. I'd never work again. What the hell else could I do? Everything in my life would change now. This one moment of passion would shatter my entire world like an earthquake.

But the worst thing was, it hadn't been worth it for her. I hadn't satisfied her.

"Morning." I kept my head down and swerved past them to the sink.

Skylar kept her gaze on me. "How are you?"

Uncaffeinated. Horny. Unethical.

"Fine," I said. "Have you eaten breakfast? I can make you something. Eggs?"

"We're already fueled up." Elliot's muscular biceps bulged as he stretched his huge arms over his head. "I've got myself a new running buddy."

He crossed his arms over his body and his shoulder muscles rippled. No doubt the bastard was flexing like that on purpose. Ballet had given Elliot an incredible physique. He wouldn't have looked out of place on a plinth in the Vatican Museum. The trouble was—he knew it. My brother was every bit as arrogant as he was spectacular.

I stared into the dark fridge. The light had gone off and I still hadn't had the chance to fix it.

Skylar shot me a casual glance. "Do you want to come with us, Reece?"

Elliot stretched his sculpted arms above his head. "Reece only runs if he's being chased."

Why was he touching her like that? When had these two become best friends? It was enough to put me off breakfast.

Elliot flashed Skylar a goading smile. "Do you think you can keep up?"

Skylar returned his grin and raised a mocking eyebrow. "I'm going to leave you in the dust."

I grabbed the milk bottle, only to find it empty. In fact, the whole fridge was empty. I hadn't had a chance to do the shopping, and of course it wouldn't occur to anyone else in this house that we needed to buy food in order to eat it. Fine. It would have to be black coffee. If only I could find a clean mug.

A horrible warm blast of old food stench hit me as I pulled the dishwasher open. Everything in there was still filthy. Every muscle in my body screamed with tension. All I wanted was one fucking cup of coffee. How difficult was that?

"For fuck's sake," I muttered under my breath.

Elliot's head snapped to me. "Say something, Reece?"

I ran my tongue over my lip, fighting to quell my rage. Getting angry about it wasn't going to help anything. Anger was like any other emotion. It was information. It didn't mean I had to react.

"Everything's fine," I said.

"Oh. I forgot my Fitbit." Skylar dashed to the door. "I won't be a minute."

Elliot dipped his head, his gaze unashamedly trained on Skylar's retreating backside. He shot me a smug look and kept his voice low. "How angry do you think Miri will be if I fuck her friend? She'll get over it, right?"

My jaw clamped. "Skylar is going through some stuff at the moment. She doesn't need you messing with her."

"I know, it's perfect timing. She's been dumped by Sean Wallace." Elliot cracked his knuckles. "I love being the rebound guy. That's when they want it dirty and no strings."

"That's great. Good for you. Take advantage of a vulnerable woman so you can get what you want. The rebound guy? Have you heard yourself? You do know there's more to life than meaningless hookups."

Elliot snorted. "Says you. I've never seen anyone more in need of getting laid. Did Megan take your dick along with all your fucking furniture?"

"While we're on the subject. You need to get me off that dating app."

Elliot watched me with a goading expression. "Talk to Frankie. She set it up, not me."

Another flare of temper gripped me. I took a breath and counted to ten. This was just anger. I could deal with anger. I was angry with myself. I'd lost control and compromised my ethics and my integrity. I'd messed with Skylar's head. She was already going through so much. I'd disappointed her. In my eagerness to get what I wanted, I'd been a lousy fuck. No. Not angry. I was furious with myself.

I shook my head. "Consider your behavior, Elliot. She's a guest in our house. Have some respect."

Elliot sighed. "I know, but you've seen her, right? What's a little awkwardness if I get a piece of that? Miri will get over it."

Something hot and angry snapped inside of me. "Keep your hands off her. You're like a walking erection. It is possible to have an attractive woman in this house without sleeping with her. Stop being so fucking juvenile."

Elliot stared at me for a minute before he frowned.

Miri sauntered in, yawning and rubbing sleep from her eyes. "What's going on?"

Elliot glided to the sink and washed a mug, probably for the first time in his life. "There's something wrong with Reece. He got angry with me. He even used some special grown-up bad words. I think he's malfunctioning."

Miri shot me a wry glance. "Have you tried turning him off and back on again?"

Very fucking funny.

I tried to take deep breaths, but a hot, scratchy sensation dug deeper inside like talons. What the hell had I done? I'd been so weak. I'd let a client give me a blow job in my own office. I'd fucked her in my kitchen. Now she was here in my house, and I felt sick with jealousy at the thought of Elliot making a move on her. This woman wasn't for me. I couldn't have her. How had it got to this point?

Miri yanked the fridge door open. She stared at the empty shelves. "Why is there no food?"

"Oh, I don't know. Maybe because the food fairy that fills up the shelves didn't come last night," I said.

Miri's eyes widened with shock. She studied my face. "Jesus. Reece. Was that your attempt at sarcasm?" She shot Elliot an amused look. "He *is* malfunctioning. What did you to do him?"

"Here." Elliot poured me a coffee and put the hot mug on the island. "Drink this, Reece. I think you need it."

I gave him a grudging nod of gratitude. My younger brother might have been annoying, but at least he knew when to take a step back, unlike his twin. Why hadn't Frankie taken me off that app? Was the whole team laughing about me? Skylar swept into the kitchen, fiddling with a black strap on her wrist.

"Just in time." Elliot put his arm around Skylar's shoulder to shepherd her out of the room. "Reece is malfunctioning. He needs to get laid before his head explodes and his balls drop off. Let's get out of here and leave him to it."

Skylar flashed me an embarrassed look. My teeth itched with humiliation.

I'm in control.

She disappeared out of the room with Elliot. I pressed my forehead to the cold fridge door.

Nope. Who am I fucking kidding? I'm not in control. Not even a little bit.

"Honey, I'm home." Gabe's clipped voice drifted to my ears.

I turned to see him leaning in the doorway with a smirk and a briefcase in his hand. Miri beamed and melted into his open arms.

His gaze transferred to me. "What's up with you, Doc?"

Irritation rippled every inch of my skin. "Oh, fuck off, Gabe, and stop fucking . . . leaning everywhere, will you?"

His shocked laugh chased me out of the room as I stormed down the hall.

Chapter 21

SKYLAR

Back home, I ran myself the hottest, deepest bath. My muscles loosened as I sank into delicious soapy water. The scent of black-pepper bubble bath filled my nose. My mind drifted to Reece Forster. The memory of his cool, calm voice crackled over my skin like electricity. I couldn't stop thinking about the delicious sensation of when he'd hoisted me up against the wall so masterfully.

I let my hands glide through the suds and over my hips and waist. Reece Forster with his geeky glasses and crisp white shirt had driven me wild. A couple of weeks ago I hadn't known him, and now every second was consumed by thoughts of him. I wouldn't get out of this bath until I'd made myself come. Even if the water was stone cold and I turned into a prune, I'd get the job done.

I closed my eyes and let my mind drift. I didn't have much to draw on with Sean. He was rough. Most of the time, it had been a relief when it was over. I let my mind fill with Reece Forster: his handsome face, those full, sensual lips, the tortured noises he'd made when he moved inside me. I let my fingers drift low between my thighs, rubbing and circling in a slippery massage.

Arousal built as my fingers worked. I fondled my soapy nipple, imagining it was Reece Forster touching me. A little shiver of pleasure went through me. The hot throb between my thighs became a desperate ache. My breath came in sharp pants. The water swished in the bath as I moved my fingers around the bundle of nerves between my thighs, experimenting. All that mattered was Reece Forster and all the ways I wanted him to make me feel good.

I submerged myself to my chin in the hot, silky water. My breath quickened. Hot, tight tension curled like a snake in my lower belly, ready to unleash—

A noise downstairs made me jump. The slam of the front door. What the fuck? Shock held me rigid before I mastered my fear, got out of the bath, and wrapped myself in a towel. I tiptoed to the bathroom window and peered out for the source of the noise. Sean's car sat on the drive. Tinny whirring and crashing filled my ears. I pulled on a robe and followed the sound downstairs. Sean's trainers sat on the entrance mat and his football jacket, still wet from the rain, hung on his peg. Seriously? I hadn't even bothered to change the locks because I couldn't imagine he'd have the audacity to show up when I'd told him to leave me alone.

I followed the racket down to the basement gym. Sean stretched out his long, powerful legs on the rowing machine. He wiped sweat from his brow and shot me an affable glance.

"Hey. How are you? I thought I'd get some training in before the match this afternoon."

Confusion made my heart pound. What the hell was he doing back here? Why did he have that smile on his face as if nothing had happened?

He stared at me. "Were you having a bath?"

I pulled my robe tighter. "What's going on?"

Sean went back to rowing. The metal chain snapped with his long, fast strokes. "I can't stay with my parents anymore. They are driving me mad."

"Tough luck. You can't stay here."

He kept his voice light and his gaze fixed on the small screen in the rowing machine that tracked his time. "It's my name on the mortgage."

He couldn't be serious? This had to be a sick joke. A buzz rang out and Sean's phone flashed at the side of the rower. He snatched it and shoved it into the pocket of his gym shorts.

"Lana? Or is this a new one?"

He shook sweat from his blond head. "Nothing happened with Lana." He panted, picking up his pace on the rower. "Girls message me. It means nothing. You know how it is when you're the captain. I made some mistakes, but it won't happen again. If you want to give this another go, then I'd be willing, but you're going to need to get off my balls about the other girls."

A wild, hysterical laugh rose up in me. "Are you fucking kidding me? You've treated me like shit for years. There is no way back for us, Sean."

He shot me a cold look. "I've treated *you* like shit?"

He stopped rowing and wiped the sweat from his brow with a towel. He got up and planted himself in front of me. Resting an elbow on the exercise bike frame, he leaned into me. Sweat assaulted my nostrils. He traced a line over my lips with his thumb. "I'm willing to try couples therapy if you are. Maybe we can get that geeky doctor from school to help us figure things out."

I tilted my chin, gathering as much dignity as I could muster. "Don't talk about Reece like that."

His mouth spread into a thin-lipped smile. "Right. Reece. The two of you looked cozy in that library. Anything you want to get off your chest?"

"It's none of your business. You're a liar and a cheat. There is no amount of therapy in the world that will make me want to give this another go."

His expression grew hard and resentful. "I have needs, Skylar. The other girls make me feel wanted. What do you expect? Sex with you is so . . ."

My resolve hardened and I stood straighter. "So what?"

He shrugged. "Dull."

"And what if that isn't all my fault? What if it's both of us? What if it's *you*?"

"Of course it's not me. I've had plenty of girls. They don't have any problems getting off."

I folded my arms. Nausea rolled in my gut. "Plenty of girls? I've been faithful to you since school. All this time . . ."

He turned and went back to his rowing. His expression was taut and derisive. "Regardless of what goes on between me and you, this is my house. I'm not leaving."

My head pounded. I stormed out of the gym and upstairs to the bedroom. Hangers screamed on the metal rail as I rifled through my wardrobe, throwing clothes into a case. Fuck Sean. How dare he? Half of me wanted to march downstairs and argue with him, but my heart hurt too much. I bit back my tears. I didn't fall apart. The captain needed to be strong.

In a daze, I stumbled downstairs and out the front door. Cold air hit my face and I tried to take deep breaths. What now? I needed a plan. I could go to my parents, but they'd have so many questions. I didn't want to be grilled like a squid by my mum. I couldn't bear to talk to anyone. I'd have to go to a hotel. My heart ached. How long could I do that for? I needed a place to think straight.

I threw my bag in the boot of my car and set off for the training pitches. Hot panic sizzled over my skin. Only one thing could help me when I felt like this. I needed to calm down. My breath snapped hot and sharp in my lungs. Reece's voice drifted to my mind.

Your feelings will make themselves heard however they can. They won't always choose the most convenient times.

Reece was right. I didn't need distraction. I needed to talk to somebody. I needed Reece. But first, I needed to kick a ball as hard as I could.

Chapter 22

REECE

Skylar hadn't looked at me once since she entered the office. She wore her football kit: a blue jersey, shorts, and knee socks. I leaned back in my seat, getting comfortable, seeing if she would mirror my movements and relax. She didn't. She could probably see I was faking. No part of me could relax in her presence. She looked so different from this morning. Her hair tumbled in a messy lilac waterfall to her shoulders. Dark hollows shadowed her pretty eyes. Had I made her feel like this? We hadn't even talked about last night. I shouldn't have let her walk out of my house.

I tried to stop my gaze from drifting to the bookcase. A couple of the spines protruded at odd angles. It made my skin prickle with the need to straighten them. An ache blazed right between my shoulder blades, but I fought to sit still and composed. After a night tossing and turning, my spine was the only relaxed part of me, and it was supposed to be supporting my entire body.

I took a breath. "How are you? Have you come straight from practice?"

She shrugged and adjusted her football socks below her knees. "No practice. I just needed to kick things. I was heading for the pitches, and I ended up here instead . . ."

Hot air licked over my skin. Skylar chewed her lip and smoothed her hands over her toned thighs.

I cleared my throat. "About last night . . . You don't need to feel bad or any guilt about what happened between us. This was my fault. It's my responsibility to manage the boundary. This is my failure, but—"

"He's such a prick," she said quietly.

"Sorry?"

"Sean."

Sean? Had she seen him? Had something happened since I'd last seen her?

Her shoulders quivered and she sniffed. "Sorry." She swiped her cheeks. "I don't cry."

"You don't have to apologize for crying." I nudged a box of tissues across the coffee table. "Cry all you want with me."

Her fingers quaked as she took a tissue and dabbed her eyes. I wished we weren't in this office, in this situation, because I longed to just hold her in my arms, stroke her back, and kiss her tears away.

She folded her tissue into a tiny square with quivering fingers, then took a shuddering breath. "He was at the house. I was having a bath and I heard him downstairs. He was there on the rowing machine, pretending like nothing was wrong . . ." Her voice broke off and she turned her face to the window. "I phoned Miri. She invited me to stay, but I thought you'd be more comfortable if I don't. Gabe is letting me stay at the Beaufort."

"No. You should stay with us. I can go elsewhere for a while."

"The hotel is fine." A bitter smile trembled on her lips. "Just when I thought I was making some progress. The worst part is that he's right about all of it."

131

"Right about what?"

The silence grew so thick it smothered us. I fought every compulsion to break it. That wasn't the way to help her in this room.

"You know, the worst part is that I've never asked for much. I want someone who I can love, and who will love me back. I've got a lot of love to give. Do you know what I mean?"

Yes. I know what you mean.

Skylar had a huge heart. She had big feelings because she wore her heart on her sleeve. She was brave and fierce.

She licked her lips and her eyes searched mine before they darted away. "It doesn't matter. I don't even know why I'm telling you any of this." She stared straight ahead with a sad, faraway gaze. "You don't want me, either. Last night . . . You see the problem. I can't . . . It's the same with Sean. I can't orgasm. I was so turned on. Still, it doesn't matter. I can't let go and enjoy it even when I want it the way I wanted it last night." She shook her head and raked a hand over her face. "I'll leave you alone. I shouldn't have even come here."

She stood and moved to the door. Instinctively, I got up and followed. I wrapped my hand around the door handle.

"Last night was . . . I couldn't last, Skylar. I'm sorry. It was me. Not you. It surprised me, that's all. I got too . . . It was a little . . ." My tie suddenly felt too tight, like a noose around my throat. I loosened the knot. ". . . Overwhelming. If I didn't satisfy you, then that's all on me, not you. Don't run out of here like this. Please. Let's keep talking."

Tears glistened on her proud, pale face. "I don't want to talk anymore. I'm done. Don't worry about me. I won't bother you again."

My heart thumped erratically, and I should have let her go, but my fingers gripped the door handle so tightly they ached. Her blue, tear-filled eyes reflected glimmers of light. They were full of expectation. She made me feel the way I did when I walked through the park full of crocuses pushing their heads above the dirt in spring. There was so much ugliness in the world, but some things could still be so beautiful they made you ache.

I'd never wanted more than for this to be out in the open so I could just stare at her like this without feeling guilty that I was doing the wrong thing, or that people might see us together.

I carried this heaviness inside of me all the time from trying to do the right thing. From always trying to be in control. Always trying to be perfect. I didn't want that anymore. I just wanted her. I wanted to feel myself moving inside of her. My gaze froze on her soft mouth. I needed to trace the outline of her lips with my thumb. I'd never wanted anything so badly. Sean Wallace might have been a selfish lover, but I couldn't think of anything I wanted more than this woman's nails clawing my back and my name on her lips when she was so twisted up with need she could only cry out.

My heart pounded so hard she could probably hear it. I met her longing gaze with my own and traced my thumb over the soft line of her jaw. Her eyes fluttered shut and she shivered with anticipation. Oh God. I was touching her. Why was I touching her again? What did it matter now? We'd already crossed the line. It had already gone too far.

She hesitated, measuring me for a moment, before she leaned up and whispered in my ear, "The only time I've ever got close to getting myself off, I was thinking about you."

A rush of adrenaline went through me. I couldn't let her walk away thinking there was something wrong with her. Sean Wallace might have been an ace on the football pitch, but it didn't take muscles to please a woman. It took listening, consideration, patience, and a willingness to learn. Skylar Marshall was perfect. I had to show her.

I pulled her toward me and my lips found hers. She gave a shocked gasp, then her arms encircled me and her hands locked against my spine. I didn't have Sean Wallace's muscles and I'd never understood the offside rule, but I'd show this woman how perfect she was if it was the last thing I ever did.

Chapter 23

Skylar

Reece's lips crashed down onto mine. His tongue thrust its way between my lips, and I succumbed to his devouring kiss. His lips seared a path over my neck and he spoke between hot, fervent kisses. "You said you were thinking about me when you touched yourself. What were we doing in the fantasy?"

I opened my mouth and closed it again. I'd never been shy, but I'd never spoken so directly about what I liked with anyone before. Sean had never asked.

Reece's lips blazed a path along my jaw. "Tell me. Whatever it is. I won't judge you."

"You . . . Your voice. You're talking to me."

"My voice? Dirty talk?" His words were a hot whisper against my jugular.

"No . . . not dirty . . . I hate that. Sean says things like that, that I'm a filthy girl and a slut. I don't like it. I don't want to be a bad girl. It doesn't make me feel good. I want to be . . ."

Warmth stroked my cheeks. These things felt so unnatural to talk about. I coughed to cover my embarrassment.

Reece stopped his amorous assault. He studied my face and frowned. "You don't want to be a bad girl?" His dark eyes locked with mine. "A good girl?" he said softly.

My body flooded with heat at the sound of those words on his full lips. I nodded. "Yes."

He drew away from my neck. His expression darkened. "Get on the couch."

I blinked to hide my confusion. "Pardon?"

Slowly, he removed his blazer and hung it on the back of his chair. He rolled up his sleeves to the elbows in his slow, controlled way. I couldn't tear my gaze from the dusting of dark hair that smattered his muscular forearms and his long, elegant fingers. His masculine, self-confident presence made my heart hammer.

With one smooth step forward, he towered over me. My back hit the door and he boxed me in with a hand either side of me.

He leaned in to whisper in my ear. "You heard me. Be a good girl and get on my couch."

He reached around me to snick the lock on the door. Then he crossed to the windows and pulled the cord. The blinds raced down in a resounding whoosh, making the room dim. A shiver of anticipation shot up my spine. He didn't need to tell me a third time. My knees were weak as I moved to the other side of the room and sat on his cool leather couch. He loosened the knot in his tie and his steady demeanor took on an even more serious edge.

"Lie back." His voice was calm and composed but his eyes blazed with fire behind his glasses.

If anyone else had stood and issued orders at me I would have played hell with them, but not Reece. I wanted to please him. To do whatever he wanted. I wanted to come undone for him.

"Show me how you touch yourself."

A twinge of embarrassed panic went through me. "I can't. You don't want to see me doing that."

He tilted my chin, forcing me to look in his dark eyes. "Trust me, I can't think of anything I want to see more."

"I can't."

"Yes. You can."

His fingers danced up my inner thigh, teasing under the hem of my shorts. Heat flooded my body. His lips found mine as he tugged my shorts down and off. Planting his elbow by the side of my head, he leaned over me, and his lips met mine in a slow, drugging kiss that made my skin tingle with desire.

"Show me," he murmured into my mouth. "You don't have to feel any embarrassment with me."

This is where we both came to work. Nobody here could have expected what was going on. It only made it more exciting. A desperate ache took root between my thighs. A strange fear gripped me, like I was standing at the edge of choppy waters preparing to jump in. The water would be freezing, but it would be so liberating to swim. Fuck it. I didn't do fear. A captain can't be afraid.

We both watched as I slipped my fingers down below the waistband of my thin cotton knickers and rubbed in slow, slippery circles. Waves of pleasure spread from my core at my gentle massage. Every nerve was heightened. Even the cold air on the apex of nerves between my thighs left me weak.

He slipped his fingers over mine. His lips brushed my ear as he whispered into my hair. "Guide me."

I did as he asked, moving his fingers beneath mine in firm strokes on my slick tender flesh.

His clean manly scent filled my nose. "You think about me when you do this alone?"

"Yes."

A quiver surged through me at his tormented groan.

His voice was a velvet murmur. "I keep having these dreams. I can't get you out of my head. It's like being a teenager with a crush again. This longing I have for you is torture. Do you know what you do to me?"

"What do I do to you?" My voice barely broke a whisper.

"You make me feel out of control, like I'm losing my mind for you."

I arched my spine on the couch, my backside squirming into soft, buttery leather. My breath came hot and sharp and we were panting into each other's mouths between hungry kisses that were somehow both slow and urgent. Still he kept up his relentless, torturous massage between my thighs.

"You're so beautiful. So perfect." His hands were cool as they slipped under my jersey. He eased down the zip at the front of my sports bra and palmed my breasts. "So good . . . such a good girl."

My body ached at the loss of his touch between my thighs.

"This might not happen for me, Reece . . . I know you're expecting it . . . You don't have to do this . . ."

He moved his hands from my breasts to cup my face. His face was its usual stoic mask; only his smoldering eyes betrayed his ardor. "Listen to me. It doesn't matter if it happens or not. I've got all the time in the world to watch you like this. Don't spend the whole match focusing on scoring a goal. Just enjoy the game."

He lifted my jersey up and I helped him take it off. He sucked my nipple into his mouth. I moaned and arched against him, digging my fingers in his soft hair. His lips trailed over every inch of my breasts, then he was moving lower, planting hot, open-mouthed kisses on my stomach. The throb between my thighs became a desperate ache.

Slowly, his large hands skimmed my hips and he kissed through the fabric of my knickers. Sean had never gone down on me and I'd always wondered what it would feel like. Reece held my gaze as he tongued through thin cotton. "Do you like that?"

"Mm-hmm."

"You're going to be a good girl and tell me everything you like, and I'm going to give it to you. I'll give you anything you want."

He pulled up a chair to the end of the couch. Then he took hold of my hips and dragged me down so his face was positioned between my legs. His hands grazed my hips as he slid my knickers down and off, leaving me bare apart from my socks pulled to the knee. I moved to take my shin pads and socks off.

He shook his head. "No. Leave them on."

"You want me to leave my socks on?"

"Yes."

"But I've got shin pads on."

His voice was as gentle but uncompromising as ever. "Leave those, too. I've always imagined you wearing them when I make you come."

His tone was so matter-of-fact and his face so impassive that I couldn't help but laugh.

"Are you judging me, Miss Marshall?"

"No, Dr. Forster." I put a hand over my heart and flashed a sardonic smile. "This is a safe space."

His stare was unwavering before his gaze dropped and froze between my thighs. I lay spread and exposed for him. Instinctively, I moved my hands to cover myself.

"Don't do that." Gently, he took my hands away and put them by my sides. His voice was a reverent whisper. "You're perfect. I knew you would be."

Embarrassment coursed through me to be so exposed, but a thrill ran through me too. Reece had made no secret of the fact he wanted me. It made me feel confident in a way I never did with Sean.

He smoothed a hand up the back of my leg. "We're going to experiment. You're going to tell me what feels good. There is no right or wrong answer."

His head bowed and he planted teasing kisses on my inner thighs. I cried out at the first firm lap of his tongue against my wet heat.

"Oh God, Reece." My voice came out a desperate whimper.

"Good?"

"Mm-hmm."

His tongue flicked against my clit. A jolt of electricity went through me. My thighs clenched. I cried out as he buried his face and his glasses bumped against me. My toes curled, and I clamped my hand over my mouth to stifle another cry. Someone could be walking past in the corridor outside, but Reece seemed so completely lost to his work, he didn't care.

His tongue swirled, licking, probing, tasting in ever more determined strokes. My knees buckled and my thighs trembled. I wanted to be quiet, but my surrendering groans couldn't help but broadcast my need for him. His eyes lingered on mine while he worked, adjusting his pressure and rhythm according to my moans. With his hands on my hips, he dragged me to the end of the couch, spreading me wider and hooking one of my thighs over his shoulder. Divine pleasure radiated from his determined probing. My fingers buried into his soft hair as he lapped. Then his mouth covered my clit and he sucked. A shockwave of pleasure sizzled up my spine. Everything tightened with need. My breath came in gasps.

"Like that?" he murmured against me.

Somehow, I found words to speak. "Like that."

I rocked senselessly against him, but a warning bell rang in my head. What if he was getting bored down there? What if I couldn't get there? What if Sean was right about me and there was something wrong with me?

As though he could read my mind, Reece's eyes connected with mine again from between my thighs. "Don't get in your head. Just breathe. Just this breath."

140

My body tensed; still it didn't feel like I could let go enough to get there. Frustration made my shoulders bunch. "I don't think I can do this."

"Take the pressure off." His murmured words against my clit made me arch against him. "Let me give you pleasure. It doesn't have to end in anything. I can do this all day. There's nowhere else I'd rather be."

His soothing voice crackled over my skin like icy flames. Closing my eyes, I sucked in a slow breath. My body tightened like a fine silken thread pulled too taut. I fought to draw deep breaths and let my muscles soften. Heat raced from his touch. He moved his long, elegant finger up through my slick folds, parting me. "So pretty and perfect." His fingertip teased my entrance. "So delicious. So wet and warm."

He slipped his finger a little further inside me and held still. I couldn't contain my moan.

"Good girl. You're so good at telling me what you need."

He filled me with his finger, curling upward, hitting a spot that sent shudders through me. Heat flashed all over my body. Sweat dripped down my neck. I squirmed and writhed my backside, tightening around him.

His eyes met mine. "More?"

"Yes."

He slipped a second finger into my slick heat, moving in delicious strokes while his thumb still traced circles on my clit. I ground against him, pressing closer. He watched me with an expression of awe. "That's right. Just let it come. Don't chase it."

My hands clenched into fists. A desperate need for release gripped me, as torturous as it was divine.

He studied my face. "It's okay. You can let go with me. I've got you."

Sweat collected at my temples and my heart thundered. He stood, holding his tie out of the way as he leaned over to kiss me, and I tasted myself for the first time. I'd never felt more desperate for his kiss. I'd never wanted anything more. The fact that he would do this for me—that he wanted to satisfy me in a way that Sean could never be bothered to—meant everything.

With one hand, his sure fingers worked their magic between my thighs, and with the other he smoothed back my hair. "I've got you. You can trust me. You're so beautiful. Every inch of you is perfection."

His praise stoked my desperate need to come undone for him. "Faster," I whimpered.

He responded instantly, his expert fingers rubbing firmly where I needed him most as he analyzed my reactions. "Good girl. You're doing so well."

"Fuuuck . . . I just need more." My fingers fisted into his shirt and I jerked him toward me. I needed to hear his voice. "Talk to me."

"Do you know how much I've craved you?" His calm, considered words were hot against my ear. "You have no idea how badly I've longed to see you like this. I want to see you lose control. You can do that with me. It's easy. I'm going to take care of you. Just let go."

I sucked in a breath. It was easy. With Reece it was easy to let go. His poised, solid demeanor made me feel safe. He pressed his forehead to mine; his warm breath fanned my face. I gripped his shirt so hard my fingers burned. "Oh . . . I think . . . Oh . . . I'm going to . . . Oh . . . Don't stop . . . Ah . . ."

The tension inside built to fever pitch. An elastic band about to snap. My breath came in high-pitched pants. A series of rough cries left my mouth and I bucked my hips against his hand, desperate for the friction. My backside lifted half off the couch in urgent whimpering need. Still he wouldn't stop his relentless slippery massage.

More.

Reece moved back to the end of the couch. He bowed his head between my thighs and replaced his fingers with his mouth. Our eyes met and held as he sucked my clit, hard. The sensation was almost unbearable in its intensity. A cry left my mouth and I was too far gone to pleasure to bother trying to smother it. I raked my hands through his soft hair. Release exploded through me, sending rippling crests of euphoria racing through my body. I surrendered to the mastery of his tongue and it was like diving into the deepest, clearest lake and finding that I'd been waiting my whole life to take the plunge. Delicious waves of satisfaction carried me away. Reece's dark eyes were my only tether as I lost myself in the explosion of pleasure.

He kept working until he'd wrung every last quiver from me. I collapsed back, savoring, shuddering, trying to come back to my senses. Tingling aftershocks sparked from the base of my spine to the soles of my feet. My panting filled the silent office. Reece watched my face with an expression of fascinated awe, like a scientist who has just made a paradigm-shifting discovery. He'd changed everything. The small smug smile on his full lips told me he knew it.

"Oh my God." I sat up, dazed and half-drunk with pleasure. "I'm pretty sure they didn't teach you that at Cambridge."

"No." His brow lifted a fraction, and he raked a hand through his dark hair. "That kind of thing is extracurricular."

Chapter 24

REECE

The city flashed by outside in a blaze of bright lights in the darkness. Skylar's scent of grass and mud filled my car. I had to stop my gaze from drifting down to her muddy football boots and the mess they made in the passenger seat footwell. My hands tensed around the steering wheel and I tried to breathe through it. What would Laurel say? A little bit of mess doesn't matter. I could clean it once I'd dropped Skylar at Gabe's hotel. The scrape of the windscreen wipers filled my ears. We'd hardly spoken since I'd offered her a ride. This had gone too far.

She stretched her arms above her head languorously. Huskiness still lingered in her tone. "I want you to take me out on a date."

"A date?"

"We've never been on a date. I want you to take me out to dinner."

A date? I'd spent so many hours practicing a way to say something to this woman, anything, never mind asking her on a date, and here she was throwing the possibility out so casually. What would it be like to take Skylar Marshall out for dinner? To pull up at a restaurant, take her hand in mine, and escort her inside. Every pair of eyes would track her, and then their curious gazes would land on me. The luckiest man in the world who got to bathe in Skylar's glow for a night.

I'd take her to this beautiful little Italian place that Gabe had introduced us to. It was all cozy nooks, checkered tablecloths and candlelight glinting on wine bottles that lined the walls. Gino, the chef, had given us a tour of the kitchen, and shared his tiramisu recipe. Skylar would love it there. It was charming without being pretentious.

I'd get the booth by the window, a nice bottle of red. No expense spared. I'd be just as happy staying in, eating takeaway pizza and watching TV together. Maybe even happier that way. Skylar might be too. Some of the girls on Miri's team liked to party, but Skylar had always seemed more of a homebody.

No matter where we went, if she was mine, I'd treat her like a queen. I'd keep telling her how beautiful she was, how funny, how kind, how smart. How lucky I was to be with her. I'd make it my mission to undo all the bad thoughts that Sean had put into her head, so she never doubted herself again.

A cold feeling spread through me. It was just a fantasy. Skylar couldn't be mine. We couldn't have a normal relationship. I shouldn't have done any of this stuff with somebody I'd been trying to help.

I cleared my throat. "None of this should have happened."

She rolled her eyes. "Don't start all of this again. If you think I'm not going to pursue this after what just happened between us, you can think again."

A muscle jumped in my jaw. We couldn't keep going with this. I'd wanted to show her that there was nothing wrong with her. Now she was free to pursue a relationship with someone better than Sean Wallace.

"Nothing has changed. We can't see each other outside of my office."

She laughed and it came out hollow. "Nothing has changed? Everything has changed. Unless you normally get women off on your couch as part of your process. This is not therapy, Reece. You need to get this out of your head."

A ball of ice swirled inside. "I want what's best for you."

"And what if you're best for me? I like you, Reece. I like you a lot. I know you're panicking and backpedaling, wishing it hadn't happened. But I don't wish that it hadn't. Meeting you is the best thing that's happened to me in a long time. You're not like anyone I've ever met. You're kind and you're clever and funny. You listen to me. And you gave me my first orgasm. I'm not letting you get rid of me so easily."

I wanted to help Skylar, not add to her problems. It wasn't even true. I didn't want to get rid of her. I wanted her more than ever. Did she think this was easy for me? It wasn't. Even if we kept things a secret, I knew what we were doing. How could I look myself in the eye knowing how I'd compromised my ethical standards? It was damaging for Skylar, too, if it was making her feel like this. She wasn't fucking up. I was.

I parked in the lot across the street from the grand, soaring Beaufort Hotel. I switched the engine off.

Skylar unbuckled and twisted in the passenger seat to face me. "Look, I get it. We work together. You don't want to get into anything with me. It's fine. I'm not looking for anything deep here, either. I just got out of a relationship. My focus has to be on getting us promoted. I don't want this getting out, either. I'm just asking for . . ."

I glanced at her. *What? What was she asking for?*

"Some no-strings fun." She arched a brow. "Like you said you wanted in your profile."

A pulse beat in my head. "I didn't make that dating profile. My siblings think this kind of thing is funny—"

"Fine, but so what if you did do it? You're allowed to date. You're allowed to have sex."

Yes, but not with you.

It was unethical and it was damaging for her. I'd made a huge mistake. The best thing to do would be to get her out of the car and go home. I couldn't continue this, no matter how she made my heart thump. I dared a glance at her. Her elegant face drew my gaze like a magnet. My fingers ached to touch her, to feel something good and beautiful instead of the restless tension that consumed me.

I'd been restless for so long. Burned out from looking after everyone all the time: my mum, my patients, my family. Agitation always crawling under my skin at all the mess in the house and things beyond my control. I needed something . . . different. Something fun. Something *wild*. But at the same time, I wanted someone to relax with. Someone to let me rest my head in their lap, or rub my back.

Skylar wasn't an option—it was selfish and stupid to get involved with her—but God, I wanted her. I wanted her the same way I'd wanted her when we were both fourteen. Except the teenage me wouldn't have had a clue what to do with a woman like this.

I knew now.

She reached for my hand and her warm fingers intertwined with mine. "I can see you fighting yourself. It doesn't have to be so deep."

Her eyes were gentle and contemplative. I didn't want her gentleness. Heat tingled where her fingers touched mine. I should have let go, but I couldn't. She leaned into me, tilting her face upward. My body ached for her. I wanted to pull her onto my lap and take her right there in the parking lot. I wanted to bury myself in her, to lose myself. Every day was a struggle to maintain control over myself when I was so desperate to drown in her.

More than anything, I just wanted to be with her . . . anywhere, in any way that she'd have me. I longed to go back to Gabe's library and watch the fire dance on her beautiful face as I read her poetry, or cuddle with her on the couch watching trashy TV. I wanted us to do normal things. To get away from this feeling that we shouldn't be together. To just spend time with her because being with her made me feel more . . . myself than I ever had before. More alive.

She glanced at the hotel across the street. "You should see these rooms. Can you believe Gabe owns this whole thing?"

Her sweet watermelon perfume filled my senses as she moved closer and rested her palm on my cheek. "We've crossed the line, Reece. Stay with me tonight." Her voice was a soft murmur. "What's the point in denying yourself now?"

The touch of her hand was unbearable in its tenderness. She gazed into my eyes and I felt my pulse everywhere, my throat, my wrists, my eyelids. This was the third time I'd had the woman I was infatuated with asking me to spend a night with her. The difference was, now I'd had a taste of her, how was I supposed to go back to before?

A torrent of filth filled my mind.

The caress of her soft mouth on mine. Her kiss, rushed and urgent but devouring and all-consuming. Pulling her roughly onto my lap, freeing her perfect breasts from her sports bra and feeling the beautiful weight of them in my palms. Slipping my fingers into her shorts.

She watched my face in the dim light of the car and a smile curved her lips. "You're thinking about it, aren't you? Come inside. Gabe insisted I stay in the penthouse. Apparently, there's a gold-plated Jacuzzi. It sounds like a bloody porn set."

Her eyes clung to my face. I shook my head. "It's my fault that things went so far between us, and it's my responsibility to put a stop to it."

"This is bullshit. You want me. I'm yours. Be brave, Reece. Take what you want."

She reached for the door handle. "Stop overthinking this. I'm asking you upstairs for a shag in a gold-plated Jacuzzi. I'm not asking you to marry me. Don't you want some porn-star sex in your brother-in-law's porny hotel room?" There was a trace of laughter in her voice. "Live the dream."

I couldn't help but laugh at her bluntness.

Her eyes riveted to my face. "I don't think I've ever seen you laugh." She nudged me in the side. "Life doesn't have to be so serious, you know. Are you coming or not? I'm not going to beg."

This had to end. I had to get out before I messed up even more. But tonight, I couldn't say no. The fact of the matter was that I was weak, and Skylar knew it. Tomorrow, I'd hand in my resignation. Tonight, I needed porn-star sex with Skylar Marshall in one of my brother-in-law's porny hotel rooms.

Chapter 25

SKYLAR

I lay back in the enormous circular Jacuzzi. Delicious heat soothed my sore muscles, and everything relaxed inside of me like a full-body sigh. The low hum of the Jacuzzi filled my ears, and silky rose-scented bubbles vibrated and splashed against my bare skin. Reece's hands were everywhere, skimming my thighs, gliding over my hips, stroking my stomach.

Steam misted his glasses. He removed them and placed them on the side with a gentle click. Without his glasses, he looked more boyish, but not more handsome. I liked him either way.

"Can you see without them?"

He kissed along the yellow rose tattoo on my collarbone. "I can see enough."

My fingers dug into his shoulders and he shook his head in wonder. "Do you know what the teenage me would be thinking if he knew that one day I'd have you naked and at my mercy? Look at you." He gazed down and his hand disappeared under the bubbles and smoothed over my stomach. "It doesn't matter how often I go to that gym, I'll never have abs like this."

I ran my hands over his lean, muscular arms. "I like your body."

He studied my face, a half-smile on his full lips. "You don't have to patronize me. I've seen that gym. All those football players posing and flexing their muscles . . ."

"You're not jealous of those guys, are you?"

"No." His voice was calm, his gaze steady. "None of them have made you come like I have."

I couldn't help my laugh at his matter-of-fact expression. It was a fair point. No man had ever made me feel the way Reece had. It wasn't just the orgasm. It was the way he looked at me as though I was fascinating. The way he gave me every scrap of his attention when I spoke. I sat up on the ledge that lined the Jacuzzi and walked my fingers up his hot chest. "Are you getting cocky now, Dr. Forster? I suppose that one orgasm you gave me was impressive, but for all we know it was a fluke."

A faint smile pulled at his serious lips. "That sounds like a challenge."

I cocked a teasing brow. "Does it?"

His fingers danced over my hips, but he didn't touch me where I needed him, where the hot tingling ache made my thighs clench. Every nerve was heightened in the intense bubbling heat that engulfed us. He parted my lips with his tongue and kissed me. His thumb brushed between my thighs and I couldn't control the moan that escaped my lips.

"Are you going to be a good girl for me again?" he murmured against my mouth. "Tell me what you need and I'll give you anything."

I lowered my lips to his ear and gripped his hard shaft under the water. "I'll tell you what I need when I feel you inside of me."

"This is about your pleasure, not mine. Nothing turns me on more than satisfying you."

"This is about both of us."

He reached up to caress my face. "The captain gets whatever the captain wants."

He perched on the ledge next to me. His fingers dug into my hips as he dragged me through the water onto his lap to straddle him. A shadow of unease went through me. Sean had never liked me on top.

He studied my face. "You look worried. What's the matter?"

"I'm not confident on top."

He cupped my face, his voice calm and level. "This is about experimenting, not performance. We're going to find out together what feels good. It's not an exam. You can't get it right or wrong."

He palmed my breasts. Heat seared from his touch and my muscles softened again as the hot water beat against me. The ache to feel full of him left me breathless. Warmth spread through me at his earnest expression. What did Reece see when he looked at me? Not whatever Sean had seen. With Reece, I felt like a goddess.

He hissed and held perfectly still as I ran my hands up his erect length. He lifted my hips. I hovered over him so that the thick head of his shaft pressed against my wetness. He groaned but neither of us moved. The press of him was divine torture. The desperate urge to slam down onto him made my hips jerk and my body ache, but I wanted to tease him. His thumb moved to circle my clit in gentle then firm strokes, the way he'd learned. Waves of pleasure spread from my core. I gripped his broad shoulders. My head fell back on my neck with pleasure as I rocked over him.

He reached up and cupped my face with both hands. "You're going to look so beautiful riding me."

We both groaned as I lowered myself onto him. I held motionless, adjusting to the size of him, then I rolled my hips, grinding, finding an angle that worked well. Water splashed over the side of the Jacuzzi onto the tiled floor. My heart thundered. A sudden fear gripped me. What if I couldn't come? What if it had been a one-off in his office?

Reece watched my face, his eyes narrowing as if he could read my mind. "It doesn't matter. Stay with me in this moment. Take the pressure off and relax. If you don't get there, we try something different. There's no rush."

His hands explored the slippery hollows of my back and I trembled as I drew myself up before gliding back down onto his length. I pitched forward against him, grinding, working him deep inside of me. My breasts hovered near his face and his tongue traced out to suck my nipple into his mouth. A shiver of desire raced through me. My hips bucked erratically. All that mattered was the intense, soothing heat that enveloped my body and his firm strokes filling me. I bumped up and down carelessly. Blood pounded my ears.

He watched me with a smoldering intensity. "Yes. Like that. You're so beautiful." His free hand scorched a path down my arched spine. "Such a good girl when you ride me like this."

His praise and awestruck look lit a fire in me. Waves of ecstasy throbbed from my core, leaving me panting. All thought left my head. I surrendered to molten heat, to the vibrations massaging my muscles, soothing every inch of tension, and to the intense liquid pleasure where our bodies joined.

His head fell back, resting on the edge of the Jacuzzi. His mouth parted with pleasure. "Fuck . . . Ah . . . Oh . . . This feels incredible . . . Fuck . . . Skylar."

His hoarse words pushed me over the edge. My fingers dug into his shoulders as the tension inside gripped me in an unbearable need for release.

A choked cry left my lips. "Oh God. I think I'm going to . . . Don't stop . . . Please don't stop . . ."

He held my backside, spreading me wide and thrusting into me. "I'm not going to stop."

The involuntary tremors of my climax ripped through me. My legs trembled but he wouldn't allow me to collapse. I came apart on his lap like dandelion fluff swirling and scattered to the breeze, shaking and crying out—an intense, shuddering climax that had me whimpering and digging my nails into his shoulders. He nursed me through it, whispering his praise and encouragement in my ear. Not that I could listen. I was too lost to raw sensation.

My body trembled, my limbs like jelly. I molded against him, slick and hot. We lay spent and still, taking heaving breaths. He lifted me gently away and reached for his glasses.

"You need to drink some water." He scanned me with concern. "Let's get you out before we cook."

He got out of the tub, offered a hand, and hauled me out. Softness cocooned me as he wrapped me in the warmest, fluffiest towel I'd ever felt. In silence, he dried me carefully and toweled my hair. Then he filled a glass at the tap and watched me gulp beautiful, quenching cold water. Then, I was weightless. He lifted me into his arms and carried me into the bedroom.

I couldn't stop my startled laugh. "What are you doing?"

"I'm not finished with you yet."

Gently, he laid me down on my back on the huge four-poster bed. Cold air licked over my burning skin. He lifted the towel up over my hips and buried his face between my thighs. The hot press of his tongue was almost unbearable on such tender, raw sensation. I still hadn't stopped trembling from my orgasm. His dark hair was soft between my fingers as his tongue swirled and probed at my swollen flesh. His hands gripped my thighs, spreading them, pressing them flat. My body arched against him.

He lifted his head. "Tell me that you're beautiful and desirable. Tell me that you know you can bring a man to his knees."

I laughed to cover my embarrassment. "What?"

"I mean it. I want to hear you say it. You know that you're an incredible captain, but do you know how powerful and sexy you are?"

I rolled my eyes. "Don't go over the top, Reece."

"I'm not. Wasn't there a whole YouTube show on this very topic? Miri told me about it. How many people would risk it all just to be where I am now?" He lapped between my thighs, one slow stroke of his tongue that parted me and sent an electric jolt of pleasure through me. "You're incredible. Everybody sees it. I want you to see it. Say it properly, like you mean it."

I gasped. His hot breath against my too-sensitive clit had me arching up against him. "I can't."

"Why not?"

Hot tears pressed at my eyes and I didn't even know why. My fingers ached where I gripped the sheets.

"Sean made you feel bad about yourself, but it's not what I see. You've always been trying to prove that you're good enough, but you are. You need to see it, because when I look at you, I see perfection."

"I'm not perfect. I'm so far from perfect, Reece. You need to take me off this pedestal. It's going to hurt us both when I fall."

"You're perfectly imperfect. I don't see anything wrong with you. I want all of you. Even the bits you don't like. Just as you are."

He smoothed a hand over my stomach and my body writhed under his touch. "Never forget who you are. People look up to you because you were born a leader. You have this energy about you. You shine. Everyone that meets you can see it."

I could almost believe everything he said. The way he looked at me and worshipped my body. "You make me feel like I'm beautiful."

"Good girl." He rewarded me with a swirl of his tongue that made me whimper.

I moaned and dug my fingers into his shoulders.

"I'm not going to leave any part of your body undiscovered. I'm going to know it all by heart and then I'm going to learn how to make you come so hard you're going to beg me not to stop."

"You've already figured that out."

His words were a murmur against my tender flesh. "There's always room for improvement."

Chapter 26

Skylar

Hot, senseless pleasure made my body tight with need and I ground against Reece's tongue. I moaned and he watched my face before he ceased his probing. He took hold of my hips and dragged me to the end of the bed. I was too turned on to even think about how exposed I looked on all fours. He positioned himself behind me. With a knee, he nudged my thighs further apart, spreading me. His shaft pressed at me and then he entered me in one slick thrust that made us both moan.

I needed him faster, but he held me in place as he thrust lazily in slow, maddening circles. Every slow stroke was torture when I'd been so close to the edge. I groaned and bucked against him to hurry him, but he held my hips still.

"If you want me to go faster, then you'll have to tell me," he murmured.

The words wedged in my throat. It was too embarrassing to tell him what I needed. He thrust into me in deep, delicious strokes, but it wasn't enough. He wrapped his arm around me, pulling me up so my back pressed against his damp chest.

"If you don't tell me what you want, how will you get it?" His voice was a rough whisper in my ear. "Ask for what you need."

"Faster," I whispered.

"You want to come?"

"Yes."

He took my hand and moved it between my legs to strum my clit. "Then take it. A captain doesn't ask permission. She just takes what she wants."

With one arm around my waist, he pumped into me in fast, forceful strokes that left me breathless. My legs trembled so that it was only him holding me up around my waist as I bucked desperately against him.

"Do you see what you are in this moment?" His lips brushed my ear. "You're a goddess."

At his whispered words another orgasm tore through me, harder and more intense than the first. I cried out and collapsed back onto my hands. Still he kept grinding into me as I bucked against him, riding the trembles and waves of my climax. His fingers dug into my hips as he pulled me hard against him and thrust in a succession of quick hard strokes. I turned to watch his face as he groaned and found his own release. Breathing hard, we collapsed back down together in a sweaty tangle.

"We're going to break this bed if we carry on like this," I said.

Reece hauled me into his arms. A smile lit his tired eyes. "I'm sure Gabe can afford a new one."

◆ ◆ ◆

The next morning, birds sang sharply in my ears through the open bathroom window. I showered, wrapped a towel around myself, then raced back to the warmth of the bed and Reece's arms. He pulled me tight against him.

He placed a kiss in the hollow of my neck. "I don't like it when you shower. I miss you too much."

"But you must prefer me clean?"

"I like you every way."

He flipped me over, his lips trailing over every bump of my spine and across my shoulder blades. A shiver of pleasure ran through me. His hands roved worshipfully over my back and down my arms. He traced his fingers over the faint silvery lines etched into my hips.

I chuckled and swatted his hand away. "Don't touch my stretchmarks."

"I adore them. I adore every inch of you. It was like a punch in the gut that first time you walked into my office. You were so confident, striding around like you owned the place, and I knew I was powerless again." He lifted my hips, propping me on all fours. I groaned as his tongue lapped between my thighs. "You have me under a spell."

I threw a glance over my shoulder to watch his dark head bob. "I wish I'd known you when we were younger."

"You wouldn't have liked me then."

"Yes. I would have. I wasted so many years with Sean. I didn't even know what it was like to be with a man that cares about satisfying me."

"And now you do. Don't accept second best."

His tonguing became more insistent. My back arched and my fingers dug into the sheets.

"We have to get ready for work," I said.

"One more orgasm."

I couldn't help my chuckle. "Don't you think I've had enough?"

"No. You have so many to catch up on."

I let my body relax. If Reece wasn't worried about being late, then I didn't need to worry either. His glasses bumped against the back of my thighs as he licked me from behind.

I couldn't help my groan of pleasure. "How did you get so good at this? How many women have you been with?"

Silence swirled. Would he reply? He didn't like to speak about his personal life, but if he wouldn't open up after this, then when would he?

"My ex worked as a doctor at the same hospital as me."

"What happened with your ex?"

He spoke between hot open-mouthed kisses on my hips. "Caring for Mum took a lot of my free time." Sadness edged his words. "I didn't have much of that anyway with work at the hospital."

I didn't want to pry because every time he spoke, it meant he stopped tonguing at me, but curiosity wouldn't allow me not to ask. There was much I wanted to know about him, and for the first time, the conversation was a two-way street.

"I'm sorry."

"Sometimes relationships are about infatuation and poetry, but sometimes they are about actions and difficult conversations. When we hit a rough patch, she didn't want to invest the energy to work through it. I want a partner that will stick it out with me in the long term. No matter what."

I turned my head to watch his handsome, somber face over my shoulder. "You deserve nothing less."

A small smile of enchantment touched his lips, but his eyes were dark and unfathomable. A pang of unease pulled at me. This was happening fast. I hadn't even got Sean out of the house yet and I was already falling for another man. My life was chaotic. I was living in a hotel, and that paled into insignificance compared to the challenges I was about to face in my professional life. The news about Sean was sure to be spreading by now. I didn't want people to be gossiping about me and Reece.

My shoulders stiffened. "How are we going to play this at work?"

He ceased his tonguing. "I don't . . . I can't . . . I need to figure out my next steps."

His expression was tight and grim. It didn't benefit either of us if people were talking about this.

"We'll talk about it another time. Not now." He stroked my backside in slow circles, then dipped his head between my thighs again. "I'm busy at the moment, setting a world record for orgasms given to a football player in twenty-four hours."

Amusement bubbled up inside of me, but his wicked tongue turned my laugh into a moan. I let my body relax and surrendered to his sure hands. Reece Forster was a man on a mission, and I was happy to help him achieve his goals.

Chapter 27

Skylar

Somehow, I made it to practice without being late. We'd lost count of the orgasms after a while, which was a shame because the committee awarding world records would have been impressed. The rest of the team had hit the showers, but I stayed behind to take a few more shots. I blasted a ball into the empty goal.

"Nice shot."

Miri's voice made me spin around. She was with Gabe and Evan Lewis—the American I'd run away from at Gabe's party. I'd probably come across as rude, but not rude enough to send him packing. Why hadn't he gone home yet? When Claire had mentioned that transfer nonsense, I'd shut her down. There was no way I'd leave my team. If this man thought there was a chance I'd leave this team, he was mistaken.

Miri ran a hand over her pregnant belly and hitched her shoulder. "I'd volunteer in goal if I could, but you know . . ."

Gabe put an arm around Miri and pulled her in close. "You'll be back on this pitch before you know it. I'll be on the sideline with the stroller."

She smiled and reached up to kiss him. He wrapped his arms around her and they kissed like two people who thought they were alone.

The American coughed and flashed me an amused glance.

I matched his smile and rolled my eyes. "Can't you two get a room?"

"We have a hotel full of rooms. Miri just can't keep her hands off me. It's not my fault I'm irresistible." Gabe's gaze flickered to me. "This is Evan Lewis. Director of the LA Halos. Evan, meet our captain, Skylar Marshall."

"We've met, briefly," I said.

Evan held out his hand. "Good to see you again, Skylar."

I held my hands up and flashed an apologetic smile. They were far too muddy to shake with a man that looked this pristine. "You too."

His smile was wide. "Gabe's been telling me you're taking this team to the Women's Super League."

It was impossible not to return Evan's disarming smile. "That's the plan."

It was strange that he would even think about a transfer. What did the WSL matter to an American?

Gabe picked up the ball and did some impressive kickups. Gabe always looked so smart in his expensive suits, I forgot that he still knew his way around a pitch. "And we're not just getting into the WSL. We're going to the top of the table. This team is going to be the best in England."

"England's fine, I suppose." Evan's voice was casual, but his bright eyes shone with purpose. "The people are friendly enough, but the weather is so shitty. The WSL is fine too, but it's not much of a development opportunity for a player of Skylar's caliber."

He had a teasing look in his eyes as he flashed a glance at Gabe. "Unless your captain is happy to be a big fish in a small pond?"

Gabe's mouth twitched with amusement, but he kept his eye on the ball as he bounced it from his shoulder back to his knee. "Some of us like this pond."

Evan nodded thoughtfully. "But a bigger pond would be a greater challenge. Maybe across the pond . . ."

Gabe stashed the football under his elbow and flashed an amiable smile. Why was he even entertaining the idea of a transfer? Didn't he want to keep me? First Claire and now Gabe. Did anybody actually want me to be here?

"Are you trying to get rid of me, Gabe?"

Miri reached for my hand. Maybe I hadn't managed to keep my hurt from my voice. "Of course he's not. Evan is an old friend of Gabe's. There's no pressure. This is a development opportunity, something good for you and the team."

Evan's brogues squelched as he lifted his foot from the mud and glanced at it with disdain. Gabe might have been happy to get his Armani muddy, but from the look on Evan's face, he didn't feel the same. "We've been discussing a short-term arrangement—an exchange of talent and ideas. You do a year or two with us. We'll send a player over here."

I would never leave the team, but I had to admit Evan's interest was flattering. It was one thing to play in the Women's Super League, but to play in the States? The LA Halos were one of the best teams in the world. If I had a mind to leave, I couldn't deny it would be an incredible opportunity.

Evan shielded his face from the drizzle. "We have blue skies, beaches, and mountains. This could be a gentle ocean breeze in your face."

And what of all the things I'd leave behind? My team. My family. Reece. A pang pulled at my heart. Last night had been one of the most amazing nights of my life. Still, what future could I have with Reece if he insisted on keeping a professional boundary?

A phone buzzed in Evan's pocket and he smiled politely. "Excuse me. I have to take this." He stepped away to take the call.

Gabe shot me an encouraging smile and passed me the ball. He glanced at Evan and the empty pitches beyond and lowered his voice. "Is everything okay for you at the Beaufort?"

"Of course. It's a five-star hotel. It couldn't be any better."

Especially with the company I'd had last night.

"And have you heard anything from Sean?"

My teeth gritted at the mere mention of his name. I shook my head. PR was issuing a statement today. They'd advised me to stay off social media for the week until it blew over. I didn't have a problem with that. I'd always hated social media anyway. It was Sean who had insisted I keep it up.

Gabe dropped his voice even lower. "You need me to beat Sean up for you?" He rocked back on his polished brogues and his bright eyes twinkled. "Technically, I'd have to put my security guy on it. I can't risk a punch to my face. I'm too pretty for fights."

Miri nodded and stroked his cheek with an indulgent smile. "It's true. Look at him. He's too pretty."

I laughed. "If anyone's beating Sean up, it's me."

"Stay at the Beaufort as long as you need. Although I'd avoid the mushroom soup." Gabe smiled and raised a sardonic eyebrow. "Mother suspects it's from a tin." He bent down to kiss the top of Miri's head. "I'm going to take Evan back to the office. Call me if you need me."

He transferred his gaze to me. "We'll talk later. Think about the opportunity, Skylar. We don't want to lose you, but I'm thinking about what we'd all gain. When we get into the WSL, we're playing at a whole new level. We're going to need new skills, new strategies. It's a different game at that level, and I need us to stay ahead. You're an amazing captain. No one is doubting you, but if you're in the US, you're going to learn so much. You'll come back stronger, and be the leader we're going to need when we're playing at a world-class level."

Miri's eyes burned into me.

"I suppose you think the same?"

She shrugged. "It makes sense to me. It's a skill swap. We're going to benefit here too with a new player to teach us." Her face softened. "Nobody wants to see you go. We'd miss you so much, but it's just temporary and then you'll be back. Think of it like a lovely long vacation."

I sighed. When she put it like that, it didn't sound bad. Still, I wasn't sold. These were my girls. I wasn't about to abandon them. There were other ways we could improve our game when we got into the WSL. We'd all just have to work harder. Maybe we could get in some new coaches.

Gabe gave me an expectant look. I'd have to give him something just to keep him off my back. If there was one thing about this man, he didn't leave anything alone.

"Fine. I'll think about it."

"You do that." He nodded with satisfaction, before he gave Miri one last kiss then headed toward Evan. Evan—still with the phone pressed to his ear—flashed me a smile and a wave before the two of them walked back to the training suite. Miri smiled as she watched Gabe's retreating back. A little pang pulled at me. It must be nice to find your person and have it be so uncomplicated. Why did things have to be so complicated with Reece?

Miri wrapped her coat around her huge bump and transferred her gaze to me. "Are you going to kick a few more balls?"

Drizzle misted my face. "You don't have to do this with me, you know. It's cold out here. I'm fine alone."

"I know, but I like the company." Miri pulled up the hood of her raincoat. "Gabe said that PR is doing a statement about you and Sean today . . ."

"Yep."

"Do you want to talk about it?"

"Nope."

I found a nice piece of grass and laid the ball down before firing it into the top corner. Practicing penalty kicks was important, but it was never the same. You'd never be able to recreate the pressure and tension of a match day. Still, it was a necessary evil.

"Hope Reece isn't getting too heavy with you?"

My football boot skidded in the mud on my run-up and I nearly went flying. "What?"

"The meditation classes? He's been coming home late."

"Yes. Meditation. It's great. I'm so fucking Zen, I'm levitating."

Miri chuckled. "I wish Reece would take his own medicine and find some bloody Zen. It's hard when we're all in the house together. Don't get me wrong, we all love each other, but my siblings are a constant pain in my backside."

I shrugged. "Tell me about it. I have three older brothers. I know all about annoying siblings."

"I hope getting out of the hospital helps him. I'm worried about him."

I tried to keep my voice casual. "Worried why?"

"I shouldn't tell you this, but he didn't come home last night. I mean, that's fine. We were all at the house and Mum is doing so much better. She has a nurse on call so he doesn't need to fuss as much, but he said he was staying with a friend."

My shoulders tensed from talking about Reece behind his back, but I needed to know if I had to give him a heads-up. Clearly, he wasn't ready to tell his family what had been going on.

"So? Maybe he *was* staying with a friend. He's a grown man, isn't he?"

"Whenever he used to say that, it always meant Megan."

"Megan?"

"His ex. She was awful." Miri grimaced and shook her head. "I don't want them to get back together."

"Why? What's wrong with Megan?" I asked the question tentatively. I didn't mean to pry, but curiosity got the better of me.

Miri sighed and toed at the pitch. "They worked at the hospital together."

"She's smart, then? Like him?"

Miri nodded. "Ambitious, too. Reece wants to make people happy, but she bossed him around and took advantage of his good nature. He gave so much to her, but when he needed her, she disappeared. I think she broke his heart, although you'd never know. He doesn't talk about it.

"We all tease him, but Reece is the rock that holds the family together. He got us all through last year with Mum." Miri shielded her gaze from the rain and looked up into the stadium. "He bottled everything up after we lost Dad and he took on the burden of being the man of the house. He's more like a dad to the twins. Grief affects everyone differently. Nobody could get him to talk about how he felt back then. He became so controlled and uptight." A wry smile twisted her lips. "Now he won't shut up about people's feelings. Anything to not talk about his own, I suppose."

Poor Reece. My heart sank. I'd caused him more trouble. I hadn't meant to. He spent all of his time taking care of other people, but who took care of him? I wanted to, if only he'd let me. Sometimes I caught him looking so stressed and tired. Maybe next time I could offer to give him a shoulder rub or a massage. He'd probably freak out at the idea, but I loved taking care of people.

Maybe I could bring him round some dinner tonight? I'd found this lovely pad thai recipe. Would he be receptive to that kind of thing? He'd mentioned before that he didn't like his siblings messing up the kitchen, but he hadn't seemed to mind when it was me in there.

Miri rolled a ball underfoot thoughtfully. "I'm sure he's just burned out. I'm hoping that working here will help him lighten—"

She frowned and grimaced. Her hands flew to her lower belly and her face creased with pain. She opened her mouth to speak but a grimace stole her words.

I took her by the shoulders. "What is it? Pain? Contractions?"

She doubled over, her face pale. She put a trembling hand between her legs and it came back red. A spreading patch of crimson stained her light leggings. Her terrified eyes met mine. I grabbed her, holding her upright. The endless expanse of green and white chalk sprawled around us. We were miles from being able to call out for help.

Fear gripped my stomach, but I kept my voice calm. "Can you walk? Can you get off this pitch?"

She grimaced, then nodded.

I slipped an arm around her waist. "Good. Everything is going to be okay. I've got you. Let's get you to the hospital."

Chapter 28

REECE

Lana twisted the ring on her finger in a wild circle. "Well? What should I do? What can I say to her?"

My eyes burned with exhaustion. It had been impossible to relax with Skylar next to me in the bed. We'd hardly slept. I hadn't wanted to close my eyes and miss any of it. I snapped my head back to Lana. I had no right to sit in this chair and counsel anyone. How was I supposed to offer advice on this? Lana had hurt the woman I cared about. If Skylar knew we were in here together, she'd be pissed off. Not that I'd ever say anything. I wasn't about to add breaching confidentiality to my list of wrongdoings.

Lana readjusted her shin pads beneath her socks. "Sean told me that things had been over for a long time. They hadn't been sleeping together anymore. They didn't love each other. Skylar won't even give me a chance to explain. She doesn't reply to my texts. I think there's something going on. Maybe she has a new man."

I pasted on my most noncommittal expression. "How do you feel about your relationship with Sean?"

She frowned and swiped at her cheek with the back of her hand. "We don't have a relationship. It was a few flirty texts and a couple of kisses. I shouldn't have done it." Lana dropped her head into her hands. "I've fucked up. I couldn't stop. It was Sean Wallace. I knew I couldn't have him, but that made it more exciting, so much harder to resist. He's a tosser, but he's so hot. I've always liked him. It was an infatuation . . . an obsession. It's a kind of madness when you want someone like that. You lose all sense of reasoning. Do you know what I mean? Some people have this power over you. I can see now what a prick he is, but it's too late." Her voice broke. "Skylar will never forgive me."

"You're being hard on yourself."

"We're best friends. More than friends—I'm her second in command. I'm the one she can rely on, whatever happens. I should have had more control. I have to make it right with her. I don't know how. She won't even speak to me."

Guilt made my shoulder blades itch.

I should have had more control.

My gaze fell on the pitches outside. Skylar would be in this building somewhere. I shouldn't have even been in this office doing this job. I'd lost every right to help people when I'd overstepped the boundary with her. I'd wanted to help Skylar, not complicate her life more. I'd had zero self-control.

"Are you okay?"

I jumped at Lana's voice. I had to get my head in the game. This wasn't fair on Lana. She wanted to repair her friendship with Skylar. At least I could have one positive impact on the team and help with some restorative work between the two of them.

A frantic knock sounded on the door. Lana's gaze flashed to the clock and she folded her arms. My next appointment wasn't for another half an hour. I opened the door a fraction to see Gabe. He was breathless, pale, and crumpled. Completely un-Gabe-like. I knew something bad was happening without having to ask. It was the face Mum had worn all those times we went back and forth from the hospital to visit Dad.

171

"Miri." The word fell from his lips and then he ran off, eating up the corridor in long strides.

◆ ◆ ◆

I caught a flash of Skylar's purple hair in the crowded maternity waiting room and raced to her. Gabe got there before me. He grabbed Skylar by the elbows and swung her around to face him. "Where is she?"

"It's okay. She's okay. She's in labor. They wouldn't let me stay."

I kept my voice level, despite the churning in my guts. One of us had to stay calm. "What happened?"

Skylar ran a trembling hand over her pallid face. "We were on the training pitches and she doubled over."

I swallowed, my heart beating a rhythm. Miri wasn't due for another month. The eggshell-blue hospital walls closed in around me.

Somehow, I managed to keep my voice even. "Is she okay? Is the baby okay?"

Skylar chewed the skin around her thumbnail. "The doctors said everything is still okay with the baby."

"But Miri? Is she okay?"

Gabe shook his head, his face pale. "No. We have a birthing suite at a private hospital. This isn't supposed to be happening yet. I need to speak to whoever is in charge. It's too soon. This isn't good enough."

Skylar took Gabe by the arm. "Miri is okay. It's okay. Calm down. I'll take you to her."

I made to follow.

Skylar flashed me a glance. "Only one birthing partner allowed. Wait here. I'll be back."

Skylar shepherded a frantic-looking Gabe away. They disappeared together down the corridor. My knees buckled and I sagged into a hard green plastic chair. The din of the crowded maternity waiting room filled my ears as I tried to relax and slow my heartbeat.

"Reece?"

My heart stuttered at the familiar voice. I looked up to see a petite blonde woman in blue scrubs. For a moment, I could only stare at her. Her pale-yellow hair flowed from a center part down to her rounded chin—a much shorter style than when I'd last seen her.

Megan.

I blurted the first thing that came to mind. "What are you doing here?"

"Maternity placement." Her intelligent eyes met mine from behind her delicate glasses, and she hitched a blue folder under her elbow. "I thought you left the hospital?"

"I have. I'm here with Miri. She's in labor."

Megan's high arched brow soared upward. "I didn't know she was pregnant. Congratulations."

No. You wouldn't know . . . or care.

My stomach felt like it was being scratched with sandpaper. "It's early. She wasn't due for another month . . ."

This hospital held nothing but pain and trauma: all the times we'd been in and out with Dad as kids, the horrible time after Mum's stroke, coming to work day in and day out trying to help so many wounded people. I'd been drowning. Now, all those horrible memories flooded back. I'd thought I could help my patients, but I'd been flailing and stressed for so long. For the sake of my mental health, I never wanted to come back here. It had taken time away to realize that.

Megan flashed a tentative smile and dropped down next to me. "Miri and the baby will be fine. It's a great team here. They'll take care of her. Women have been giving birth since the dawn of time."

The chatter of the waiting room filled the silence. I gazed at the ambulance bay outside. I couldn't stand being back here. I'd hated it at the end. Really fucking hated it.

I felt Megan's eyes burning into the side of my head. "How have you been?" she asked softly. "I heard you've been working at a football club?"

She wrinkled her nose and her smile relaxed into a grin of amusement. Was that funny to her? I supposed it was. Megan had always been focused on a career in medicine and climbing the greasy pole. She'd never see any appeal in changing direction and trying something new. Whenever I'd talked to her about my garden or the book I'd always wanted to write, her eyes had glazed over. She saw me as a failure. Maybe she was right. I'd hardly made a success of my career. The hospital had been too much and then I'd trampled all over my own ethics.

I kept my smile bland. "Not so bad. How have you been?"

A neat row of ambulances sat in the bay outside. People darted around the fountains under a rain-choked sky. I closed my eyes because I didn't want to look at Megan. The sudden onslaught of emotion from being back at the hospital, being back with the woman who I'd loved and who had let me down, overwhelmed me.

Megan cleared her throat and she darted a glance at me. "I bumped into Frankie the other day. She said you'd met someone . . ."

I sighed. "That was Frankie being Frankie. You should know better than to listen to my siblings."

Megan chewed her lip and observed me through lowered lashes. "So, you haven't met anyone?"

Skylar flashed through my mind. Where was she now? Why were they taking so long? Thank God she'd been with Miri and got her here safely.

Megan smoothed her scrubs over her thighs. "Do you want to get a coffee? I was about to go on a break. We could talk?"

Talk about what? We'd spent months and months talking. We had nothing left to say to each other. "I'd better stay here. In case there's news."

"When Frankie told me you'd moved on, I realized . . . Well . . ." Awkwardly, she cleared her throat again. "I've been meaning to call. I miss you. I've been wondering if maybe . . . if there was any chance we could give it another try . . ."

A sudden pain speared my heart. Megan was still talking but I couldn't listen. "You really think Miri will be okay? You're sure it's a good team? If anything happens to her . . . to the baby . . ."

A sharp antiseptic odor filled my nose and made my eyes water. Exhaustion slammed into me. My shoulders slumped. Heat pressed behind my eyes.

"Hey," Megan said softly. "Come here. It's okay."

Her arms wrapped around my shoulders and she pulled me into her soft embrace. The familiar scent of her spearmint ChapStick filled my nose and, for a moment, it gave me comfort in the memories of when things had been good between us.

She pulled back to look at me, her hand still resting lightly on my back. "Shall we grab that coffee?"

My eyes burned with tiredness. I had enough on my plate without a trip down memory lane with Megan. "Everything that happened between us . . . It's fine. I don't bear a grudge. I respect your decision."

"*My* decision?" She glanced around and lowered her voice. "You didn't give me time to make a decision, Reece. You dropped everything on me: your mum, selling up, moving back home. You told me that it would be better for me if I walked away—"

"And it is better, isn't it? You didn't want to jeopardize your chance of promotion. You'd worked so hard. I understood. I wanted to spare you my drama."

She wrinkled her nose. "It all ended so . . . quickly."

"I had to be there for my family. You didn't have time for it."

She winced. "I didn't handle it as well as I should, but you didn't fight for me, either. You shut yourself off, buried yourself in work, pushed everyone away . . . the way you did the whole time we were together. How was it that I was with a psychologist and I had no clue what you were feeling?"

"How do you think I was feeling? My mum was gravely ill. Everything was falling apart. You wanted to go. You didn't want to be with me like that."

Tilting her head back, she peered at my face. "I wanted to be with you, I just didn't know *how* to be with you like that."

Was that true? Maybe I had pushed Megan away, but I'd been trying to protect her. She was doing so well in her job, and she was happy. I hadn't wanted to drag her down with me. We hardly had time to spend together as it was, and I'd known how involved it would be caring for Mum. If I hadn't been open enough then I was sorry. I talked about other people's feelings all day. It should have come easy to talk about my own, but I'd never wanted to burden my friends and family with them. I had my supervisor, Laurel, to talk things through with.

I took Megan's hand. "I'm sorry if I hurt you. I didn't mean to."

"I'm sorry, too. You were probably right. I wouldn't have been able to give you the support you needed." She tapped the folder on her lap. "Work has been . . . a lot." She studied my face. "Don't you miss it at the hospital?"

I closed my eyes and let the chaotic sound of the waiting room fill my ears. It was a sound that triggered an onslaught of bad memories. "No. I don't miss it. Not in the slightest."

A cough sounded overhead. I drew away from Megan to see Gabe and Skylar. Gabe beamed in a dazzling display of white teeth. Skylar stood behind him, her arms folded across her chest. Her gaze moved between Megan and me and she frowned.

"Miri's fine. It's all fine." Joy shone in Gabe's emerald eyes. "Do you want to come and meet your new nephew?"

Chapter 29

SKYLAR

Reece wore a tired, faraway expression as he drove us through the dark city. We'd left Gabe and Miri at the hospital. I couldn't strike the memory of how he'd looked holding his tiny nephew. Warmth had lit his normally stoic face and he'd held the baby with so much love and care. I'd never met a man like him—so powerful and commanding when he needed to be, but also so soft and loving.

But it had been tainted by the fact I'd seen *her*.

Her smile had been polite, but I'd caught her skeptical glances at my hair and tattoos. I could spot disapproval a mile off. She'd looked at me the way Sean's parents always had. Reece had introduced me as Miri's friend. That had done nothing to shift the gnawing jealousy in my gut.

Megan and Reece looked perfect together. She was prim and stuffy and full of long words too. That was the kind of woman that suited him. What did he even see in me? He was so buttoned up and starchy. He needed someone posh and refined like Megan, not a purple-haired loudmouth covered in tattoos and piercings. Nobody would place us as a couple. We were two pieces of a jigsaw that didn't fit together.

"Back to the Beaufort?"

Reece's voice rattled through the stillness.

I didn't want to go back there. It was lonely and boring. It made me feel adrift and lost at sea. "Will you stay with me?"

I'd tried to keep my voice light, but it came out shakier than I'd intended.

He cleared his throat. "I can't. I'm sorry. I can't leave Mum on her own in the house."

"Miri said you have nurses on call overnight."

"We do, but it's been a long day." He spoke in a low, composed voice, but he wouldn't look me in the eye. "Besides, Mum is desperate to hear from me. I can't wait to tell her everything."

Silence swirled between us again as the night flashed by outside, neon lights flaring in the darkness.

"Megan seemed nice. The two of you look . . . good together." My voice cut the silence. It sounded strange and faraway.

"Looks can be deceiving."

"You were hugging."

His voice held level. "I was worried about Miri. Megan was comforting me."

"Are you getting back together with her?"

"You don't need to be jealous of Megan."

"That's what Sean used to say to me. You don't need to be jealous . . ."

He frowned but didn't speak. He was doing that annoying thing where he left a long silence so I'd be the one to spill my guts, as usual. Fine. If he wanted me to spill my guts, I'd give him both barrels. I folded my arms and words poured out of me, hot and angry.

"You don't tell me anything. I ask you questions and you change the subject. You won't let me in, even though I've told you every single tiny detail about my life and about the way I'm feeling.

I don't know what this thing is between us. Is it just sex? Do we have to stop now? Is there any way we could ever be together and it would feel okay for you? Because I know you're going to leave me, and I can't bear that. I need you too much."

I clamped my mouth shut, biting my lip until it throbbed like a pulse. Sudden heat pressed behind my eyes. I hadn't been enough for Sean and now I wasn't enough for Reece. He'd go back to his ex. I had to end this now before he hurt me.

Reece flexed his fingers around the steering wheel and pressed his lips together.

I threw my hands in the air. "Give me something, Reece. For God's sake. Tell me something about you. I'm sick of talking about me."

He cleared his throat. "We lost Dad in that hospital. I watched him get sicker and sicker."

A muscle worked in his jaw. "When you're a kid, you don't think people will die. You don't have that concept. You don't know what it means that when somebody is dead, they are gone forever. I felt so guilty when he died because I'd never let myself imagine it. I wasted all the time I had with him at the end. I hated visiting hours. I used to slip away and go to the cafeteria instead of being with him."

My throat ached to hear the sadness in his voice. I kept my tone soft. "You were just a kid."

"When he passed, everyone fell apart. I vowed to be the strong one for my family. I vowed to help other people with their pain, because I knew how it was to hurt. I didn't want anyone to ever feel the way I did. That's back when I was a good person."

"What do you mean? You *are* a good person."

"This isn't just sex for me, Skylar. I shouldn't have touched you. It doesn't matter how much I want you. I can't have you. The first rule in healing is that you do no harm. We shouldn't have made this

179

relationship sexual. You were hurting after Sean, and you needed a safe space and someone detached to listen to you."

"How many times? I don't want detached. You're not my therapist."

"You sat in my therapy chair."

"It doesn't matter. I'm not your patient. This is just a way for you not to let me in, and I'm tired of it."

He frowned. "You don't think I want to let you in?"

"You don't act like it. Whenever I feel like I'm getting close to you, you freak out and push me away."

"You've told me things you wouldn't have told me unless you'd come to my office. I'm the team psychologist. My role is to counsel the team. I have a genuine worry for your welfare, and for my reputation. I've overstepped a professional boundary. I've behaved unethically."

"Have you? Or is this a great excuse for you to keep me at arm's length? I don't know why you keep pushing me away. I don't want to hurt you, Reece. I care about you." My voice rose an octave higher and I took a breath. "I don't find any of this easy either. The last thing I want after Sean is to jump into things with another man. I have no time for distraction. All that matters is getting to the end of the season, but it feels . . . right between us. I've never met anyone like you before. I've never felt anything like this before . . ."

He swallowed and kept his gaze fixed on the road ahead. He checked his mirror. The click of the indicator filled the silence.

"I don't want to be with Megan. I want to be with you." His brows drew together. "That's all I've ever wanted. I can't stop feeling like this about you." His voice was resigned. "But I can't shake this feeling that I should have put a stop to this sooner. That I'm doing something wrong. I wanted to help you, and I don't think this is the right thing for you now. This job was only a temporary thing for me. I'm not a sports psychologist. I don't even understand the offside rule."

Despite the grim conversation, I couldn't help but chuckle. "How can you not understand it? You're so smart. It's not difficult."

"Because every time somebody has tried to explain it to me, we've been at a match and all I can focus on is you."

The drizzle misted the windscreen and I watched the raindrops running all over in different directions.

"I can't go back to the hospital. I need to do something different, like travel or study or write. I don't know. I just know I can't stay at the football club. Not if it means fighting the way I feel for you every day."

Unease still niggled at my gut. I couldn't shake the image of Reece with his arms around his ex. Sean had really done a number on me, but it wasn't just the jealousy that made me uncomfortable. It was the barrier that Reece insisted on putting between us. He didn't want to let me in. I wasn't enough for him. I definitely wasn't enough compared to his ex-girlfriend. What would it take to convince him that we could be good together? That he should let me be with him?

"Megan is a doctor. She's smart and well dressed. I spend all day covered in mud. Seeing the two of you together . . . you're so perfect for each other—"

"I like you covered in mud. I like everything about you. When I'm with you, I'm fourteen again. You're the most beautiful girl I've ever seen, and I'm praying you'll notice I'm alive. Stay with me tonight. I'll have to check in on Mum, but she's in the annex. We'll have privacy." He cleared his throat, his voice hoarse. "If you want to . . ."

The seatbelt snapped against me as I jerked to sit up straight. Last time I'd been in his house he hardly dared hover in a room with me for a moment before he'd run away. Did he want things between us to be out in the open now? I'd convinced myself I didn't want that because it wasn't good for the team, but being with him tonight and hearing him open up had made me feel more strongly about him than ever.

I kept my voice light, because my heart hammered so hard and I didn't want him to know how much it meant to me that it was him asking me to stay for once. "I don't know, Reece. The Beaufort has a gold-plated Jacuzzi. I'm not sure how your place is going to measure up."

He lifted his elegant fingers from the steering wheel, stretching them before wrapping them tight again. "I've got lime-and-coconut cake."

"Home-made?"

He wrinkled his nose. "Of course."

I couldn't help my chuckle at his prim, serious expression. "Fine. You twisted my arm."

◆ ◆ ◆

Reece watched me tuck into my cake with a little smile of satisfaction. He inclined his head in my direction. "Good?"

I nodded. "Amazing."

Today had been a long, exhausting blur. Tiredness pressed over me like a heavy blanket. I hadn't realized how starving I was until I'd been presented with food.

"You're an amazing cook. Like, *really* amazing. Is there anything you can't do?"

Pink tinged his cheeks and he waved a dismissive hand. "I'm not good at sports."

"You don't need to be when you can do this with a coconut."

"I'll teach you next time we have a 3 a.m. baking session." He gave a significant lift of his brows and a faint smile graced his lips.

My body flashed with heat as the memory came to me. The last time we'd been in this kitchen, he'd had me against the wall. Was he going to make me sleep in the spare room? I hoped not.

I cleared my throat. "They haven't thought of any names yet?"

"Not yet."

I blew steam from my tea then took a sip. "We might have to intervene to make sure Gabe doesn't get the final say. You know what celebrities are like when they name their children."

Reece's lip twitched and a twinkle flickered in his tired eyes. "You're a celebrity. You have almost as many followers on social media as Gabe."

I snorted. "Me? No. I'm just a footballer. I don't care about any of that. I've been keeping away from it anyway. The whole world probably knows about me and Sean now."

A yawn escaped me and I smothered it with my hand.

Reece watched me. "It's late. You must be exhausted. I have to go and check on Mum and see if she needs anything."

A sudden awkwardness came over me. "Shall I sleep in the spare room then, or . . . ?"

He pulled me into his hard body and pressed a soft kiss to my temple. Warmth enveloped me as he held me, stroking my back. His hands cupped my face. "I want you in my bed. That's where I always want you."

Chapter 30

Skylar

In the dim light of his bedroom, Reece undressed me and eased me down on to his bed. The sheets smelled like him, cotton fresh and clean. His hands roamed over my hips, and his eyes fixed on my breasts.

I ran my hands through his soft hair. "I want you to tell me things."

He fondled my nipple before he dipped his head to caress me with his tongue. "What do you want to know?"

I couldn't help my moan. "All the things. I want to know everything. What did you want to be when you were a kid? What is your biggest fear? What is your deepest regret? What is your favorite food?"

He peppered hot kisses around my belly button. "Should I stop doing this?"

Despite the currents of desire spreading through my body, I tried to keep some rational thought in my head. This was important. He'd opened up to me in the car about his dad. It had felt like progress, like something shifting between us.

I stilled him with a hand on his shoulder. "I want us to talk."

He froze, considering me for a moment, before he shifted to lie so we faced each other. The gentle tap of rain on the window and the tick of the clock on Reece's bedside cabinet filled the silence.

"Tell me something." I brushed a lock of his hair from his forehead. "Pretend I'm the therapist, and this is a safe space."

Moonlight spilled in through a crack in the curtains, painting his strong serious profile in blades of silver. A line formed between his brows.

I couldn't help my chuckle. "You don't have to look so worried. Just tell me anything. What did you want to be when you were a kid?"

He smoothed a hand over the blanket. "I wanted to be an author. I've always loved to read. I wrote stories all the time."

"Do you still write?"

He pushed his glasses up his nose and pressed his lips thoughtfully. "It's not something I've considered for years. I had no time to do anything fun when I worked at the hospital. I don't think I'd be any good at it."

"Does it matter if you're good? If you enjoyed it when you were a kid, maybe you'd enjoy it now?"

"Maybe." A faint smile pulled at his generous lips. "Is that enough? Can I go back to ravishing you now?"

"Ravish away, but keep talking. What's your biggest fear?"

He planted kisses along my collarbone. "That's easy. Flying. I've never been on an airplane."

"Never? Why not?"

"You just sit there and have to trust that you're not going to fall out of the sky. Airports are so busy. They herd you like cattle."

"Is it the lack of control? You like to be in control."

Gently, his hand circled my breast. "Yes. I like to be in control."

His low seductive voice made heat crackle through my limbs.

He bowed his head to suck my nipple into his mouth. "What about you? What's your biggest fear?"

My skin prickled with pleasure. "We're not talking about me."

"Old habits die hard. Tell me."

"I don't like enclosed spaces."

He licked his thumb and traced a slow, slippery circle on my nipple. "Why?"

"I just don't. My brothers played this prank on me when we were little. We were supposed to be playing hide-and-seek. They made me hide in a toy-box, and then they didn't come and find me. I was in there in the dark for ages, and it makes me feel all breathless and weird to think about it now. I'd always rather take the stairs than an elevator."

His intelligent eyes shone with empathy. His voice was tentative. "That was a cruel trick. How did it make you feel that they did that to you?"

I laughed. That bland innocent expression was such a smoke-screen. I wasn't about to fall for that. "Oh no you don't. This isn't about me. Tell me, what would be your ideal date?"

His hands moved down the length of my back. "Anywhere with you. Where do you want me to take you? Somewhere fancy? Do you like Italian?"

"I'd just want to do something . . . normal. I could never do anything normal with Sean. People always stop us for autographs, and there's nothing Sean loves more than posing for selfies."

"You wouldn't have that problem with me. Nobody wants my autograph. No matter how many times I offer it."

I couldn't help my bark of laughter. "I like your sense of humor. It's so dry."

"I like your sense of humor, too." His lips teased my nipple, making my back arch. "Where would you go on a date? What's normal to Skylar Marshall?"

"I don't know. Something like . . . bowling."

He stopped his licking and teasing, and peered up at me. "Bowling?"

"I love bowling. I used to go with my family."

He pinned my arms above my head, and kissed along my jawline to my chin. "Bowling would work. I used to go with my family, too. Forster bowling night used to be a sacred tradition. It's probably the only sport where I'd have a chance of giving you some competition."

Amusement went through me at his serious expression. "Oh, really? You fancy your chances?"

"I'm good. I even have my own bowling shoes."

I laughed. "You do not."

"Of course I do. I'm not going to wear those bowling alley shoes. How many people have worn them before?"

"They deodorize them."

The corner of his mouth twisted. "I'm not taking any risks when it comes to foot fungus."

"You're a complicated man, Dr. Forster."

A shadow darkened his face. "You wanted to know more about me. Is this conversation putting you off?"

"No. I think your quirks are adorable. I want to know them all. It's not as though you're wrong. I'm beginning to question my lax approach to bowling shoes."

His hands slipped down to my hips, then in between my thighs.

A tortured groan escaped his lips. "You're so wet."

"It must be all the talk about bowling."

His fingers worked a gentle message between my thighs. Electricity sparked through my body.

"Is that the secret? You want to know all my quirks?"

"Yes. All of them."

He covered my neck with kisses. "When the house is empty, I like to disinfect all of the door handles. It's one of my favorite things. That, and cleaning inside the oven."

"Nobody likes cleaning inside an oven."

"Because they're using the wrong cleaning products. I've done a lot of research."

I suppressed my chuckle. "Why doesn't that surprise me?"

His other hand ran deliciously up and down my spine, as his fingers worked their magic. I curled into his body, pleasure radiating from my core. "I like the idea of you killing germs. It never occurred to me that dirty talk could be so literal."

He planted worshipful kisses along my jawline. His voice was edged with humor. "Right? Is my stringent approach to hygiene doing it for you? Because I've got plenty more where that came from. Wait till I tell you about my system for loading the dishwasher. It's meticulous."

"I'm not going to be happy until I know everything there is to know about Reece Forster."

He lowered himself to kiss between my thighs. His tongue flicked over my clit, making me shudder with need.

"Do you like that?"

My heart thundered. "You know I do, but you're meant to be answering my questions."

He spread me with his thumbs and lapped a slow hot swipe with his tongue. "I am answering your questions. You wanted to know my favorite thing to eat."

My laugh turned into a moan. "Come back up here. One more thing."

He kissed his way back up my body. I shifted close, feeling the press of his rock-hard length against my thigh. Taking him in my hand, I rubbed the tip of his shaft through my wet folds. His eyes rolled back.

He groaned, a rough primal sound. "Fuck. What else? My laptop password? My bank details? I'll tell you anything. I'm completely at your mercy."

I wriggled, maneuvering myself underneath him. "How much do you want me?"

He stilled. The eagerness in his soft eyes shifted to tenderness. "You never need to ask me that."

"Don't I?"

He planted his elbows either side of me and pressed his forehead to mine. "Never. I want you so badly. I'd do anything to have you. All I've ever wanted is to make you mine."

"Then take me. Have your wicked way with me, Dr. Forster."

He arched a sardonic brow. "We don't have to talk about bowling anymore?"

I took him in hand, guiding him into position. "I'm done talking."

Reece slid into me with a groan, his hard body atop mine. I wound my arms around his broad back, urging him on with soft whispers. My body molded to the contours of his as we moved in perfect harmony, making love slowly in the darkness. He'd learned every inch of me so well that every touch was divine ecstasy. He didn't need to be guided. It was effortless. Finally, I could let go with a man because he made me feel so comfortable even if we were talking about the most ridiculous things.

I felt safe with Reece, and able to be fully myself in a way that I never had with Sean. I'd never have to fake it with Reece. There was no pressure. If it took me a long time to orgasm, he'd be patient. If it didn't happen at all, it wouldn't matter. He'd do whatever I needed and take however long it took to satisfy me. The thought brought tears to my eyes and made my heart burst with warmth. Desire spiraled through me. Everything inside me relaxed the way it had when we'd been in the Jacuzzi together.

His intense, deliberate thrusts sparked a hot tide of passion. Our eyes locked as our breathing came into unison. I couldn't contain my surrendering moans. Searing need made my legs shake. Shivers of delight raced through me as my climax gripped me. I abandoned myself to the raw sensation.

Agonized gasps escaped me. "Yes. Oh God. I love this, Reece. I love you."

Shit. What had I said that for?

Unease prickled my shoulder blades, but I was too far gone to pleasure to pay it mind. My body tightened like a spring and released in shuddering ecstasy. I collapsed, sweating and panting.

Reece pulled me into his arms and held me snugly. Echoing silence wrapped around me. I'd let myself get carried away and declared myself so freely. It was true, even if it was said in the heat of the moment. It had happened fast, but I had fallen in love with him. I couldn't help it. Maybe he didn't feel the same. Maybe this was all in my head. I shouldn't have said anything. I shouldn't have—

"I love you too, Skylar." For the first time his voice was a little awkward, and uncertainty crept into his normally inscrutable expression. "I've loved you since the first moment I saw you. I always have. I always will."

Chapter 31

Reece

The next morning, I returned from the bathroom to find Skylar on my bed, spooning cereal into her mouth.

"Oh, shit. Sorry." She laughed when she saw me in the doorway. "I was so hungry. I couldn't wait. You don't mind me eating in your bed, do you?"

No. I didn't mind. If it was anyone else, maybe, but Skylar Marshall could do whatever she wanted. Nothing could bring me down today. Last night she'd told me that she loved me.

"As long as you're in my bed, I don't mind what you do in it."

She gave me a suggestive smile. "Are you coming back to your bed?"

She gazed up at me. I already knew her face by heart. I'd long since committed every green fleck in her blue eyes and every cinnamon freckle to memory. An aching foreboding burned in my gut. How would this work? What would be left of my reputation when it got out that I'd taken a job at a football club and then slept with the captain? What the hell would people think? Miri? Gabe? Mum? I'd never be able to look anyone in the eye again. This was costing me my reputation, my career, and my self-respect, but with

Skylar by my side, all of those things felt like a small price to pay. This wasn't just sex. It never had been.

I trailed my lips along her neck, breathing in her watermelon scent. My hands traced up her bare legs and she shuddered against me. Where I expected to find material was the smooth skin of her perfect backside.

"You're not wearing underwear."

"What's the point? You're always so eager to tear it off."

Her devilish eyebrow raise made me stiffen. So confident. So cocky.

Good girl.

I kissed the warm hollow of her neck. "Have you had an orgasm alone yet?"

"What?" She laughed nervously.

"Have you got yourself off?"

She lowered her gaze in confusion. "Why are you asking me that?"

"Because you need to know that you can do it for yourself. You can take it whenever you want."

She fiddled with her nose ring, but she wouldn't look at me. "I don't know if I can . . . I guess because I haven't needed to. I haven't thought about it . . ."

I stroked my palm under her T-shirt, over her taut stomach, resisting the urge to ravish her. This was about her pleasure. "Why don't you have a go now."

She laughed. "Don't be ridiculous."

"Why is that ridiculous?"

She swallowed and her hand fluttered to fiddle with the silver bar in her eyebrow. "You don't want to see me doing that."

"I don't want to see you writhing in pleasure naked on my bed?" I tapped my lips, pretending to consider. "It's a struggle to think of anything I'd like to see more."

"You really want to see that?"

"Yes."

She licked her lips. "Really?"

"More than anything."

She frowned and lowered her hand gingerly down her stomach and under the covers. Her face softened with pleasure. A current of desire shot through me. Nothing turned me on more than watching Skylar Marshall learn how to satisfy herself. I needed her to know that she could take all of this for herself whenever she wanted. Sean had made her feel deficient, but she was anything but. She was perfect. My fingers burned to touch her, but I lay next to her, stroking her silky hair back from her head.

A soft moan escaped her lips as she chased her own delight.

"Take off the T-shirt. I need to see you bare," I said.

She laughed and pulled her T-shirt off. "I thought this was about me."

"It is, but I'm not a saint."

She gave a delicious whimper and wriggled her backside into the bed. "It's nice, but it's not enough. I need . . ." She bit her lip and her eyes raked over me. "You're going to make me say it?"

"You're allowed to ask for what you need."

She spoke between soft moans. "I need you."

"What do you need from me?"

She laughed and it turned into another moan. "You know damn well. Don't torture me . . ."

I had to torture her a little bit. She needed to be able to ask for what she needed with a partner. Maybe it wouldn't always be me. My heart sank at the thought of her with someone else, but at least she'd be able to get the sex life she deserved in the future. She wouldn't settle for a selfish lover like Sean Wallace again.

"You don't need me, or anyone else for that matter. You know your own body better than anyone else ever could."

"I know, but now I want you." She closed her eyes, her lips parting with pleasure. "This would be better if it was you touching me."

"And if it was me, show me where you'd want to be touched."

She put her free hand on her breast. "Here." She ran her fingers lightly over her nipples, making them firm into hard peaks. "Then I'd want your tongue."

"Where?"

She lowered her lashes and flicked out her purple hair across my pillow "You know where."

"Not unless you tell me, I don't."

I knew she was embarrassed and that I was torturing her, but if I didn't push, she wouldn't ask for what she needed.

She squeezed her eyes tighter and blurted the words. "I'd want you to go down on me. You're so good at it."

I fought to keep the smug smile from my lips. "Am I, now?"

The sheets rippled as she worked faster. "Mm-hmm."

I liked to take my time with her but seeing her in this state had every nerve raw. It was hard to be so patient with her when I was dying to get lost in her soft moans and gasps.

"You're doing so well."

Her fingers dug into the sheets and her face scrunched. Her breath came in short, sharp gasps.

"Don't forget to breathe." I kissed her shoulder and stroked her hair back. "Just this breath and the next. Don't chase it. Let it come."

Her lips parted and her toes curled.

"Look at you. So beautiful. So good at taking what you want."

She reached for me hungrily, covering my mouth with hers in a deep kiss full of need. Then she pulled away, burying her face into the pillow to smother an agonized series of cries. She jerked and shuddered as she found her release. Her back heaved up and down and it was a while before she lifted her head from the pillow. I couldn't tear my eyes from her face as she fought to regain her composure. She sniffed and buried her face into my T-shirt.

"What's the matter?"

"I didn't think I'd ever get to this point." Her voice choked on a sob. "Thank you."

A tear ran down her cheek and I kissed it away. "You don't have to thank me. You did this. Now you know you can do it whenever you want. You don't need a man to make you feel like this. You don't need anyone." I pulled her snugly into my arms where she fit so well, as though she'd always meant to be there.

She twisted in my arms, pressing her back against mine, spooning me. "I figured out what spoon I want to be."

"Oh?"

"This one." I could hear the grin in her sleepy voice. "The little one, as long as you're the big one."

Chapter 32

REECE

The sound of the front door slamming downstairs woke me. The bang was followed by footsteps on the stairs. My eyes flew to the clock. What time was it?

"Reece? Are you in? They let us out early." Miri's cry drifted from downstairs.

My blood ran cold. Miri had been discharged already? I couldn't have her walking in here.

Another knock on the door. "Are you in there, Reece?"

"Hang on!" I leaped off the bed, scouring the floor, picking up clothes.

Skylar paled and yanked her T-shirt down. I pulled her up off the bed and shoved her toward my wardrobe.

"No. Please. I don't like enclosed spaces."

"I'm sorry. Just for a minute."

She stiffened and I guided her into the wardrobe. She tried to twist out of my arms. Her voice was a forceful whisper. "What does it matter? Let's tell her. Miri won't care. She already knows about Sean."

"We agreed to keep things quiet."

Skylar's face dropped. "Why? You're ashamed of me?"

"Of course not."

I was embarrassed about myself, that I'd let myself down like this. I didn't want Miri and Gabe to know what I'd been up to at that club. They were trying to help me out. Skylar pressed herself against my shirts. I shut her inside the wardrobe then dashed to open my bedroom door. Miri's eyes met mine and she frowned. She peered over my shoulder into the room.

"What's going on in there? Were you talking to someone? Why is it such a mess?"

I stepped outside, closing the door behind me. "I was on the phone."

"Why is everyone on the landing?" Gabe's voice made my shoulders tighten.

Gabe snuggled the beautiful baby boy in his arms and smiled. God. They were both here.

Gabe presented the tiny bundle swaddled in blankets to me. "Do you want a cuddle, Uncle Reece? We're going home, but we thought we ought to see you and Mum first."

I pinned my arms to my sides, battling to keep my face level. "Give me a moment. I'll be right down."

Miri appraised me with tired eyes, before her brow lifted with surprise. "You have someone in there, don't you?"

My mouth clenched tighter. "Don't be ridiculous."

Miri searched my face, then hers flashed with triumph. "You're lying!"

Gabe chuckled. "Caught in the act, Dr. Forster. Who's the unlucky lady?"

Sweat prickled the back of my neck. I shifted my gaze to Miri. "Mum will be desperate to see you. Why don't we all go and—"

"Oh God. It's Megan, isn't it?" Miri studied my face and slapped her palm to her forehead. "You're back with Megan? Gabe said you were all over each other at the hospital."

Did he now? I flashed Gabe an annoyed look and he cocked an amused eyebrow. He was probably still pissed off that I'd told him to stop leaning.

"You may as well come out, Megan. No point hiding away. Don't be shy."

Miri reached for the door handle, but I plastered myself in front of the door. "You can't go in there."

Her shrewd eyes met mine. "Why are you being so weird? Like, even weirder than usual?"

"Because it's my bedroom. I'm entitled to some privacy in my own bedroom."

Miri's lip twitched. She held her hands up in mock surrender and stepped back. "Fine. I just pushed a human being out of my vagina. That was traumatic enough. I don't need to see Megan in lingerie."

"Have you eaten? Go and sit down. You need to rest. I'll make you something, come on."

She waved a dismissive hand. "Don't fuss." She shook her head. "I can't believe Megan would have the audacity to show her face here after how she treated you."

"How do you know it's Megan?" The words were directed at Miri, but Gabe didn't take his eyes from the sleeping newborn in his arms. "He could have met someone else."

Miri frowned. "It's not one of the girls from the team, is it?"

An uneasy feeling made my mouth dry. "The team?"

"No. Sorry. Of course it isn't. It's just . . . I overheard something weird the other day, and I didn't know whether to mention it or not . . ."

"Oh?"

She lowered her voice. "It's silly, but the girls have some kind of bet."

"Bet?"

"Don't take it to heart. It's stupid. It's about who gets to . . . you know . . . first . . ."

My brow furrowed in confusion. "Gets to . . . ?"

Miri shifted her weight. "The winner is the first one to . . ." She cleared her throat and shot an appealing look at Gabe.

Gabe covered his newborn baby's tiny ears with his fingers. "The winner is the first one to do the horizontal tango with you."

My confusion must have showed on my face because Gabe flashed an amused smile full of white teeth. "They all want to butter your crumpet. The winner is the first one who gets to play doctors and nurses with you."

I turned back to Miri. That was as clear as mud. "What is he talking about?"

"It's a bet to see who can have sex with you first." Miri shook her head. "It's disgusting. Completely unprofessional. Claire is going to discipline them. Don't you worry. Heads will roll, but we want to wait until after the final match."

Gabe pressed his lips flat, but I couldn't miss the trace of humor in his emerald eyes. "That's right, mate. It's disgusting. Completely unprofessional. All these women desperate to shag you. It's terrible. Heads will roll."

Miri shot him a poisonous look. "I thought you were taking this seriously. This is sexual harassment. Imagine if it was the other way round."

Gabe smothered his smile and lowered his gaze. "I know. It's terrible. Reece must be mortified that one minute he is so un-shaggable his sister had to create a dating profile for him, and now all these professional athletes are scrambling over each other to get in his pants."

Could that be true? A bet? Was Skylar in on it? She couldn't be. Was everybody laughing about me behind my back?

Gabe cooed at his baby and bobbed from foot to foot. He flashed me a sly grin. "Are you going to be less uptight now you're getting some?"

Miri angled Gabe away and steered him down the corridor. She called over her shoulder, "Come for some cuddles when you're ready, Uncle Reece."

Gabe chuckled darkly. "When you've stopped boning, obviously."

Chapter 33

REECE

"Is it true? The team has a bet about me?"

Skylar stumbled out of the wardrobe, gasping and clutching her throat.

"What?" Skylar's wide eyes met mine. "What the hell was that, Reece? I couldn't breathe. It was too hot. You know I don't like enclosed spaces. I told you! How could you do that to me?"

An intense sickness swept through me. A chill, brittle silence enveloped us. Disappointment flickered in Skylar's expression and she folded her arms across her chest.

"I'm sorry. I just . . . I need to know about the bet."

Her eyes flashed angrily. "It's nothing to do with me. Just some stupid thing Lana cooked up."

"But you knew about it and you didn't tell me?"

"It's just the girls being idiots. Not a big deal."

My teeth itched. "Is that what everyone thinks of me? I'm some kind of joke?"

She scrambled around the room, picking up clothes. "Don't turn this around. You're so ashamed of me you shoved me in here with a one-way ticket to bloody Narnia."

"I don't need my sister and my boss finding out what I've been doing. They wanted me to work to counsel the team, not have sex with the captain."

She threw her hands up. "They are the last people that can judge us. They were banging in that office for weeks when they were telling everyone they were just work colleagues. Everybody knew about it."

"Right. Everybody knew. Do you want everyone on the team talking about us? I can't stand to be gossiped about, Skylar. I got bullied every day at school. I couldn't go a day without Sean or one of his meathead friends beating me up or pulling some stunt on me. I lost my dad and then I got taunted every time I stepped through the school gates. Nothing has changed, has it? Sean is still laughing at me. All your friends are still laughing at me, and you . . ."

She hitched a hand on her hip, but her face softened. "I'm what?"

You're breaking me. Just your presence. Knowing I can't have the only person I want without losing everything else that matters to me.

She frowned. "Look. I'm sorry. I hate that you went through that, but this isn't school and I don't want to be your dirty little secret. This is Miri and Gabe. They wouldn't tell anyone. We're going to have to tell people, anyway. We can't sneak around forever."

I didn't want to tell people. Not yet. How could I? If Miri thought it was bad I had Megan in here, God knows what she'd think when she found it was Skylar.

Skylar watched me and shook her head. "It's me, isn't it? You're ashamed to tell people. I'm not a fancy doctor like Megan. I didn't go to university. I've never even read Keats, let alone bloody Yeats. Why the fuck is there a Keats and a Yeats? It's ridiculous."

"Where has this come from? I don't care about any of that."

"I've been in this house all night and you won't even let me go near your mother. I bet you introduced Megan—"

202

"My mum isn't well. I don't want to give her any additional stress."

"Right," she snapped. "And the sight of me might finish her off?" She exhaled heavily and shook her head. "I'm sorry. I didn't mean that. I'm just pissed off." She grabbed her leggings from the floor and yanked them up. "I get it, Reece. I'm the girl that's good enough for a roll in the sack, but when push comes to shove, you'd rather hide me in the wardrobe than own up to this thing between us. I'm embarrassing for you."

"No. You're not. Not one bit. It's not that. It's me. I'm ashamed of myself. I've broken my own ethical code. I don't know how I'm going to tell people about us. You trusted me to help you and I violated your trust. What are people going to think? I'm a terrible psychologist. I'm going to lose my reputation. What am I supposed to do? Everybody in that place is already laughing about me anyway. This has always been . . . untenable."

She frowned and narrowed her eyes. "*Untenable?* Care to explain what that word means for the people who didn't go to Cambridge?"

Exhaustion washed over me and my voice sounded hoarse. "Unable to be maintained. This was always wrong."

"How can it be wrong when it feels this good between us?" She shook her head, and her eyes glimmered with tears. "I'm tired of this, Reece. I'm tired of all your excuses not to be with me. You told me that you love me."

"I do love you. I'm not giving you excuses. They are solid reasons."

Her eyes flashed with fury. "Bullshit, Reece. This is all bullshit. Well done. You created the perfect excuse not to be with me. You were never my therapist. You've created this dynamic as an excuse. If you don't want me, that's fine. Stop lying to yourself."

My mind whirled. Lying to myself? "I want you. I told you, you never have to worry about that."

I reached for her, but she snapped her hand away. She grabbed her team jacket and shoved her arms into the sleeves.

"I have a match in less than a week that is going to define my entire career. I've been working toward this my whole life. I have one shot to get this team into the Women's Super League. One fucking shot. This is messing with my head. The team has to come first. You're right. This is untena-whatever if it's making me feel like this. I can't do this anymore."

A deep, unaccustomed pain overwhelmed me.

She kept her gaze fixed on the door. "Maybe we should stay away from each other. I need to focus. It's not fair to my team."

"Is that what you want?"

She pressed her trembling palms to her eyes. "Yes. It has to be. I have to think of them. You need to stay away from me, Reece. I have to get through this match. Don't message me. Don't call me. Forget all about me."

Despite my despair, I tried to keep my face level. "I've never been able to forget about you. I wish I could. That's the problem."

She frowned. "You wish you could forget about me?"

That had come out wrong. "No. I mean to say that I've always wanted you. Even when I knew I didn't stand a chance with you, I longed for you."

"I know. You had some schoolboy crush on me. I get it. We're adults now."

"Not just then. Always. That first time you were in my office. The times when you invited me inside your house, and I turned you down. You can't even imagine how desperate I was for you, how much it pained me to do that, but I wanted to do the honorable thing and be there for you as a professional. All I've wanted to do is help you."

204

"The honorable thing? The honorable thing would have been to be honest about how you felt about me from the start."

"You were upset. You'd just got out of a breakup. The last thing you needed was me trying to date you."

"Maybe so, but that was my decision. Do you know what I think, Reece? I think you're scared. You're scared to let someone close, so it's easier to push me away."

That wasn't true. Skylar was upset and angry. One of us could stay calm at least.

"I'll stay away from you if that's what you want. You need to walk away. I respect whatever you need to do."

"You respect it?" Sadness flickered in her eyes. "So clinical and composed all the time, Dr. Forster. Does any of this affect you?"

I swallowed. "Yes. It affects me."

It's breaking me.

She snorted. "It doesn't look like it."

She wrapped her hand around the door handle, then she turned back to me, her hands clenched stiffly at her sides. "There's a transfer opportunity. Gabe wants me to go and play in LA."

Ice swept through me. LA? She wouldn't go, would she? I kept my face level. "Oh?"

She rubbed the back of her neck. "It's a temporary thing. I refused it, but the way things are going lately, I'm wondering if I should just pack a bag and get out of here."

"Is that what you want?"

She fiddled with the bar in her eyebrow and stole a glance at me. "If I said I wanted to go, would you even care?"

More than anything. Please don't go.

She regarded me with impassive coldness, but tears glimmered in her bright eyes. I'd hurt her. I was continuing to hurt her. This had to end.

I kept my voice soft. "It doesn't matter what I think. You need to do what's right for you."

"But what do you think? Do you want me to stay?"

A pregnant silence wrapped around us. I had the sudden sense that everything hinged on my next words. I wasn't selfish enough to ask her to stay. Love is sacrifice. I've always known that. I'd given up so many things for my family because I loved them. I had no regrets about that. No resentment. It's what I wanted to do. I had to put Skylar's needs before my own. Being with me wasn't the right thing for her, no matter how much I wanted her. I'd never been right for her. I had to let her go. We'd been hurtling toward this point since the moment I'd let her drop to her knees in my office. The only way to make this better was to let her go. This was all my fault.

My heart shattered into a thousand pieces, but I kept my face level. "It sounds like a great opportunity. You should think about it."

She flinched as though I'd slapped her. "And what about you. What will you do if I go? Will you stay at the club?"

"You don't have to worry about me. I'll be fine. I have my family and my . . . garden."

Her voice was quiet and distant. "Your garden?"

"I like gardening. I like to watch beautiful things thrive and know I had some small part to play."

Her eyes met mine and her expression was thunderous.

So powerful. So beautiful. So wild.

Blood pounded in my temple, and a deep, desperate pain gnawed at me. I longed to pull her into my arms. I'd wanted to help her heal, but instead I'd made her hurt like this. I'd only made things worse. I'd fucked everything up, but I'd only ever wanted the best for her. I fought every urge to drop to my knees and beg her not to go.

Brushing away tears, she rolled her shoulders and stood taller. "You're right. Maybe this is what I need. A new beginning. The LA

Halos are an amazing team. This could be great for me. Maybe I do need to do something completely different." Her voice was thick and unsteady, her mouth twisted into a thin-lipped smile. "And you . . . I need you to stay away from me. I have to get through this final match. I've got too much to deal with."

Wild grief tore through me. She nodded woodenly and flung the door open.

I held my hands up and kept my voice low. "Miri and Gabe will be downstairs. Let me check that they've gone to the annex, please . . ."

She bowed her head and her shoulders shook. With her back to me, I couldn't tell if it was with rage or sobs. "Fuck the annex. Fuck your garden. And fuck you. We're done."

Then she was gone.

Chapter 34

SKYLAR

Colorful graffiti laced every inch of the toilet stall door. I traced a finger over the inked offerings.

Sean Wallace is a prick.

Yeah. Isn't he just? I glanced at my watch and tried to slow my breathing. I had ten minutes before I needed to be in the dressing room prepping the team for our final practice. I'd rehearsed my pep talk. This had to be the pep talk to end all pep talks. Mostly, I wanted the girls to know how proud I was. How amazing it had been to lead them this season. How honored I felt. It wasn't a time to lay on the pressure.

The sound of the restroom door swinging open broke me out of my reverie. Voices drifted from beyond the stall doors.

"Did you see the statement on Instagram about Sean and Skylar? Mutual separation to concentrate on their careers? Sounds like bullshit to me. Something must have happened."

My heart leaped into my throat. I recognized the voices: two of my girls, Jenna and Tori.

"Does that mean Sean Wallace is back on the market?"

"Rumor is he's been banging Lana. That's why they split."

"Shit."

"I know. I wouldn't be that worried about Skylar. Apparently, she's hooking up with the psychologist guy."

My guts churned. How the hell had anyone found that out? We'd been so careful. There were no secrets with this team. I should have known.

A laugh. "Skylar got there first? I've lost twenty quid. I thought I was making good progress as well. I even made him smile the other day."

Tori piped up again. "Skylar needs to get her shit together. I can't believe we got through this whole season and she's cracked at the final hurdle."

My whole body flashed with heat. I put a hand on the stall wall to steady myself. My breath came hot and sharp. Part of me wanted to go out and confront them for talking shit about me, but I couldn't move. The shock held me still. My team had lost faith in me. Tears threatened my eyes.

Reece's words drifted into my head.

Calm and still like a mountain.

This was no time to fall apart. My life might have been turning to shit for weeks now, but no matter how I felt, I had to keep it together. The team had to come first. This was our defining moment. My moment as captain. I'd go out on that pitch and show everyone why we deserved to be promoted. Because we did deserve it. Now we had to prove it.

"I don't know what she's thinking. She's messing up on the pitch and now she's traded in the captain of Calverdale United for Captain Geek."

I hadn't seen Reece all week. He hadn't been in his office. He hadn't messaged me. He was doing what I wanted. I'd asked for space. The team was too important. But part of me had hoped he'd fight for me. I didn't want to do any of this without him. When push came to shove, he wasn't that different from Sean. He'd been ashamed of me. His door was always open to the captain, except for when he'd pushed me in a wardrobe and shut it in my face.

My heart contracted. I wanted to fling open the stall door and confront them. I wanted to tell them that I'd take Reece over Sean any day of the week. At least Reece knew where to find the clitoris. But I didn't. I waited for them to go and I wept quietly, because now I knew the truth. My team had lost in faith in me. How could I lead us to victory if they didn't believe in me? I'd tried so hard to fake it and hold everything together, but it was over.

Not good enough.

Chapter 35

REECE

In the dim silence of my office, I took my books down from the shelves and packed them neatly into boxes. With each heavy tome, regret assailed me like a wretched steel bar compressing my lungs. I should never have taken this job. It had always only been a way to be closer to Skylar. My behavior had been unacceptable. I'd broken my ethics and my commitment to do no harm. The last thing I'd wanted was to hurt Skylar, but I had. I'd messed with her head and her heart. That was the unforgivable part.

Lemon polish filled my senses as I spritzed the walnut desk and polished the smooth surface. I wanted to have compassion for myself. It was what I tried to give to my patients, but it's so much harder to be kind to yourself. I sat in my therapy chair and sunk my head into my hands. If I was counseling a patient, I'd highlight all the factors that led to this point. It had been a difficult year—the breakup with Megan, moving back in to take care of Mum, burn-out at the hospital. Maybe if I was the one in the therapy chair, I'd take it back even further than that. I'd unpick the trauma around losing Dad. I'd worked so hard to process it, but with something like that it would never be done. The wounds ran deep.

Everybody told me to take a break, but I ignored them and pushed through. My feelings for Skylar had always been unmanageable. I should have told my supervisor or quit sooner, but I'd been arrogant enough to think I could handle it. I'd thought I had it under control. The truth is that life is chaotic and messy. Some things were beyond my control, no matter how much I wanted to kid myself otherwise.

I moved to the couch and ran a hand over the soft, buttery leather. I couldn't help but picture Skylar there, writhing with her first orgasm. I'd wanted to help her. I'd gone about it in the most inappropriate way imaginable and it ended in tears. Maybe she'd be laughing about me now with her teammates. The ones that had made a bet about me. No wonder everyone was so keen to do individual coaching sessions.

Humiliation made the back of my neck itch. It was the same feeling I'd had at school when Sean's gang had rounded on me in the hallway, shoving me into the lockers, laughing in my face. Skylar hadn't noticed what was happening then either. Even if she wasn't involved in the bet, she could have told me. I was repeating the same pattern. Skylar Marshall was part of my past. Maybe I'd thought I could heal that old wound by pursuing her again, but nothing had changed. We were adults now, but she was still the prom queen and I was still the geek that worshipped the ground she walked on. It made me ache. I loved her still. I'd always love her, but I couldn't carry on here. I couldn't stay somewhere where people didn't take me seriously, where they were laughing at me.

With a whoosh, I shut the blinds and slipped my jacket back on. I'd broken my ethics in this room. Passion had overtaken my sense of reason and I'd let my heart rule my head. When I reported what had gone on here, I'd lose my license to practice as a psychologist. My family would be horrified. I'd lost my reputation and my self-respect, and for what? Nothing. I'd gladly give those things away for Skylar, but I'd lost her too. She didn't even want me at her final match.

I took one last look around the office.

Goodbye, Calverdale.

I won't be back.

Chapter 36

REECE

Later that night, I ripped up a weed from the vegetable patch, but it didn't give me the usual satisfaction. My stomach felt hard and empty. At least it was quiet down here and I could hear myself think. A cough sounded from overhead. Miri hovered over me. She passed me a hot mug of tea. Gabe towered next to her with my tiny newborn nephew swaddled fast asleep in a blanket.

Miri hovered for a moment before she settled on the shed step next to me. The chirrups of the sparrows on the bird feeder filled the silence.

Miri glanced at me. "What's going on? You've packed up your office. Is everything okay?"

I tried to think of something to say to reassure her, but the truth slipped out instead. "Not really. No. I'm not okay."

Miri frowned. "Is it about the bet? Gabe is going to talk to everyone about that. We just need to get through this final match."

Silence wrapped around us and I watched the tall sunflower husks bending gently in the breeze.

I cleared my throat. "I got bullied all the way through school. Did you know that?"

Silence thickened and the sound of the wind rustling in the sunflowers filled my ears.

"I knew it was difficult for you . . . I didn't know how bad." Miri's voice was soft.

"When you told me about the bet, it made me feel like I was back there. Dad had just died. I had to keep going to school and pretending that everything was okay. The whole time I was just so . . . powerless and out of control. I can't stand to be made fun of like that. To think that everyone is laughing at me. You put me on that dating app because you think I'm a joke."

Miri paled. "No. It was just a bit of fun. We want to see you happy after Megan, that's all. I'm sorry. You know Frankie gets out of hand sometimes. Her heart is in the right place."

Gabe stepped forward, his expression unusually earnest. "Nobody is laughing at you, mate. It was just some daft joke from Lana that escalated."

Miri nodded. "That's right. That team is a bunch of messy bitches sometimes. Life is messy, Reece."

Yes. It's definitely that.

I took a breath. They'd find out sooner or later. Better coming from me than someone else. "When you came home from the hospital and you thought I had Megan in my room, it was Skylar."

Miri chuckled. "Skylar?"

I nodded.

The smile died on her lips when she saw that I wasn't laughing along with her. Her eyebrows shot up. "Skylar? As in Skylar Marshall?"

"Yes. Skylar Marshall."

Miri frowned in confusion. "Really? But Skylar's so . . . the two of you are so . . ."

A muscle worked in my jaw. "You don't think somebody like Skylar could be attracted to me?"

Miri held her hands up. "I didn't say that. It's just . . . does she know you line up the mugs in color order in the cupboard?"

"Yes. She knows, and she likes it. Skylar agrees with a lot of my household management policies. Just because you lot love to ridicule me doesn't mean everyone else does. Some people like things to be neat and tidy. It's not going to kill you to hang the towels up after you've used them. How else are they going to dry?"

Gabe snorted. I turned my face away. Nothing about this situation amused me. I couldn't strike from my mind the stricken expression Skylar had worn when she'd burst out of that wardrobe. I'd hurt her by trying to hide this thing between us because of my own guilt. I'd damaged her by not maintaining the boundary between us. She'd needed a safe space to talk, not a hookup.

Miri picked up an old watering can and twisted it in her hands. "How long has it been going on?"

"I don't want to talk about it. It was a mistake. Skylar came to me for help and support after her breakup. She was in a vulnerable place. I knew that, but I still let this thing happen between us. You brought me to the club to counsel the team, not become romantically entangled. I've behaved unethically. I'm resigning. I can't work at the club anymore after this."

Gabe swayed to and fro, rocking the baby in his arms. "I'm not accepting your resignation. We need you at the club."

"Get someone properly qualified. An actual sports psychologist. You don't need me."

"You've been doing some great work. The team has been playing better since they lost that first game. They're working better together. They seem calmer now they're doing the meditation routines after training. You've had a positive impact. We're not letting you go. There's no point arguing with me. I always get what I want in the end." He inclined his head toward Miri and flashed a smile full of white teeth. "Just ask your sister."

Fine. I didn't have the energy to argue with Gabe. I wasn't going back to that club.

I looked up to find Miri watching me. "And you and Skylar? Is it serious?"

"We're done. She doesn't want to see me anymore."

Miri studied my face intently. "You've completely blown this out of proportion. I don't understand. The football club isn't the hospital. Skylar wasn't your patient. If it's the fact that you work together that's bothering you then leave the club. You can be together if you want to be."

"Skylar needs to concentrate on the final match. I pissed her off when I hid her from you. Besides, it's not right. She came to me in the middle of a breakup, vulnerable and sad. I should have met her in that space and helped her. I've behaved so selfishly."

Heat pressed behind my eyes at hearing myself speak the words out loud. I'd let myself down. I'd let everyone down. Miri and Gabe fell silent. They probably couldn't believe what they were hearing. I'd spent my career counseling people through their problems, and I'd let my own life get so out of control.

Miri reached out and caught my hand in hers, then she pulled me into her arms. "Hey. It's okay. You're being so hard on yourself. You're human, Reece. Just like the rest of us. You're a good man. You're kind and thoughtful. You've held this family together through so much. I know you're beating yourself up for this, but don't do that too much. Dad would be so proud if he could see you now. I know we all give each other a hard time, but it's from a place of love. We're all proud of you."

"Thank you." My heart contracted, and I buried my face into Miri's shoulder. "The worst part is that I love her so much. I've always loved her. She told me to stay away. I didn't want to tell anyone what was going on. She was so angry with me. I hate the way we left things."

Miri held me at arm's length. "The pressure is intense at the moment. Everything is riding on one game. You should talk to her. Maybe she's calmed down."

"She needs to focus on the match tomorrow, not on me."

"What about a text? Wish her luck. You can talk properly afterward." She leaned back, sizing me up. "She's probably so stressed about tomorrow. It will let her know that you care about her."

Warmth spread through me. Miri was right. I didn't want to distract Skylar or bother her, but the thought of her running out onto that pitch thinking that I didn't care about her didn't sit right either. At least I could clear the air.

"Fine. I'll do it."

"Good." Miri brightened and stroked the baby's head. "We thought of a name, by the way."

I braced myself to maintain a neutral expression. "Oh?"

"Simon."

A pang pulled at my heart and I stroked my nephew's smooth cheek. They'd named him after Dad.

"Simon," I said. "It's perfect."

Miri smiled.

Gabe squeezed my shoulder. He raised an impressed eyebrow. "Skylar Marshall, though? Really? I didn't know you had it in you." He transferred his gaze to Miri. "And you lot put him on that dating app. You needn't have bothered." A hint of laughter edged his voice. "The doc's got game."

◆ ◆ ◆

I went to my room and sent a text.

I'm sorry for all of it. I know you don't want to talk to me, that's fine, but if you need me at the match for moral support, I'll be there.

I waited as three blue dots appeared.

Then disappeared.

The minutes ticked on. A chill black silence enveloped me. My throat ached with defeat. She didn't need me. Then the dots appeared again.

Please come.

Chapter 37

SKYLAR

Rain lashed in thick sheets as we charged around the pitch. My body ached. My legs threatened to collapse, but we had another ten minutes of play. Neither team had scored. Reece's eyes burned into me from the sideline. I felt his solid, soothing presence even if I hadn't dared to stop and drink him in yet. I glanced at him standing stiff and composed next to Gabe, an oasis of calm in the tensest ninety minutes of my life. I tore my eyes away. He was a distraction I couldn't afford.

Sophie had the ball at her feet, charging to the goal. I got in position for a cross, but an opposition player sliced along the grass, clattering into her. Sophie went down, hard. The ball flew out of play.

Agitation rippled the length of my spine, but also excitement. The tackle had clearly been a foul. That meant we were owed a penalty.

"Ref," I cried.

I dashed to the referee and the crowd of players that had already gathered, shouting and pleading their case. It could go either way. I knew this ref. She'd made questionable decisions in the past. A sharp elbow dug into my side as the opposition player nudged me out of the way. I fought to stand my ground in the skirmish. Unmoved by our protests, the referee glanced at the chaotic scene where Sophie lay on the floor, grimacing and surrounded by medics. Thankfully, she looked more angry than pained. The referee waved us away to consider and I waited, holding my breath for her decision. It was so late in the game, but if the ref awarded a penalty, we had a chance at winning.

My heart pounded. Adrenaline made every nerve jumpy and raw. I peered over the ref's shoulder to the sideline. I allowed my gaze to hover on Reece just for a moment. My eyes needed their fix. I couldn't help but be drawn to him, wherever he was. I swallowed, trying to quell the frustration that gripped my throat. For fuck's sake. What was taking so long? It had been an aggressive slide tackle. Definitely a foul.

A great shiver ran through me as the sweat evaporated from my arms. A shrill whistle rang out. The referee pointed at the penalty spot. That was the signal. She'd awarded the penalty. One goal would end this now. Victory hovered so close I could taste it. I bent down to scoop up the ball, but hands appeared from nowhere and grabbed the ball before I had the chance. Lana's red ponytail bobbed as she trotted with the ball to the penalty spot. I chased after her.

I grabbed her wrist. "What the fuck are you doing?"

Lana's fingers shook as she laid the ball down on the penalty spot. She wouldn't look at me. "Claire told me that if there's a penalty, she wants me to do it."

No. I always took penalties. "Are you kidding?"

Lana gave a taut shake of her head. She worried her bottom lip between her teeth. "I'm sorry. I have to do what Claire tells me. I don't want to do it either. What if I fuck it up?"

A pulse beat in my temple. I should have been the one to shoulder this responsibility. "Why would Claire do this?"

The stadium's roar filled my ears like a wild beast.

Lana flattened her lips, but her voice choked. "I told Claire it should be you."

There was no point pressuring Lana. It wasn't her fault. She had to follow the manager's direction. I'd have to appeal to Claire and hope I had enough time before they restarted play. A huddle of medics crouched next to Sophie with the stretcher. We couldn't restart play until she was off the pitch, but I wouldn't have long. Better be quick. I raced to the sideline and planted myself in front of Claire.

Despite my effort to stay calm, anger bubbled inside of me like hot lava. "What the fuck, Claire? I always take the penalties."

Claire's icy gaze met mine. "It's not personal. The pressure is high. This is about the team."

I tried to keep the tremor from my voice. "Is this because of what happened before? Because that was a one-off. It won't happen again."

Claire's eyes glinted in the sunlight like two pieces of porcelain. She smiled benignly as if dealing with a toddler. "Let Lana do it. You don't need the pressure."

She turned her back on me. The anger that boiled inside of me became a twisting ball of barbed wire in my gut. My team had lost their faith in me and so had my manager. The roar of the crowd became screaming white noise. How could she make this call? I was the best penalty shooter in the team. Apart from that one fuckup, I'd never missed. Everybody knew my stats. I'd messed up last time because of how things had been with Sean. It wouldn't happen again. I could do this. Couldn't I?

Numbness smothered me. A year of work, and I didn't get to see it through. Lana was the second-best penalty scorer. She had a chance, but she was also one of the youngest on the team. It was so much pressure on young shoulders. This was the captain's responsibility. She shouldn't have to bear that terrible burden if things didn't go our way.

I tipped my face to the sky, trying to calm myself. My hair dripped with water, but at last the rain had stopped battering us. The clouds parted, revealing the faint wash of a rainbow against pale blue. I allowed my gaze to find Reece's. Dark tendrils of hair curled on his forehead. We were too far apart to speak, and I wouldn't be able to hear him over the racket anyway, but we didn't need words. His face had always been so inscrutable, but he offered me a smile that was unmistakably warm and encouraging. Reece believed in me. He'd always seen something in me, even when I couldn't see it in myself.

His gaze clung to mine as he drew exaggerated breaths, his full lips parting to inhale and open as he exhaled.

Deep breaths. Calm and solid like a mountain. You've got this.

He tipped his head in a nod. A sudden spaciousness filled me. I'd got us here, hadn't I? Sean had trampled my confidence, but I had to have my own back. This wasn't a time for self-doubt. I'd never been like the other girls at school. The ones who knew all the words to *Frozen* and wore pretty fairy costumes on dress-up days. I'd spent my childhood in shorts and football boots with the roar of the wind in my ears and the taste of mud on my tongue. I'd clocked up hours of grueling training in every weather condition. Injuries. Defeats. Blood, sweat, and tears. I'd given everything to football. I'd fought my entire life. Everything had been building to this one moment. A single penalty. I wasn't a teaspoon. Not anymore. I was the only girl that had been good enough to play with the boys. I'd always been good enough. Somehow, I'd forgotten myself.

I could do this.

I'd always been able to do this.

Planting myself in front of Claire, I forced myself to settle and spoke with quiet but determined firmness. "I panicked before, but it won't happen again. I've worked with the psychologist on it. You have to trust me now. I won't let you or this team down. I'm taking that penalty, and I'm getting us into the Women's Super League."

Claire's gaze pierced mine, and I detected the slightest thawing in her eyes.

I stood taller. "I'll get it done because that's what I do. This is no one else's responsibility but mine. I'm the captain. Let me do my fucking job."

A small smile played on her lips. She tapped her pen against her clipboard thoughtfully and gave a grudging nod. "Fine. Off you go then, Marshall." She waved a dismissive hand. "You're right. You're the captain. Do your fucking job."

I found a nice patch of grass. A few cheers rang out. Then clapping. Then stomping. My hands were sure and steady as I placed the ball on the penalty spot. Once, I might have trembled, but not now. I had a job to do. I'd been training my entire life for this one moment. I straightened. The wind slapped my face and screamed in my ears, but a voice rose up in me. A cool, calm voice that enveloped me in comfort.

You are strong and steady like a mountain. Just this breath. And the next.

Reece had told me he was a terrible healer, but that wasn't true. I was still angry with him, but he'd helped me believe in myself again. Sean had broken me, and Reece had put me back together. Maybe it hadn't been the way he should have done it. He hadn't healed me with bandages or medicines. He'd loved me, and with his love he'd fixed the cracked parts inside of me.

I blocked out all of it: the clapping, the stomping feet, the howling wind. I'd been a little girl that the boys didn't think was good enough. I'd shown them. I'd show everybody.

I'm the captain.

The whistle blew. Adrenaline coursed through me, but I didn't move. No rush. A mountain stands still and composed, regardless of the weather. One breath and then the next. With every ounce of strength, I aimed for the top-right corner. The keeper jumped and time moved in slow motion. The tips of her orange gloves grazed the ball as it sailed over her head. It hit the back of the net. The stadium erupted with wild screaming.

Lana dove on me and I was weightless as the girls lifted me into the air. My heart soared, wrapped in the love of my team, where I knew it would be safe. We'd done it. We'd made it into the Women's Super League.

Sometimes, even captains miss.

But not today.

Chapter 38

SKYLAR

When my feet finally hit the pitch again, my face ached from grinning. There would be interviews and photos to pose for, but first I needed to find Reece. I scanned the sideline, but there was no trace of him. As I headed for the tunnel, a familiar voice held me in place.

"Skylar?"

I twisted, hoping to see anyone but the man who stood in front of me. Sean raked a hand through his golden hair and hitched a shoulder.

"Sean? What do you want?" This wasn't a time to go toe to toe with my ex.

His smirk was as smug as ever. "You did well."

I stared at him, unable to hide my annoyance. "What?"

He rubbed the base of his spine. "I mean it. It's not easy taking a penalty under that kind of pressure. I had to do it last week against Liverpool."

"Right. Thanks."

I tried to dodge past him. Sean was the last person I wanted to speak to.

"I heard you had an offer to play in LA?"

What was it to him? I should have walked away, but his eyes seemed to plead for friendship.

"You heard about that?"

He nodded. "When are you leaving?"

A chill swept through my body as the sweat from the game began to evaporate. "I'm not."

He frowned. "What do you mean?"

"I can't leave. The team need me."

"But this is a chance to play at world-class level. You dreamed about this. This is what you've worked for, Sky. They do things differently over there. Think about what you'd learn."

I opened my mouth to protest, but all of the reasons seemed feeble. Sean was right. This was an incredible opportunity. I couldn't deny the appeal of going somewhere where no one knew me. The team was gossiping about me behind my back. They'd lost faith in me. I couldn't go on social media because everybody in England was obsessed with theories about what had gone on between me and Sean. I didn't even have a home anymore. My best friend had betrayed me and kissed my ex-boyfriend. But worst of all, I'd lost Reece.

A heavy feeling had settled inside me ever since he'd shoved me into that wardrobe. Reece didn't want me. He'd come here today, but it didn't mean anything had changed. Every time I walked past his office, my heart ached. How could I ever move on from any of it if I stayed here?

Sean shot me a knowing look and pointed to my black captain's armband. "Is it because you can't give it up? You won't be captain over there."

A heavy realization settled inside of me. No. That was the least of my concerns. If anything, it would be a relief to put down such a heavy weight. When Lana had tried to take that penalty, there was a part of me that had wanted her to. It had fallen on my shoulders, but it would have been such a relief to step aside for once. To let someone else carry the responsibility.

I twisted the cuff around my arm. "Don't you wish you could take a break from it sometimes?"

He gave me a grudging nod. "Sometimes. I miss how it was at the start, when you just got to play the game."

That was it. I missed playing the game. Being part of the team. I'd had to take that penalty, because I'd had to prove myself, and now I'd done it. I'd scored the winning penalty, and I'd got us into the WSL. I had nothing left to prove.

Maybe Miri was right. LA could be a glorious vacation. If I was training with stronger players, I'd have a chance to relax and fall back in love with the game. I wouldn't always be carrying everyone on my shoulders. I didn't need to do all this on my own anymore. I'd done everything that I'd promised this team. I could walk away with my head held high. A fresh start.

Sean's expression filled with impatience. "If you're going to LA, I need you to come and get your junk out of the house." He wrinkled his nose. "It's a mess."

And just like that, any moment of reconciliation with Sean was quashed. He was still an arsehole, even if he'd unwittingly helped me make a difficult decision.

"I'll do it when I can."

I made to move past him, but he grabbed my elbow. "Don't take too long."

I eyed Sean with a calculating expression. Of all the times he could have come to me with this shit, he'd chosen now. He couldn't even let me enjoy my victory.

No way would I give this man the power to ruin this victory for me. I plastered a smile onto my face.

"You think you've won, but I've got you figured out, Sean. I know what you were trying to do to me. You wanted to make me feel small, because that made you feel better. Deep down, you know that you're the problem. You're an egomaniac, and I can guarantee that all those girls you were with behind my back were faking it too."

His mouth formed a grim, tight line. "What?"

"You heard me."

I turned to march away, but anger held me in place. I spun back around to face him. "The problem is, you forget who I am. You thought you could bend me out of shape, but you can't. Getting over all of your bullshit made me something better. You made me into a fucking dessert spoon."

He stared back in confusion. "You're weird, Skylar."

Warmth spread through me. Nothing Sean said would ever hurt me again. I had nothing to prove to him, or anyone.

"There isn't a single thing wrong with me. I'm great, just the way I am."

A flash of tweed in the crowd caught my eye. I squinted into the stands and my heart took a perilous leap.

Reece.

I darted away, leaving Sean and all of his bullshit a distant memory.

Chapter 39

Reece

I moved with the crowd into the foyer. It was time for Skylar to enjoy her victory. She'd wanted me here for the match, but I wouldn't encroach on her need for space. If she wanted me, she knew where to find me. I wouldn't make a joyous time for her uncomfortable. An elbow landed in my back as a group of supporters waving scarves in the air and chanting passed by. It had probably been a good game. I wouldn't know. I hadn't been able to take my eyes off Skylar long enough to concentrate.

Drizzle misted my glasses as I moved with the surging crowd through the exit.

"Reece?"

The familiar soft voice held me frozen. I'd expected her to be in a press conference by now, enjoying her victory. Instead, she was standing in front of me in the crowded foyer of the stadium. Mud splattered her face. Her hair was pulled up in a ponytail that revealed the shaved edges of her undercut.

She fiddled with the ring in her nose. "You're going?"

"I thought it would be for the best."

She swiped mud from her arm and cleared her throat. "Right."

We stared at each other for a moment. Then I came to my senses and remembered why we were here. "Well done. You had an incredible game. You've got everything you wanted. You're in the Women's Super League."

She chewed her lip. "Not everything I wanted."

Silence swirled between us. People swarmed around us, throwing us curious glances. Skylar frowned and took me by the elbow. She led me back inside the stadium until we found a quiet corridor nearer the pitch.

We both blurted out words at the same time.

"You were incredible out—"

"I'm going to take the offer to play in LA."

Pain squeezed my heart. "What?"

Her gaze came to rest on my questioning eyes. "It won't be forever. It's more like a vacation."

"Is that what you want?"

"Yes. No. I don't know. It would be amazing for my career, and maybe I need something different after everything that happened with Sean."

It was a good decision for her, even if it made me want to weep. I could never be so selfish as to keep her here. "I'm sorry for everything. The wardrobe thing was terrible. If I ever made you feel like I was ashamed of you, then you couldn't be more wrong. You came to me in the middle of a breakup, vulnerable and sad. I should have met you in that space and helped you. You need time to process everything that's happened without me. It will be good for you to go."

Her head bowed, but she held perfectly still. "I can't take this anymore from you, Reece. I don't know what it's going to take to get through to you. I'm not your patient. I never have been. I had a bad breakup with Sean, but I handled it. This was never about me being vulnerable."

Sadness filled her eyes. "You're scared to let me in, so you've put so much energy into pushing me away. I have so much love to give. I want to give it to you, but you won't accept it from me. I'm not going to force you to let me love you. If you've taught me anything, it's that I deserve more than that. I won't demean myself in that way.

"Sean always tried to make me feel like I was the problem, but I'm not. I've given you all the love I have. If you don't want that from me, then that's on you."

A pang pulled at my heart, and for once I had no answers. Megan had accused me of pushing her away, too. All I'd ever wanted was the best for Skylar. I still wanted that.

Her palms cupped my cheeks and the muddy scent of the pitch hit my nose. "I want to stick this out with you. All I know is that it makes sense for me to go. I need to get away from all of this and get my head straight. This year has been so intense."

She wiped her tears with the back of her hand. "Thank you. For everything. You helped me so much. I love you more than I have ever loved anyone. When you're ready to let yourself feel that from me, come and find me."

She flashed a tentative smile and I was a breathless boy of fourteen again.

"Goodbye, Reece."

I could have stopped her. I could have dropped to my knees and begged her to stay, but I wouldn't stand in the way of such an incredible opportunity if that's what she wanted. Skylar deserved the best. Better than me.

So, I let the woman of my dreams walk out of my life.

Chapter 40

REECE

"Let's go. The gym is calling."

Elliot's voice drifted through my bedroom door.

I turned the page in my book. "Tell the gym I'm on another line."

Elliot hammered on the door and adopted his drill sergeant voice. "It's leg day. We don't skip leg day."

I rolled out of bed and opened the door. Elliot scanned my room with a frown, his eyes lingering on the heaps of clothes and the dirty plates piled on the bedside cabinet.

My younger brother wrinkled his nose. "When did you last shower?"

I ran a hand over the stubble on my jaw. "None of your business."

His disparaging gaze dropped over my crumpled T-shirt and sweatpants. "It's my business if I have to look at you in this state. This is not you."

I tried to shut the door, but he danced past me into the dim room. He picked up a dirty mug and examined it. "Are you ready to talk yet?"

"No. I just want to be left alone."

He drifted to the door. "Miri," he shouted. "Reece is malfunctioning again. We're going to need a full system reboot."

"So hilarious. You're wasted on ballet. You could be doing stand-up." I tried to shove him out of the door. "Please leave me alone."

Footsteps drummed on the stairs, before Miri planted herself in front of me, a muslin cloth draped over her shoulder. The smell of milk and baby powder clung to her. "You're not still moping, are you? Come and hang out with Simon. There's no time for moping with a baby."

Gabe trailed after Miri, planting himself at her side. "Let the man mope. We all need a good mope sometimes."

Simon nestled happily in Gabe's strong arms. I braced myself, ready for Frankie to turn up. I couldn't go a day without a family intervention. Yesterday, Mum had been the ringleader. Today, it looked like Elliot had taken it upon himself to lead the charge.

"What's going on? Why are you all here without me?" Frankie's voice boomed from down the landing. "I thought we weren't doing this till this afternoon."

Frankie elbowed her way past Elliot and squeezed my shoulder. Her voice was unusually sympathetic. "We get it, Reece. There isn't a man on this planet who wouldn't be bawling into their bran flakes if Skylar Marshall had dumped them. We're here if you need to talk."

A devilish look crossed her face as she pulled her phone out of her pocket. "I think we should put you back on the dating app. It's the best way to move on."

I lurched to grab the phone from her hand, but she was too quick. Anger rippled under my skin, but I kept my voice calm and level. "If you put me on that app again, I swear to God, Frankie—"

"Leave him alone." Miri shot Frankie a warning look. "No one is putting you on that stupid app. We're just worried about you. You can't spend your whole life in this house. We want you back at the football club."

"I can't go back to the club."

Miri shook her head. "No one is bothered that you hooked up with Skylar. It was interesting for an afternoon, and now everyone is back to work. We're training for the big league now. Nobody has time to care who is doing what with who. Just come back to work."

I had no interest in returning to the football club. Every inch of the place reminded me of Skylar, and what I'd lost. "I'm not ready."

I moved to close the door, but Miri stuck her foot in the jamb. "What is it going to take? Have you tried talking to her? They have phones in LA, you know. Can't you work this out?"

"Skylar has a chance at a fresh start. LA was the right call for her. I'm not going to bother her. She doesn't need me."

Miri frowned. "Is that what she told you?"

Skylar's hurt face drifted through my mind. Her parting words rang in my head every day. She thought I was rejecting her, when I'd just been trying to protect her.

"She said I'd been finding excuses not to open up."

Frankie folded her arms and nodded sagely. "That does sound like something you'd do."

Shame iced my shoulder blades. "I also made her hide in a wardrobe even though she doesn't like enclosed spaces. I'm not proud of it."

Elliot stared at me for a moment, then he threw his hands up. "I'm out. There is no helping this man."

Frankie hooked her arm into her twin's elbow and hauled him back before he could make his escape.

I ignored them both, and kept my gaze fixed on Miri. She'd understand where I was coming from. Miri had once worried so much about keeping her relationship with Gabe professional. "I don't think it was an excuse. The fact was, she'd been going through a difficult time, and I'd been trying to help her. Anyway, Skylar is happy playing in LA. She's better off without me for the same reason that Megan is. I have too much going on to burden her when she's doing so well."

Miri and Gabe shared a look. Miri gave him an encouraging nod that suggested whatever he was about to say had been carefully coached.

Gabe cleared his throat and stepped forward. "Do you know how difficult things were when I fell in love with your sister? I had the whole British press on my back, not to mention we were trying to keep things professional."

A rueful grin graced Miri's lips and she stroked Gabe's arm. He returned her smile and continued. "The point is that life is going to happen, but when you love someone, you don't mind. Whatever the drama is, you're willing to insert yourself right in the middle of it because you want to share your partner's burdens. You help each other."

I let the words sink in. Miri had put up with stuff about Gabe's life in the public eye that would have sent a lot of people running for the hills, but they'd got their happy ever after. I'd thought a lot about Skylar's words. It was all I'd done in the two weeks since she'd been gone.

The truth was so hard to accept. Maybe I *had* pushed Skylar away. She'd had to beg me to open up, and maybe I *was* being too uptight about the whole situation. As much as it felt like I'd been trying to counsel Skylar, she'd never asked me to. It wasn't a formal arrangement. Skylar had been going through a tough time, but she wasn't vulnerable. She was the strongest person I knew, and she'd never looked stronger than when she was calling me out on the way I'd treated her.

Had I really screwed this up so badly? This was Psychology 101. I'd spent a lifetime trying to advise other people, but I'd failed so miserably with my own issues. I'd loved Skylar from afar for so long, and when she actually returned my affections, I'd panicked. I didn't need a psychology degree to work it out. This was all my own baggage. I hadn't felt worthy of Skylar's love, so I'd created barriers in order to relieve the pressure to receive it.

"I panicked and pushed Skylar away. She wanted to be with me, and I wouldn't let her get close."

Frankie's eyes shone with sympathy. "Skylar Marshall is the hottest woman to ever breathe in your direction. You were obsessed with her for years. Of course you freaked out. The point is you are worthy, Reece. You're a brilliant man. We all know it."

Miri smiled. "That's right. You have a lot to offer. You're kind, and smart. You're a good listener."

Miri nudged Gabe. Gabe's smile turned up a notch. His bright eyes sparkled with humor. "You're a catch. If I've learned anything from spending all this time with the women's team, it's that emotional intelligence and a willingness to fold laundry are sexy as hell."

I kept my voice deadpan. "Says the billionaire with the movie-star looks."

Miri laughed earnestly. "No. Gabe's right. Emotional regulation is an underestimated trait in a partner. So is knowing how to separate the recycling properly." She shot Gabe a dark, layered look, and he chuckled.

Skylar had told me she found my quirks endearing. I'd been so uptight and frightened. I'd pushed away the love of my life. Another surge of regret assailed me.

"I want to fix this. What can I do?"

Frankie beamed and flicked an imaginary speck of dirt from her dungarees. "This is easy. Let me break this down for you. You drop to your knees and explain all the ways in which you've been a complete idiot, and why you're madly in love with her. Then you beg her to forgive you. This is why you shouldn't have skipped out on our Thursday night rom-com marathons. You would know all of this."

Gabe rocked back on his heels. "This is the part where you grovel, mate."

Frankie nodded her approval. "See, Gabe knows. He never shirks on movie nights."

"Or leg days," Elliot chipped in.

No. This was bad advice. Skylar was settling into her new life. The last thing she needed was me bothering her and messing her around. "Skylar is in LA. This is the opportunity of a lifetime for her. I'm not going to ruin it."

Frankie threw her hands up in exasperation. "You're not ruining anything, you're just telling her how you feel, and you need to be open to how she feels about you."

A surge of determination went through me. Maybe I needed to pay attention to one of these ridiculous interventions. My family had been right about me getting away from the hospital. It had been the best decision I'd made, even if I had messed things up with Skylar.

"Fine. Point taken. I'll call Skylar." I shooed them back from my door. "Now you can all go away."

Miri's amused eyes came to study my face. "You can do better than that."

I raised a questioning eyebrow.

"Your brother-in-law owns a private jet."

My sister dropped the words lightly, like small pebbles into a stream. She knew full well I'd never flown. That I had zero desire to ever fly.

"Several jets, actually." Gabe looked down with awe at the sleeping baby in his arms as he rocked from side to side. "They are all at your disposal."

238

Anxiety crept over my shoulder blades. The flight would be awful, but I couldn't just sit around here cultivating new species of mold in my coffee cups while the woman of my dreams thought I didn't want to be with her. I wanted Skylar more than anything, but I'd been so blind. After years training to be a psychologist, I thought I had a good grip on my issues, but they'd come to bite me so hard. I'd do the work to deal with this, and I'd open my heart. I'd do whatever it took to give Skylar Marshall everything she deserved, and everything I deserved, too. If that meant surrendering control, and sitting in a box in the sky, then so be it.

"Fine. You can all back off now." I gave my meddling family a smile. "I'm off to get my girl."

Chapter 41

SKYLAR

Heat beat down on my face as I left the Halos training ground. I tipped my chin to the sun's warmth. The weather was the best part about getting out of England. There was still so much to adjust to, but the football helped. I had so little time to dwell on the things I'd left behind. Being on the pitch helped me to ignore the huge Reece-shaped hole in my heart.

I headed for my car. Nobody walked anywhere in LA. That was another thing I missed about home. A couple of kids hovered by the stadium exit, waiting for autographs. I usually got out without anyone bothering me. The other girls on the team were better known than me. I was a nobody here, and it was the biggest relief. I could go out and do whatever I wanted without being recognized or followed.

I said goodbye to some of the girls who had stopped to pose for selfies and sign football jerseys. With my cap pulled low, I headed to a row of cars.

"Skylar Marshall? Can I get an autograph?"

The English accent alone would have stopped me in my tracks, but the low, composed timbre of Reece's voice sent a jolt through me. I twisted on the spot. Reece was wearing his usual immaculate white shirt. His sleeves were rolled to the elbow, showing his arms, which looked so pale by LA standards. Not that it mattered. He always looked so delicious.

I strode toward him, my heart hammering. "What are you doing here?"

"I came to see you."

"I thought you didn't fly?"

"I don't, but I shut you in a wardrobe. It's the least I can do." He pushed his glasses up his nose and gave me a tentative smile. "I came to ask you something, and I need to do it face to face."

A shiver of pleasure went through me to be close to him. I'd tried to block him out of my mind, but I'd thought about him every minute since I'd left. I was hoping so desperately that he'd call. It had never crossed my mind that he'd actually show up.

He peered around and took my elbow, guiding me to a shady spot away from the autograph-hunters.

"First, I need to say that I'm sorry. Everything you said was right. I was scared to let you in because I didn't feel good enough for you. I pushed you away, and I don't want to do that. I want to be with you. I'm going to do the work, so I never hurt you like that again."

He took a breath. "I want to let you into my life . . . all of it. If I could move here and be with you, I would do it in a heartbeat. I don't know how we are going to do this, because I have responsibilities, but I have to be with you—"

"I'm only here for six months. We can do long distance until then, if you'll wait for me . . ."

"Of course I'll wait. I've waited my whole life for you. We'll figure it out. You are my person. I'm not letting you walk away from me. I'll never make that mistake again."

My fingers ached to touch him, but his expression stopped me from dragging him toward me. His brow was creased with worry, and a pink flush rose on his cheekbones.

I took his trembling hand and squeezed it. "What is it? Why do you look so worried? I accept your apology. You're my person too, Reece. We can work on this together. I'm going to do therapy out here. This next six months can be about healing all of this stuff that kept us apart. Whatever it takes."

"I'm worried because I have something to ask you." He raked a hand through his hair. "I rehearsed this question so many times in the past, and even in the fantasies you said no."

He gave an awkward cough. His dark eyes glimmered with raw emotion. "Skylar Marshall, would you do me the honor of accompanying me on a date?"

A lump rose in my throat. He'd flown five thousand miles to ask me out on a date, even though he was scared to fly. I smothered a smile and pressed my lips to the back of his hand. "Of course I'll go on a date with you. In what universe would I say no?"

A smile graced his beautiful lips. He pulled me into his arms and studied my face, feature by feature. "I love you, and I want to be loved by you. All I want to do is give you everything I have, and whatever you want to give me, I'll gladly accept it. Things are going to be different. I've loved you so much for so long, but I wasn't ready for you to love me back. I see that now."

His eyes searched my face, seeking permission. He leaned in, giving me a chance to close the gap. "Can I kiss you?"

"You better had."

His mouth covered mine. Tingling pleasure raced through me, and I wanted to get lost in him. It didn't matter if I never resurfaced. His hands locked around my waist and his forehead pressed to mine.

Somehow, I found my voice to speak. "Where are you taking me on our date?"

Softly, his warm breath fanned my face. "We're going bowling."

My lips trembled with the urge to laugh. "Bowling? You flew five thousand miles for me to beat you at bowling? I feel so bad for you."

His laugh was a deep, rich sound. "We'll see. I told you, this is the one sport I'm actually good at."

"As long as you understand that I always play to win."

His smile was full of admiration. "I understand. I wouldn't have you any other way." He inclined his head and pointed in the direction of a parked silver BMW. "I hired a car. Our carriage awaits."

I slipped my hand into his. "I can't wait to see your bowling shoes."

His nose wrinkled. "I forgot them, but it doesn't matter. The bowling alley shoes will be fine."

A glow warmed my heart. I wrapped my arms around him, resting my head on his shoulder. "You're willing to risk it all to take me bowling. Now I know this is true love. We can work on the rest."

Epilogue

Skylar

Six months later

Reece moved closer in the Jacuzzi, wrapping his arms around me. The heat of the water relaxed my muscles and I sank lower so the bubbles came up to my neck. "This is nice."

He pressed his lips to my temple. "It is."

"It's handy having a billionaire who owns a hotel in the family, isn't it?"

Humor laced his tone as he planted kisses along my shoulders. "It has its pros and cons."

He passed me a glass of champagne and took a strawberry from a silver platter. I opened my mouth to let him feed me. Sweetness and fizz burst on my tongue. Long distance had been tough, but we'd managed. Reece had loved me from afar for so many years that it seemed only fair to return the favor.

The past six months had been the best of my life. Playing in the States had helped my confidence no end, and Reece was more relaxed. He had been working on a book, and the writing settled him. It seemed to make him genuinely content. LA had been an amazing experience, but I was so glad to be home and in Reece's arms where I belonged.

He cleared his throat. "Do you remember once when you were staying here, you invited me back to your room?"

I rolled my eyes. "One of the many times you said no, I take it?"

"Do you remember what you said to me, about Gabe's gold-plated Jacuzzi?"

"What did I say?"

"You said you were inviting me up for a shag in a gold-plated Jacuzzi, not asking me to marry you."

A laugh bubbled up out of me. "Yeah. I remember."

He didn't laugh with me. His face took on a solemn, stern expression.

"What's the matter?"

He took a breath. Water sloshed over the sides as he got out of the bath and wrapped a towel around his hips. He fiddled in the pocket of his jacket hung neatly on the chair and pulled out a small box.

"Well, you see, I invited you up here for a shag in a gold-plated Jacuzzi."

He dropped down to one knee, holding the towel in place to protect his modesty. He flicked the lid of the box open. My gaze fell to the sparkling diamond ring and my mouth fell open.

"But I also wanted to ask you to marry me."

Surprise stole my breath. "Seriously?"

A faint smile played on his lips. "Have you ever known me not to be serious?"

I couldn't help my roar of laughter. "We're both naked. I never imagined we'd both be naked when you proposed to me."

"You imagined me proposing to you?"

I chuckled. "Only once a day."

"Is that a yes?"

I wrapped my arms around his neck and pulled him down to my lips. "Of course it's a yes. Now, get back in here. Asking me to marry you is fair enough. Don't forget the rest of the offer."

THANKS FOR READING!

Ready for more Calverdale Ladies? Check out the next book in the series! I can't wait for you to get to meet my sexy Scottish kilt-wearing goalie, Alex.

Have you read the prequel novella, PITCHING MY BEST FRIEND? Sign up to my newsletter here, and get it for free! https://BookHip.com/RVXCHSB I send newsletters once a month with book updates and recommendations of other books you might like. I promise to keep the boring photos of my garden and my dog to a minimum.

LET'S HANG OUT!

All I've ever wanted from life is a crew to hang around with so that we can all wear sunglasses, look cool, and click our fingers in an intimidating fashion at rival crews. We can chat all things romance and occasionally you might be called upon to become involved in a choreographed dance fight. I will also be your best friend forever. NB: Dance fighting skills not mandatory (but encouraged).

Join my reader group:
www.facebook.com/groups/979907003370581/
Follow my author page:
www.facebook.com/profile.php?id=61553872688253
TikTok: Sasha Lace Author (@sasha_lace_author)
Instagram: www.instagram.com/Sasha_Lace_Author

Psst! Hang on! I'd love a review if you've got a sec? If you enjoyed this book, please consider leaving a review wherever you like to leave them. Amazon, Goodreads, or BookBub. Reviews are the life-blood of authors, and are very much appreciated! Thanks so much.

ACKNOWLEDGMENTS

This is my second run at writing these acknowledgments. The first time, I was a fresh-faced indie author leaping into the unknown. I had no idea if anyone would pick up my story, or whether (more likely) it would be lost in a pile with a million others. What I didn't expect was to find so many people willing to take a chance on an unknown author.

Writing has brought so many wonderful women into my life. Thank you to all the readers who have supported me, whether it was taking the time to message with words of encouragement, leaving a thoughtful review, or shouting about my books. You helped me find my confidence as a writer. You made me feel like my words have value. It means the world, truly.

Thank you to everyone in the Montlake Romance team for all of your hard work on these books. It has truly been such a brilliant experience, and I've loved every moment. I'm so excited to relaunch these books with an amazing team of professionals. Thank you to Victoria Oundjian for giving me this chance, for your passion and enthusiasm for the series, and for making my lifelong dream to be traditionally published a reality.

Thank you to Victoria Pepe for taking this series on and bringing so much energy and enthusiasm to it. I feel so confident that it is in wonderful hands, and I'm so grateful. Thank you to Lindsey

Faber for your brilliant development editing insight, and for helping me to dig so much deeper with these characters. To Jenni Davis, thank you for giving these books such a beautiful polish, and helping me to banish the word 'quirked' from my vocabulary. I don't know how many books it will take before I can rid myself of it completely, but I live in hope.

Thank you to Laura and Clare at Liverpool Lit. You are amazing agents and lovely human beings. It is genuinely an honor to be represented by an agency so committed to breaking down barriers in publishing.

To my beta reader/editor/mentor Angela, I sent out a plea for help with my first story and the universe overshot the net and sent me you—the best friend I've never met! You have always been so accepting, so generous, and so insightful. You understood what I was trying to say with that weird first story (better than I did) and you helped make sense of it. Not only did you help me become a better writer, but you showed me that people can be miraculously kind.

To my lovely writer bestie, Heather G Harris. I have long suspected the 'G' stands for genius. You've always believed in me, and encouraged me, and you've been so generous with your time and knowledge. Thank you for being my very first beta reader, and for giving me the confidence to go for it with this story. I appreciate you.

To Jo, Tamymanne, and Kat. You are a wildly accepting bunch of fellow smut-butts. Thank you for all the laughs, and the log-ins. Jo, seriously, thank you. What would I do without the log-ins!? Please don't ever change your password, or this is all over for me.

To Helen, I'm so grateful to have a lovely friend to share this writing and publishing journey with. I really appreciate your talent for finding the perfect shocked-doll expression for every occasion, and your dedication to uncovering Rhysand fan art. Whatever happens, we'll always have the Willywahs and that street team of Ken dolls from Sainsbury's.

Thank you to my precious friend Katie. You have always brought so much joy into my life. Whatever I'm doing, no matter the hour, I'd always rather be on a boat with you, playing table tennis, and stuffing my face with free sushi and peanut M&Ms at 5 p.m., directly before our five-course meal is about to be served.

To Ruchi, my twin flame, all my literary aspirations began with you. Your West Midlands project spoke to me of beauty. The letter to Thom Yorke helped me to refine my prose. All that time spent doctoring BT phone bills honed my attention to detail. The environmental rap taught me how to dig deep. The hole in the ozone layer isn't even an issue anymore. Coincidence, or the power of rap?

Thank you to my mum for always encouraging my passion to read. Even when we had so little, you made sure I always had books. Thank you for your unconditional love and support. The past couple of years have been tough, but your selflessness and strength leave me in awe. Better times are coming, I know it. Thank you for being you. I love you.

To James, your support makes my writing possible. Your support makes everything possible. You've made me laugh every day for the past twenty years. The best part of writing about football is that I get to talk about these books with you. Why are you so randomly good at plotting? It's like that time we went windsurfing and you just knew how to stand up and do it straight away, and I was covered in goose shit and crying. It makes no sense, but I'm into it. You're better than all the book boyfriends put together. They should make a trope about you.

Last, thank you to my kind, beautiful, bright, funny, smart, wonderful boys. I became a writer when I became a mother. You gave me the will to be the best version of myself. Please know that you are the greatest joy in my life, and I love you more than anyone has ever loved anyone EVER. Now get out of here. Go on. Clear off! Do not read these books. Not even when you're grown-ups. I cannot afford the therapy you will need from reading your mother's sweary, spicy books. I have given you fair warning.

PLAYING FOR KEEPS

Turn the page for an exclusive teaser chapter from *Playing For Keeps*, the next book in Sasha Lace's Playing the Field series . . .

Chapter 1

LANA

Dad's glassy eyes met mine. He propped himself up in the hospital bed. "Lana? You don't have to be here. Everything's fine."

Blood smeared Dad's face and crusted the strands of white hair that fell over his lined forehead. His skin looked ruddy over the gaunt ridges of his cheekbones.

Sure, Dad. Everything looks super fine.

Mel gazed out of the window at the dark city skyline. My older sister hadn't spared me a glance since I'd walked in. She looked as put together as always—her red hair gleamed in the bright hospital lights, her chic ruffle-collared blouse and stylish pencil skirt hugged her slim frame perfectly—but tension radiated from her in waves.

Dad shook his head ruefully. "I was gardening, and I tripped over a gnome. A bloody gnome, of all things!" His Scottish burr was slow and slurring. Even after all these years in England, he'd never lost his accent. "I bashed myself on the wall."

He turned his head, and his overpowering stench of tobacco and liquor filled my nose. I did my best not to recoil.

Oh, Dad. Not again.

I can't go through it again.

Mel kept her gaze fixed on the window as she traced a finger over the rain-streaked glass. I had no idea what she was thinking when she went still and quiet like this. This had to be freaking her out, too. The fact that she'd bothered to call and ask for help was evidence enough of that.

Mel would always be a mystery. It was so late, but she still looked perfectly polished and ruthless, as though she'd just stepped out of the boardroom after having dismissed her entire staff without notice. I had no idea what she did at the job I'd swung for her at the football club that meant she had to be power-dressing after midnight. It was to do with contracts, or finance, or something involving spreadsheets. She'd explained it before, but it always went over my head, and now I couldn't ask without looking like an arsehole who didn't know what her sister did for a living.

Dad poked a cut below his eye and grimaced. My stomach sank. Five years of sobriety and now this. He'd had the odd slip and got back on the wagon, but he'd been doing well. Why now?

I held his clammy hand. "It's okay to tell us if you've been drinking."

"Not you, too." Grimacing, he snapped his hand away to prod the bandage wrapped around his head. "Your sister has already been on my case."

Mel turned to look at me for the first time since I'd stepped into the room. Her unimpressed gaze traveled over my outfit. A bridal veil flowed from a plastic jewel-encrusted tiara on my head. A black and pink sash emblazoned with the words "Same Penis Forever" was draped over my teal slip dress. Silver kitten heels completed the look. The bloody things were giving me blisters. I always felt more comfortable in football boots than fancy shoes.

Mel's critical appraisal made me feel self-conscious. I shrugged. "Skylar's bachelorette party."

"I see you've kept things classy," she muttered.

Of course Mel wouldn't approve of penis-related sashes. My sister had studied fashion in London before she'd had to drop out. She should have been in New York or Milan now, living a life of catwalk shows and starry galas, not working a corporate job at a football club, and definitely not stuck in an overcrowded hospital with her screw-up sister and alcoholic father.

Mel moved to Dad's bed and smoothed the blanket. "Remember what they say at Alcoholics Anonymous. Relapse is part of the process. Recovery is not linear, it's a cycle. You think about what triggered this and you learn."

Mel had the thin, strained voice she used when she was about to explode and snap over the slightest thing. God. I hated that voice. I hadn't heard it in so long. Memories of all the times we'd had to deal with Dad's drunkenness flooded my brain. At his worst, he'd disappeared and slept rough on a park bench. He'd been so much better since then. Why now?

Mel shot me a sidelong glance. "I shouldn't have bothered you. I didn't realize you had something on. You can go back. I've got it under control."

Nope. It had been a while since we'd done this dance, but I hadn't forgotten the steps. Of course my older sister wanted to be the martyr and bear the brunt of a relapse.

Dad rolled his eyes. "Got what under control? Me? She's always been a worrier, this one. Not like me and you." He reached for my hand and squeezed it. "We know how to have a good time, don't we, lass? A chip off the old block."

He gripped my hand tight and brought it to his lips. "I haven't seen you in a while. Any word on *the call*?"

Not this again. Could we have one conversation where Dad didn't ask about *the call*? As if he wouldn't be the first person I'd tell. I'd been waiting for *the call* to play football for England since I was twenty. It still wasn't impossible at twenty-six, but every year that flew by made it less likely. The stupid tiara on my head felt suddenly too heavy. I slipped it off and pulled out the little plastic penis earrings that Miri had insisted we all wear.

I kept my smile breezy. "Not yet."

He let go of my hand and turned his face away. "Not to worry. Still time. Some players are . . . late bloomers." Dad cleared his throat. "Anyway, don't either of you worry about me. When Logan Sinclair leaves this world, it won't be at the hands of a bloody gnome."

Mel sighed. "Let's get him home." Her disparaging gaze fixed on the veil I held low in my hand. "I'll take it from here. You can get back to whatever you were doing."

"I'm here now, aren't I?" My voice came out sharper than I'd intended. "I'll help you get him home and then I'll head back."

She tossed her shiny hair haughtily. I got it. Mel had always been better than me at all this stuff. She was the golden girl and I was the screw-up. Mel had kept us going after we'd lost Mum. Everything had fallen apart when Mel left for university.

I'd tried not to disturb her perfect life, but then Dad's drinking spiraled. He'd go missing for days, forget to pay the electricity bill or get the groceries. I kept showing up for lessons and football practices with a smile on my face. I'd lost one parent; I didn't want to be taken away from the other one.

In the end, everything unraveled. I fell in with some older kids in the area. From the outside it looked like I'd gone off the rails, and maybe I had, but I hadn't meant to ruin Mel's plans. I was just a stupid teenager doing stupid things that I regretted now. I'd needed the escape.

When my sister came home after that first term at university, she didn't go back. Mel sacrificed her dreams to save a sinking ship. I'd never be able to shake this feeling that Dad and I were the anchor weighing Mel down.

Dad threw his arms open and burst into song at the top of his voice.

I straightened the sash over my dress. "At least someone is having fun."

Mel approached Dad in her detached, no-nonsense way, as though he were a wild beast in transit and she just needed to find the right spot to aim the tranquilizer dart. "Well, come on then. Don't just stand there. Let's move him. If you're sticking around for a change, make yourself useful."

ABOUT THE AUTHOR

Sasha Lace used to be a very serious scientist before she ditched the lab coat and started writing kissing books. Sasha lives in the North of England and is a mom of two young boys. Everyone in her family is soccer mad, so she knows way more about soccer than she ever wanted to know. As a scientist and mom, her hobbies include: mulling over the complexities of the universe, treading barefoot on Lego, chipping dried Play-Doh from fabric surfaces, dried flower arranging (because you can't kill something twice), and writing about herself in the third person.

Follow the Author on Amazon

If you enjoyed this book, follow Sasha Lace on Amazon to be notified when the author releases a new book!

To do this, please follow these instructions:

Desktop:

1) Search for the author's name on Amazon or in the Amazon App.
2) Click on the author's name to arrive on their Amazon page.
3) Click the "Follow" button.

Mobile and Tablet:

1) Search for the author's name on Amazon or in the Amazon App.
2) Click on one of the author's books.
3) Click on the author's name to arrive on their Amazon page.
4) Click the "Follow" button.

Kindle eReader and Kindle App:

If you enjoyed this book on a Kindle eReader or in the Kindle App, you will find the author "Follow" button after the last page.